# A Poisoned Garden:
New World Magic Book Four

Kim Alexander

ISBN: 979-8-218-11709-2

**Edited** by Carly Hayward of Book Light Editorial

**Cover Art** by Pretty AF Designs
**Formatted for print** by Pretty A.F. Designs

# Praise for Pure: New World Magic Book One

"I love this story! It rivals the best urban fantasy books that I have ever read." —Diana, Audible Reviewer

"Kim embraces the writing style of Ilona Andrews and Jeaniene Frost with snarky heroines, exciting plotlines, and of course mythical creatures"—Nerd Girl Official

"Captivating Read! Fantasy/Romance/Mystery writers, move over in a big way for the new kid on the dark street who can write plot and dialogue as clever and quick as Nora Roberts" —Rad Dad, Amazon Reviewer

# Praise for Kim Alexander

"Kim Alexander's The Sand Prince is a thrill ride of fantastical proportion. Can hardly wait for the next wild installment." — David Baldacci, New York Times and International Best-Selling Author

"The Sand Prince is a wonder — full of magic, drama and sly humor. Kim Alexander might just be a wizard." — Daniel Stashower, New York Times Best-selling Author

"I love these characters (even the horrible ones) and their growth and depth; I love the world(s)-building and the not-quite-hereness of it and the utterly beautiful and unique story."—Tracet, NetGalley Reviewer

# Dedication

This one is for Cait, Gen, and Other Jenn: you are my favorite.
*(Don't tell the others.)*

# A
# POISONED
# GARDEN

# 1

*March*

The woman walked right past the unicorn.

"Can I get you another?" The bartender smiled at March, his hand already on the tap. He was about to agree when something caught his attention. A smell—delicious and familiar. Was it rosemary? Here, surrounded by plastic and metal and cold light, a delicate reminder of life and warmth. March raised his head in time to catch the woman wearing the fragrance reflected in the mirror behind the bar. She rolled her suitcase to a stop at an empty barstool and plopped down with a sigh.

He went tense all over, but it only took a second to realize she was just a random traveler sitting down for lunch. Not Ruby.

After all, why would Ruby be day-drinking at the Home Team Sports Bar in Terminal Two of Phoenix Sky Harbor Airport to begin with? And why was he?

"Was that a yes?" the bartender asked.

He'd forgotten to answer. "No, I'm fine. Thank you." He kept one eye on the woman, in case she turned out to be Ruby after all.

"Don't want to miss your flight. Sure." There were other people waiting for their drinks, but the bartender lingered. "Where are you off to? Someplace good?"

"Um, not really. I'm not sure where I'm going, honestly."

The young man leaned on his elbows. "Yeah? Well, if you need a place to stay or anything..."

"Thanks, but I'm fine. Maybe you ought to..." he indicated the waiting customers, looking increasingly impatient. The bartender reluctantly left to wait on them.

He thought about how he'd gotten here; this bar, this place. Once, it would have been almost impossible for him to follow a map of time and place—points A, B, and C. It would all be happening at once. Now, he could picture each step in order, back to the beginning of this journey.

After the Unseelie king Sasha "gifted" him with his sanity by fixing him in time, he decided the thing to do was to get back to his old life, and that meant the solitude of his forest. He hadn't said goodbye to anyone, not even his old friend, the demi-goddess and therapist Bel. Not even Ruby, not that it would have mattered, because Sasha took her memories away. Her memories of March, the rocks blocking his river.

He didn't want to be distracted by human things.

He started walking, away from the city, away from the cars and buildings and humans, but mostly away from Ruby.

He told himself it was out of concern for her well-being—what would happen if she should see him again? Would it hurt her? But thinking of their last moment together, when thanks to Sasha's intervention she no longer knew him, the way she'd glanced at him with the blank, dismissive eyes of a stranger—he finally had to admit that it was his own heart he wanted to protect.

For a while he put his own body back on and slid through the nighttime streets like mercury, until there were no more streets, and briefly, his journey was over. But once home, he found he couldn't keep still, and before long, his forest was far behind him again.

Turning back into a man, he caught a ride on a ferry and crossed the big river. Then he walked, and when he got tired, he stood by the road until someone stopped their car. Then he'd sit in the passenger seat while they drove and try to keep their eyes on the road and off of him. It didn't always work out that way. Once a man driving a truck stopped for him, and he let the man give him a blowjob. Afterward, the man gripped the steering wheel and cried, saying he had never done anything like that before.

"Really?" March said. "I have. Lots of times. It feels good though, right?"

The man wiped his face with the heel of his hand and said, "I need to pray now."

March nodded. He was used to worship. "That's a good idea."

"You should leave."

March looked out the front window of the truck. The

road shot straight as an arrow dividing the endless fields of corn until it disappeared. The last thing like a town they had passed—a gas station, a motel, and long rows of storage sheds—was over a half an hour ago. He understood, though. He knew he could be a little overwhelming. Just to be sure, he said, "You mean right now? I don't—"

The man pointed his shaking hand at the passenger door. "Please get out." He never looked up.

March fished his sunglasses from the wadded up fast-food bags and random papers on the dashboard and climbed down from the truck. He walked down the road a few paces and looked back at the windshield. The mid-day sun turned it into a mirror, and in it, he could see nothing but endless green with the briefly surprising dot of a man—himself—at the center. He thought there was a good chance that the man was saying a prayer of gratitude for what had just happened to him. Or maybe he prayed that he might see a unicorn, so he took a few more deliberate steps and with a sigh of relief, turned back into himself. Every time, it was like taking off a heavy backpack, and every time, he realized he had forgotten. He looked back at the truck one last time, then plunged into the cool and quiet of the cornfield. Surely, he thought, it must have been gratitude.

After that, he avoided highways and walked through endless cornfields and cow pastures. Mostly, he was completely alone, although he opened his eyes one night to find another set of eyes looking back at him. He knew there were...entities? Creatures? Things almost as old as himself that called this place their home. The eyes held nothing he recognized—not joy or grief or mercy, only a sort of detached curiosity. After a while, they vanished. He went back to sleep.

The landscape changed as he moved west, and the trees and green, growing things grew sparser, and then green things were gone, too. He spent a long while in the desert, and if he sensed that he had been spotted by something other than the odd lizard, he ran on his four strong legs until the feeling fell away.

He stood on a hillside for hours and watched heat lightning silently tear apart the far distant sky. He listened to the love songs of the cicadas. He counted the stars, the same stars he and Ruby had looked at when they stayed at Bel's cabin. That was a long time ago, he thought. A long time. He knew what that meant now.

Solitude, he decided, was no longer what he wanted. He didn't know what he wanted, only that he couldn't stop moving.

When streets and trucks and people started reappearing, he put his human body back on, and finally found himself here.

"Where are you going?" the last woman who picked him up had asked him.

"I'm traveling," he had replied, ignoring the hunger and invitation in the woman's eyes. He pulled his hoodie over his face and pretended to sleep, and she brought him here; an airport. He liked it here. Airports were full of motion and excellent for watching people, and mostly the people were in too much of a hurry to stop and take much notice of him. He realized it wasn't isolation he'd craved after all, but he wasn't too angry at himself. He was different now and of course he would get some things wrong. New things had begun to occur to him all the time. His latest new idea was to look at people because he must have missed something. Because it made sense that if he could fall in love with one human, surely that meant he could find another? That if he paid close enough attention, he would find someone else. This idea was proving sensible and comforting and also, at least so far, wrong.

He took a closer look at the woman sitting down the bar, who had perched her sunglasses on her head and was reading something on her phone. She didn't look anything like Ruby other than having long dark hair. The bartender set a beer in front of her. March wondered what her life was like, if she laughed or cried or had someone at home. She has a phone, he thought, so she must have somewhere to plug it in. He wondered if Ruby kept the little plastic phone she bought him or simply tossed it away. After all, it didn't belong to anyone she knew.

"Maybe you should go talk to her."

March jumped in his seat, and swung around to see who had spoken. People rarely approached him, mostly waiting respectfully for his attention or permission to speak. The man lounging against the bar next to him was tall and slender. His silvery hair was neatly cropped, and he wore a jacket of some crinkly looking fabric with thin white and blue lines. His eyeglasses were small silver ovals. March relaxed a bit when he realized the man was a djinn. He had that lick of fire about him.

"I don't think so," he told the djinn. "She just reminded

me of someone I knew, that's all."

"Yeah," he said, "I can see it if I squint. 'Course, all humans sort of look alike to me." He stuck his hand out. "Mathieu."

March took the djinn's hand, which was hot, as he expected. "March." Then he frowned. "What do you mean, you can see it? How do you know—"

"Oh, sorry. Right. Yeah, I know who you are. And who you thought she was. It was a real pain in the ass finding you, friend. You have light feet." He leaned against the bar, and the reflection from the bank of televisions, each showing a different sport game, flickered in the lenses of his glasses. "You made quite an impression on some humans. Uh huh," he nodded, "you are putting off some *wild* energy. When I described you, they all asked me to make sure you were okay. I got a pocket full of phone numbers, if you want 'em." March didn't respond, and the djinn nodded again. "Didn't think so. I would have lost this bet, though, finding you here." He pulled a notebook out of his jacket pocket. "Carol sends her regards and says you should come see her if you're ever in..." he flipped the page. "Scottsdale."

March let his feet find the floor, in case he had to run. "So, you know me. Do I know you?"

"Indirectly. Doesn't matter. She's fine, by the way. If you were wondering. Or she was when I left D.C."

He stared at the djinn; he could taste panic at the back of his throat, but he wasn't sure why. "What do you want?"

Mathieu laughed. "Fine, let's just get right to it. Thought you might buy me a beer for my troubles, but okay."

"I don't have any money," March said. It sounded foolish and inhospitable as soon as he said it. "Um, I could ask the bartender to give you a beer. If you want." That had worked for him all along. Bartenders were always so friendly.

"Nah, just as well. The air conditioning in this joint makes me achy. Too cold. Listen. I also wanted to thank you. I hear you tried to find out what happened to my Michael."

Michael….oh. Doctor Mike, he must mean. Murdered for a piece of paper—the blood test that proved Marly was one of the fae. "The *kitsune*."

"Yeah. We'd been split up for a while, and I know humans are fragile, but…thank you."

"I wish I could have done more." Like take off the fox man's head. That would have been good. "What did you mean by also?"

Mathieu reached back into his jacket and this time pulled out a stiff black envelope sealed with a blob of saffron colored wax. The wax had flower petals embedded in it in an elaborate pattern. He didn't recognize the sigil. "Why I'm here. This is for you. I strongly, strongly recommend you don't make her wait. Strongly." He nodded at March and turned to go.

"Wait." Mathieu paused. "She's…you said she's okay?"

"Well, I didn't talk to her in person or anything, but yeah. Bel says she's best left alone right now. Oh, you'll want to give her a call. Bel, that is. She's expecting to hear from you."

March looked at the envelope. "This is from Bel?"

Matheiu laughed again. "Dude. Just read it. Gotta head out. Isn't it cold in here to you?"

March shrugged. "Whatever, boo. Good luck." He watched the djinn stroll towards the row of escalators, presumably heading for the exit and the blast furnace of a Phoenix afternoon.

March settled back onto his stool and tore the envelope open. It was an engraved invitation. He had never seen one before; he thought it was just a phrase humans said when they wanted their friends to hurry up and do something: "Are you gonna change the keg," Ruby would say to Claudio, who was dawdling, "or are you waiting for an engraved invitation?"

He scanned the raised golden script on the thick, silky black paper. Someone wanted him to do something, and they wanted him to hurry up and do it. He pushed away his empty beer glass and went over to the dark-haired woman.

"Hi," he said.

She looked at him, wide-eyed. "Hi, uh, hello." A faint blush rose up along her throat.

"I was wondering," he said, "can I use your phone?"

# 2

*Ruby*

**T**ime to get to work.

The Hare won't open itself, even if Claudio usually beats me to the bar. I'm technically in charge but he's pathologically early, no doubt a result of childhood trauma. Sure enough, he was already back there slicing limes. I tossed my backpack into its nook and grunted a hello in his direction.

"Uh, nice t-shirt," he said.

"Thanks." I smoothed it down. "Got it at a yard sale. Three dollars and worth every penny." It had a cartoon drawing of a blue unicorn holding up his hooved middle finger and said "*I got yer magic right here,*" in bubble letters.

"Does it remind you of anything?" Claudio was looking at me funny, but everyone looked at me funny these days. Being best friends with Magical Fairy Princess Marly probably rubbed off on me.

"Should it?" My stomach lurched, and I reached into my bag for some antacids. They seemed to help, but if I didn't feel better soon, I'd have to break down and go to the urgent care. But every time I pictured the inside of the office—fluorescent lights, ice cold air conditioning, a room full of sick people…sick little girls…it just made me feel worse. The only times I felt really well was when I was working the bar or doing something that kept my brain too busy to think. And speaking of mindless amusement, I said, "Bobby'll be here later. Can you let me know if you spot him first?"

Claudio looked a hell of a lot like he wanted to say something else, but just shrugged and said, "Sure." He usually called my not-quite-boyfriend not-quite-hookup Diet Coke Boy, so this was a cautiously optimistic step up. I didn't know what Claudio had against Bobby—he wasn't exactly a brain trust, but he wasn't an axe murderer—or worse—someone who stole from the tip jar. And to make it worse, Claudio acted like I was imagining it. It made me feel contrary, but I'd already made up my mind. "I'm going to break up with him," I said, "and I don't think he's expecting it."

Claudio's face lit up like he just won a free puppy. "I want to watch! Can I watch?"

"God, Clo, why are you so weird about this? You've been low-key shitty to him all along." Claudio shrugged and tried to look innocent. "Don't you want me to be happy?"

"I remember when you *were* happy," he muttered, turning back to the limes.

I decided to let it go, feeling another wave of nausea threaten. I felt so crappy for the last few months that I finally drove the half hour up 270 to Rockville, where no one at the drugstore would recognize me, and bought a pregnancy test—nothing, thank God. But I knew if I got my ass busy and didn't mull over the past *(something's wrong, there's a hole in it)*, I'd feel better by the end of the night. As the bar got more crowded and I let the muscle memory of pouring, serving, making change, and swiping cards take over, I was proved right. By the time Bobby finally poked his head around the corner, I felt just fine.

Was it shitty to break up with someone across a bar? Better or worse than sending a text? Better, I think. At least I was doing it in person. But then I started to back-pedal; should I make a date with him to break the news the next day? I didn't want to take him home with me that night only to make him leave, and I sure wasn't going to let him stay so I could tell him over breakfast. It wasn't like I was mad at him or that he did anything wrong in particular. He just...didn't do *anything* in particular. When I talked about it with Shanti a few days earlier, she had been quick to agree. Maybe a little too quick.

"You don't need a reason to break up with him," Shanti said over dinner. She took a sip of her margarita. "The fact that you're even contemplating it means he's not right for you."

I had a strong feeling that if I had acted like I was on the fence, Shanti would have tried to talk me into breaking up. She never really warmed up to Bobby either, and I couldn't figure out why. Maybe there was something wrong with him that I couldn't see. Anyway, it was time to break it off. There didn't seem to be any reason to drag this out.

"Hey," Claudio said. He poked me in the ribs, and I pulled my head out of the cooler.

"What?"

He jerked his chin to the right. "Diet Coke Boy's here."

"His name is...never mind." There wasn't much of a point in correcting him, since Bobby would likely never come by again. I wiped my hands and met him at the far corner of the bar. He had a strange look on his face.

"Hey, what's up?"

"You could have just told me," Bobby said. "I mean, it's obviously not working out, but why'd you have to get rude about it?"

"Um, yeah. I don't know what you're talking about." I was surprised but slightly relieved he'd beaten me to the punch. Still, this seemed weird. I hadn't done anything but ask him to come by The Hare.

He tossed an envelope on the bar. "I'm happy for you. I really am." His voice sounded anything but. "It was obvious you were never really into it. I'm just glad you didn't waste any more of my time."

"Now hang on. I was into it, for a while. I mean, yeah, I was going to break up with you but...why are you happy for me?"

"Your lover boy sent a car to come and *fetch* you. The driver said you'd drop everything to see him. I just think it's fucking rude that he had an errand boy came to my house with a letter for you."

*Your lover.* For a split second the room lurched sideways

and I thought for sure I'd puke on the bar. But the sensation passed as quickly as it struck. "I don't have a lover boy, an errand boy or any other kind of boy. Don't be gross. And how do you know it's for me if they came to your house?"

The look he gave me screamed, *Thank God I never have to see this person again.* "Your name is on the envelope, dumbass." I had to give him that one. "And the guy asked for you by name and said you'd 'been seen' with me, so thanks for roping me into whatever game you two are playing. Whatever. I'm done with you and this shitty bar." Bobby glared at me like I threw his phone into the toilet, turned, and stomped off down the stairs.

"Bye," Claudio shouted after him. "See you never." He turned to me. "Who's it from?"

I stared at him, then looked down at the envelope. It was heavy, silky cream-colored paper with no return address and no stamp. Just my name, in flowing script. "You know who it's from, don't you?"

"No. No. I, um. No." Claudio was a lousy liar.

I turned away from him and opened it. "Oh, perfect. Now this bitch." I thrust the letter at Claudio, who snatched it up and read it.

"Can you say no?" he asked. "Do you want to say no?"

I sighed. "I don't think I can turn down an invitation from Sasha."

# 3

*March*

The elevator hadn't even slid shut behind March when Shanti swooped in (even in her human, non-harpy form, Shanti favored the Swoop) and hauled him through Dr. Bel's waiting room and into her office. She often talked a little too fast for him to follow, and now she was rattling on at top speed. It seemed like she was pretty worked up.

"Nice to see you again, too," he said.

"Ugh!" She shut the door behind him.

"Above and Below," Bel cried, "Finally!" and hugged him. Well, that was nice. Then she reared back and punched him hard in the bicep.

"Ow!"

"March, you jerk. Where have you been? Do you know how hard we've been looking for you? For months!"

Now, that didn't make any sense at all. They'd gone years

without seeing each other. Decades. "Why?"

She looked at him like he was crazy. "Because you're my friend. And I am worried about you—we all are."

"Ruby isn't," he reminded her.

She sighed. "No, she's not. But that doesn't mean the rest of us...March, we couldn't figure out what happened. Shanti, Dafne, and I all left before Sasha...before he did whatever he did to Ruby. We're still not sure. And then you were gone. I thought about contacting Marly, but she's got her own thing going on, and I didn't want to worry her, and now...well." She took a breath and forced herself to settle down. "Please, sit." She paused; her mouth twisted. "Unless you have someplace more important to be." She was still angry with him. He sat on the ecru couch, and she perched on the edge of her desk.

"Well, I did get a letter..." he said.

"A what?"

"A letter. From Mathieu, he delivered it. The djinn? Didn't you send him?"

"Oh, is that why he was looking for you? No, he contacted me, since he knew we know each other, and I told him that I needed to talk to you. But he didn't mention a letter." She folded her arms, taking a longer look at him. He wondered whether he looked the same, or why she cared.

"I can understand why you'd be worried about Ruby," he said. "She's a delicate human. But why worry about me?"

She looked at him, incredulous. "March, we all thought you were about to die, or lose your mind, or get lost in time, or something. When I tried to ask Ruby what happened to you, she'd get sick to her stomach and run to the bathroom.

I couldn't even say your name. I tried to...I don't know, hint? But she acted like she didn't know what I was talking about. Shanti said the same thing—she acts like she doesn't know who you are."

"She doesn't."

Bel waited. "That's it? That's the whole story?"

He sighed. He didn't want to talk about it because that gave it substance. "Sasha removed the thing that was causing me to come unmoored in time. That thing was Ruby. He couldn't remove my memories of her, but he took away her memories of me. He said it was like pulling a rock out of the river, so the water could flow. She was my rock. So now, as far as she knows, I don't exist. I guess she came up with stories to fill in the gaps about everything that happened."

Bel nodded. "She thinks Marly got bitten by a radioactive spider or something." She shook her head. "I'm sorry. No wonder you wanted to get away."

"I love her."

Bel's head jerked up. "You what now?"

He did. He'd said it out loud—of course, there had never been anyone but the corn and a few curious cows to hear him say it. But based on what he knew—which he had to admit wasn't much—about what feelings meant and what you were supposed to do with them, he understood that he loved her. "I love her. I figured it out, but by the time I did, it was too late to tell her. I think it's possible she felt the same way."

"I think she did, too." She ran her hand through her hair. "What a mess. Well, what happened next? What have you done to fix this? Is that where you've been?"

Here came another new feeling—guilt. He didn't care for this one at all. "I promised her I would. It was the last thing I told her, that I'd try to fix this. But I haven't. I've been mostly not thinking about things." The curious, pitying way Bel looked at him now made him feel worse. It made him wish he was still alone, walking through a moonlit field. "Just...she's fine, though, right? She's well?"

"Yes." Her tone softened. "You've been going through some things, yourself. I wish you'd stuck around. You have friends here. Maybe together we could have figured—"

"No." Another new thing surfaced. This one was already in his head, waiting for him to notice it. "I..." He struggled to find the words for what he'd realized. "It doesn't matter what I want." This had begun to occur to him while alone in the corn. He'd been alone most of his life, but he'd never before felt insignificant. A lot of new things in his head, most of them unpleasant. "She's much better off without me. I have a feeling for her, but it doesn't mean I'm good for her. It should stay this way. I have a long time—a really long time—to get over it." He was stunned by the realization. "I don't always have to get what I want." This is what the corn, and the eyes in the corn, wanted him to know.

Bel gave him an appraising look. "I never thought I'd hear you say something like that. You are changing, aren't you?" She shook her head. "I'm not sure you get to make that decision for her. Also, I don't know what tampering with her memories might have done to her. I don't see Sasha as having been very concerned with side effects."

Bel was right. But then, she usually was. "I actually did

not think of that." He sat back. "So, getting her memories back might be better for her after all?"

"And then, she can decide if she's better off without you, or not. Until then, her life isn't really her own, is it?"

"You want me to try and fix this, but I'm not sure I should. I thought therapists were supposed to help you make your own decisions, not try and change your mind to match theirs."

She blew out a breath. "I'm not your therapist, March, and anyway, what do you want to happen? Do you want to spend the next thousand years being miserable?" She narrowed her eyes at him. "Maybe you do. Maybe it's the easy thing to do. After all, it's easy to say you love someone when there's no chance of having to do the work."

He lifted his chin. "I remind you what I sacrificed for her, and that your sister is still out there. Ruby is safer without her connection to me, no matter what else happened in her head."

Bel looked chastened. "That's not what I meant. I know what happened. And believe me, I appreciate that you're thinking of what might be best for her. I know this is new for you, and I'm proud of you. You've come a long way. And of course, there's the question of what would happen to you if her memories are restored."

He didn't like to remember the confusion and frustration, the fear he'd felt. There had to be another way. "Can we leave it for the moment? As of right now, I can't change it or fix it. She doesn't remember me, and that is all." She still looked unconvinced. "Is that all?"

"Well, I don't know. Like I said, I don't know what else Sasha did to her mind while he was rooting around in there. I don't even know if he created all that nonsense to fill in the blanks, or if she did it herself."

"I could ask him."

She stopped. "You could—how?"

"When I go there." He handed her the letter. "I've been summoned to the Unseelie Court."

# 4

*Ruby*

The invitation noted that time ran differently in the Unseelie kingdom, so I wouldn't have to worry about my life being too disrupted. Still, Claudio said he'd watch the bar and come around to mist my orchid if it turned out to be more than two or three days. Even so, I wasn't sure how to pack to visit the king of the dark fae. In the end, I figured a couple of pairs of jeans, some t-shirts, tights, and a dress I inherited from Shanti would do the job, and I stuffed them all in my backpack. I remembered Sasha saying there wasn't any cell service, so I left my phone sitting in its charger on the kitchen table. I decided "yes" on the allergy nasal spray and "no" on a third pair of shoes. I took a last look around and grabbed the medallion from my dresser. Tucked into the very formal invitation, Sasha included a handwritten note saying I'd need it to have it "on my person." I hung it around my neck, hiding under the "nice" jersey knit blouse I picked to travel with. I turned out the lights and wondered how long this would really take, in either world. The letter had, in typical Sasha fashion, not been clear.

"Good to see you again." James was waiting at the curb, leaning against his Rav-4. I remembered his kindness and his great taste in music at the same time I had a wave of nausea. I took a deep breath and felt it fade away.

"I thought you retired." I gave him a hug. "Are you back working for Sasha?"

"One a one-time only basis. Well, two times, since I'll be taking you home when you're done."

I got in the front, since we were friends. After all, he'd practically saved my life after I was attacked by the *kitsune*. "Yeah, about that. Do you know why I got this invite now? I mean, I'm glad I finally get to see Marly, but I was kind of wondering why the invite didn't come from her. Do you know what Sasha's got in mind?"

James both shook his head and nodded in one awkward gesture. "Can't say."

I figured that meant he literally could not say and let it go. "So, where are we going? I mean, I know we're going to the Unseelie Court. Is it off 95? Is there a lot of traffic?"

He smiled, probably relieved I changed the subject. "There won't be any traffic where we are going. Visitors to the court are highly unusual. I'll be driving a second visitor later today, which is a sort of record."

"Oh yeah? Do I know them?"

He hesitated, then did that nod-shake of his head again. I laughed. "It must be so frustrating, knowing stuff that you can't talk about."

"You could say that. I wish he would tell me less, but I think he enjoys my company."

I tried to picture Sasha enjoying someone's company. Even eating pizza in his sweatpants he'd had a stick up his ass the size of a telephone pole.

Once we got underway, we had one stop to make, one that Sasha was very clear about, and then we were back on the road.

There may not be much traffic on the road to the Unseelie Court, but it was near rush hour on the Inner Loop, and we were crawling. With reggae playing on the stereo and the AC blasting, it felt like old times. "Hey, remember—"

He glanced at me. "Hmm?"

"So weird." I shook my head. "Never mind." I rummaged around my backpack until I found my trusty antacids. They wouldn't help with lightheadedness, but they usually took the edge off my stomach trouble. Not for the first time, I wondered if something was seriously medically wrong with me. It began about six months ago, just after Marly left to go try her hand at being an Unseelie fae. While it was true that Sasha was genuinely concerned about her, and his offer to help her get used to her new fae biology probably saved her life, there was still something shifty about him. The whole business with him being tricked by the *kitsune*, there were still some parts of it I couldn't get straight in my head. I even got a new journal, thinking if I wrote it down it would help me figure it out. But whenever I tried to unknot it, it just made me feel worse. Could a memory of an event make you sick? I guessed I could have PTSD, but other than a fistfight with a fox dude, nothing happened to me that was even close to being as dramatic as Marly's trip from middle school English teacher to having something dormant in her blood suddenly activate and turn her into a fae. She should be the one throwing up, not me. I had a sudden, wild idea that I was somehow experiencing her morning sickness—that was why she was there, after all. But that was not only dumb, it opened a whole line of 'they are doing it' I was one hundred percent not prepared for. I supposed I would find out pretty soon what she was up to. Maybe she would have some ideas about me, too.

"Ah, here we are."

While I'd been preoccupied by the idea of my best friend rolling around with Sasha's scary ass, James had taken an exit off the beltway and onto a road I'd never seen before. It was two lanes wide, paved with gravel, and lined with huge, shaggy trees—beeches, maybe? Their branches met overhead and as we drove; it got progressively darker. I wasn't sure if it was the trees blocking the sun, or if we'd entered a place where our sun didn't shine, and James turned on the headlights. When we reached the other side of the tunnel, the sun was gone and I knew we were very far from home. It was quiet and almost as dark as the tree-lined road. He stopped the car in what looked like a medium sized pull-off for a scenic overlook, if you were vacationing on another planet.

I got out of the car and walked to the edge of the clearing, then looked over the edge of the stone wall and whistled. Not too far below was a sea of dark gray, churning clouds.

"I'm looking at a moat, aren't I?" Far across the chasm I could make out a sort of shoreline. It was too dark to see anything other than what looked like a broad, flat plain with a line of mountains in the distance. As I squinted at them, one of the mountains moved, like the biggest inchworm in the universe. I blinked hard several times. *Jeez, Rube, get a grip.*

I tore my gaze away from the definitely-not-moving mountains. The dark forest and the road were on one side, and on the other a hedge too tall for me to see over which stretched out of sight, broken only by a tall and delicately coiled black gate. I'd say it was wrought iron, but there wouldn't be any iron on the fae's home turf; to them it was poisonous. It wasn't exactly a parking lot, although I noted several things I figured were probably vehicles. One of them looked like the carriage from Cinderella, except done in shiny black and dull silver, and no mice.

"Is that Sasha's ride?" James nodded. "Sweet."

He looked around cautiously. "We have only a moment." He leaned in and whispered rapidly into my ear, "You must not apologize, not for anything. And you may know they can't lie? That does not mean they speak true. Watch your back. Watch your front. Watch your words." He took a step back and spoke in a more normal tone. "The king enjoys driving, he is quite accomplished." He gave me a sort of owl-eyed look, and I nodded slowly.

"Driving is very important. It's great if someone teaches you the ins and outs. Much easier to get around."

He looked relieved. I hoped that was the end of the

lecture, because someone was coming.

The frothy wrought iron gate swung open and a young man *(nope, not a man, best keep that in mind)* hurried in our direction. He was tall and slender, with the same long, silky black hair Sasha had when I first met him in Lauren's kitchen, over her dead body. New guy's eyes were all black, with pinpoint golden lights darting in my direction. He pushed his hair back, looking a bit out of breath. "Ah, you're the human. I mean, you're a human. I mean, you knew that. Sorry."

James said not to apologize, but it looks like they could do it, just not me. So noted. He put his hand on my shoulder. "I'll be seeing you soon. Don't..." he paused. "Don't worry. You'll be fine. The king is an excellent host."

The young man said, "Thank you for your service to the king. I'll let him know the, uh..."

"Ruby," I said, so he wouldn't have to keep calling me "the human."

"I actually knew that," he told me. "I will tell the king you delivered Ruby safely."

"Tell him I'll be back for her. Tell him I'll be waiting for the call." We watched James get back in his car and slowly drive away until even the crunch of gravel under his wheels was gone. The man turned to me.

"On behalf of the king, welcome to the Unseelie Court. My name is Aster."

"Aster. Like the flower?"

He shook his head. "Like the fourth runner up of the eighth season of the Australian version of *Gettin' It*. He had a most compelling story arc, starting as he did as a member of the crew..." He cocked his head at me. "Oh, I'm to see the medallion before we cross in." I lifted it out from inside my blouse, and he nodded. "Excellent. Please do not remove it while you are visiting with us. It's really quite important."

"Yeah, that's what Sasha's letter said. Why is that?"

He looked at me for a moment. "Take it off."

"Really?"

"You won't want to do it twice, but you won't understand until you do."

I lifted the chain from around my neck, and as soon as it cleared the top of my head, the assault of noise made me cry out and clap my hands over my ears, I almost dropped it. I was hearing the unfiltered sound of fae speech, I realized. I remembered the horrible car-crash noise when Sasha had tried to tell me his actual fae name—this was like that, only turned up to a thousand. Aster was saying something, and it was another layer of metallic shrieking. I fumbled with the necklace and got it over my head and down around my neck, and the noise cut off instantly.

"Outsiders to our court, they tell us our voices carry." He peered more closely at me. "Do you understand now?"

"Y...yes." I took a deep breath and tried to steady myself. The noise had been so overwhelming and so unexpected, it made me wonder what else was in store for me. This wasn't going to be like a trip to a place with a new language, like Mexico City, or even somewhere like Bangkok, where I couldn't even read the street signs. This was totally alien. "Thank you."

I must have sounded shaken up, because Aster, after only

a second of hesitation, patted my shoulder as he had seen James do.

"I've been assigned to you during your stay with us. I won't let you come to harm." He touched one of the coils on the gate—it turned out to be black glass—and it swung open. "It's time. Let us go and see the king."

# 5

*March*

**M**arch watched Bel's face carefully as she read the letter. When he handed it to her, he recognized the shock on her face and despite the situation felt a touch of pride; humans were becoming less opaque. But of course, Bel wasn't human, and his pride curdled into something that turned in on itself, pointed back at him, sneering at his own foolishness. It had a name, he just didn't know it yet.

Bel had always been good at not showing too much. He supposed that listening to human and xeno complaints and problems all day, you had to get good at not looking bored or offended. What kind of a job was that, anyway?

He thought of how Ruby had brought him to see Bel (it was one year and six months ago, and if he wanted to, he could even count the days) because she thought Bel could help him with the problem of being temporarily mortal. Of course, at the time he thought it was permanent, and Ruby hadn't known the two of them—he and Bel—had what humans call "history." Had Bel actually helped? She had moved them towards the *kitsune*, who had led them to Baba Yaga, who had plunged a knife into his chest. The old witch had wanted his horn and his immortality, and when she couldn't get that, she settled for his heart and the appearance of youth. But it hadn't worked the way she planned, and in the end, he was restored to his own immortal self.

By that measure, if hastening the death of his mortal body could be considered help, Bel had done her job. Normally, though, as far as he could tell, she got paid to listen but didn't really have to come up with any solutions. He hoped she considered this her off hours and she'd help him figure out how to respond, and maybe how to get in and then out of the Unseelie Court with his head, horn, and freedom intact. He'd heard the fae were avid collectors. He had no intention of winding up as part of Sasha's collection.

But Sasha hadn't sent the invitation.

"Why do they want to see you? Why now? And what does our friend the king have to do with this; you know he's in it up to his shiny eyeballs. He's got to be." He waited while she spoke, understanding she didn't expect an answer. Humans did that a lot, and Bel spent so much of her time around humans. "Do you know who this woman is? Madame Tournesol? I've never heard of her."

That question he could answer. "I know exactly one-and-a-half fae: Sasha and Marly. I don't know who Madame Tournesol is or why she wants to see me. When Mathieu gave me the letter, he said not to keep 'her' waiting. Until I read it, I figured he meant Marly."

Bel looked more closely at the envelope and the wax stamp. "This seal has flower petals stuck in it. See?"

"I wondered about that. Do you know what it means?"

"'These are from a special kind of lotus called Crimson Dragon Sleeps on a Golden Cloud."

"That's the name of a plant?"

She shrugged. "It's a mouthful. I've never seen one, only read about them. I read that they take a full year to fade but are almost impossible to grow. See?" She carefully prised one slim, red petal free. It curled slightly in her palm. "It's still fresh. Only those of the highest rank are allowed to touch or display them. In some cultures, if you aren't an emperor, you can't even look at them. So, I'm guessing this means our Madame is very close to the throne." She handed the envelope back. "Maybe Sasha has a sister? Or mother? Whoever she is, she wants to have lunch with you."

"I guess I'll find out." He looked back at the invitation. "What does 'formal day' mean?"

She smiled. "You're going to love it."

Three hours later, March found himself sincerely wishing Matheiu had taken a wrong turn in Oklahoma, or that he was back in his forest, or even still sitting at that stupid bar. Mostly he wished he had never heard of "formal day," or "half Windsor," or "jacquard" and particularly "let's try it a size down, bring all four shades." (He had to confess, despite his grumbling, the fabrics and colors the humans were draping over him were quite appealing.)

Bel stood behind him as he scowled at himself in the clothing store's three-way mirror. "You look gorgeous," she told him. The two salespeople who had been helping them nodded in fierce agreement.

"I'm choking," he said. "I hate this."

"Oh, stop it. It's just a tie," Bel said. "Millions of people wear them every day. And it looks good on you."

"Everything looks good on him," observed Amy, the saleswoman.

"This one is my favorite," Dan, her cohort added. "Plum is very now. The color makes your eyes pop."

March looked at the man. "Is that good?"

"You didn't like the blue?" Amy asked Dan, ignoring his question.

"Oh no, he looked like he worked at a bank," Dan answered.

"The First National Bank of Hotness," Amy replied. "I'd like to make a deposit." The two of them laughed, and so did Bel, that traitor.

He locked eyes in the mirror with the girl, and she stopped laughing. Her hand crept up to touch her throat. Her eyes widened. Her tongue touched her lower lip. *I could have her if I wanted. The boy too, probably. This is how it has always been for me,* he thought. *They come to me with desire, and I've always accepted it as my due. So why does it feel different now?* He looked away and the girl took a step back, her cheeks flaming.

"I think we're done here," Bel said. "We'll take everything. Yes, the tie also, don't listen to him."

Once the two salespeople were gone, she said, "What was that?"

He shrugged uneasily. "I can't help how people look at me."

"So, you did notice. That's new." She tapped her chin. "So many new things."

"No one ever..." He stared at Bel, suddenly cold. "Do... did people always look at me like that? And I never noticed before?" He thought of the man in the truck, how he said he wanted to pray, and maybe it wasn't a prayer of thanks at all, and then the heat rising from the woman in the car, how Matheiu said he had wild energy, and all the other humans whom he assumed were just being kind. "I have to get out of here." He walked as quickly as he could out of the shop and onto the street. With his sunglasses on and looking at his own feet, he felt if not invisible then at least innocuous. He found a spot behind a bus shelter that mostly hid him from passersby.

A few minutes later Bel came, carrying two shopping bags and a garment bag. She put her hand on his shoulder. "You haven't done anything wrong," she said.

"You don't know that." How could she, when he didn't know himself? He took the garment bag and followed her to her car, head down, making sure not to make eye contact with anyone they passed. Once in the car, he relaxed a bit. "How long has this been going on?" he asked. "Is this the only reason humans pay attention to me?"

"It isn't only humans. March, you have an effect on people. I mean, why do you think you get everything handed to you for free? Have you ever paid for a beer? Or a ride? Or wanted anything that didn't fall into your hands?"

"Paid? You mean with money?"

"I thought not."

"Wait, when they want sex from me, it's for payment? For giving me things?" He was stunned. "I thought it was worship. I think it *used* to be worship. I didn't even give all of them sex," he said. "Is that wrong, too?"

"You don't owe anyone anything," Bel told him. "And you were right, you can't control how people look at you, or how they act."

"What about you? Why do you want to help me? Those clothes—you bought them for me. Why?" He could hear a sharpness in his own voice, and marveled at it.

"Because for the millionth time, I'm your friend." she said. "But I do remember the day we met. I couldn't wait to get my hands on you, and that was with me knowing what you are." She glanced at him. "Don't worry. I can't say I'm immune to your charms, but I'm used to you. Maybe it's because I'm not human. I have to say, though, it seems like you've turned it up, like, a lot."

"Marly," he said, suddenly remembering sitting side-by-side at the bar and laughing and drinking with her. "She never acted like I was anything special. She was just my friend. Like you." He thought about it some more. "And Sasha wasn't even close to being my friend."

"Then maybe your visit to the Unseelie Court is a good thing. But I feel like we'd better get in front of the ways you've changed. Did it start with Sasha? When he changed Ruby's memories?"

"I think it started when I died. Or when I didn't die, I guess. With your sister." Having a long-bladed knife plunged into your heart would change a person, even one as changeless as himself. He barely remembered any pain, only light. Well, that wasn't quite true. He remembered the pain, but he didn't like to think about it. He preferred to recall the light and a tremendous rush of power which had taken his temporarily mortal self and shoved it back into his real, immortal body. He thought of the time he had watched a human with a dead car get it jump-started. Maybe the same thing had happened to him. "Ever since then, I've been different. I was also having time problems, so I didn't really pay much attention to it." He looked over at Bel, eyes wide. "Ruby. Did she..."

"Don't. Please. She knew what you are, and everything that comes with it. I shouldn't be telling you this, but we talked about it, and she struggled with it. Whether she really loved you or it was you wanting her to love you."

He leaned back in the car seat and closed his eyes. "I wish I had scales, or tentacles, or three eyes. Then I'd know how people really felt."

"I know plenty of people with scales and they are perfectly lovely. I don't think how you look has anything to do with it." She looked over at him again. "Maybe a little. So, we've got you some decent clothes, let's hit the shoe store and then a haircut—"

"No. Ercilia gave me these shoes and I like them." He missed who he'd been when he met Ercilia, the woman who ran the coffee/breakfast/thrift store around the corner from

Ruby's house. All he owned was one shirt and one pair of jeans and the shoes (still) on his feet, and everything was simple. "And no one's touching my hair. It's bad enough I have to walk around in that noose."

She laughed. "What a delicate flower you are. Fine, you explain to this 'Madame' why you're wearing those ugly old boots with a new suit. At least they're not brown."

He hunched down in his seat. " She won't even notice."

"Have it your way. You can change back at my office and get in touch with...what did it say?"

"I'm supposed to call a number." He paused. "Maybe I could use your phone?"

"Phones and cars and feelings," she said. He thought she sounded annoyed. "You've come a long way in a short time."

**By the time he was** dressed to Bel's satisfaction and placed the call, it was evening.

"Tell Sasha I'm waiting for my invitation," said Shanti as she closed down her computer. "He promised me a hunt. Also, you look like a complete meal plus dessert."

"We aren't talking about his appearance anymore," Bel told her. "It makes him uncomfortable."

"Is that what that meant?" he asked. "Is it good, being a complete meal?"

"Well," Shanti replied, "it's not bad but I'll use my inside voice from now on. Give Marly my love, and don't stay in that place too long." She answered the phone. "Your ride's here. Are you ready to go?"

He couldn't think of one reason to stay. "Yes, I'm ready."

# 6

*Ruby*

I followed Aster through the palace grounds, trying not to be intimidated by the fae who stopped to stare at me with their black, glittering eyes. Every one of them— men and women both—had that sort of movie-star glamor; you couldn't stop wanting to look at them. It wasn't just that they were beautiful—they were—but they were also cool and judgey-looking. The way they glanced at me, then at each other. It was like the first day of school, but with fashion models for classmates. I felt distinctly underdressed in my only slightly ratty jeans and "going out to dinner" blouse, as they all wore some variation of a floor length gown, some with slits in the front revealing brightly colored soft leggings or tight, shiny pants. Aster himself wore what looked like a cross between a bathrobe and a kimono in vivid saffron silk lined with cobalt blue. It answered the question about Sasha and his penchant for shiny black leather, and black clothing in general—apparently it was just him. I wondered if I could get one of the robes for myself while I was here. It would make me stand out that much less.

We stopped at an archway twined with vines and blooming roses. I took a closer look and realized the whole thing was made of glass. It was gorgeous work, too perfect to be real, and so was the arbor we walked under, which made a pretty mosaic of the light and dark sky above us. The path led to a hedge-walled garden, where Sasha, the only one in black, sat with a handful of fae, drinking and talking. I heard him laugh—had I ever heard him laugh before? I wondered where Marly was.

Aster approached the group and dropped into a crouch with one hand flat on the ground and the other palm face up against the small of his back. With his head bent, he said, "My lord king, I've brought the human as you required. James sends his best regards and—"

Sasha looked up, ignoring Aster. "Ruby! How delightful to see you again. Your trip was pleasant, I trust?"

He didn't rise to greet us, I noted, although I guess that when you're the king, standing is for other people. "Sasha." There was a collective intake of breath—not quite a gasp—from the collection of fae. Aster strained to look up at me without moving his head. He looked panicked. I didn't want to get him into trouble, so I added, "My lord king."

Sasha didn't seem to notice the reaction, and waved his hand at me. "Please, no need to be so formal. Oh," he glanced around, "Didn't I mention? I've decided our guest may call me Sasha, since that's the name I adopted while among the humans. And, I've further decided she may forgo my title, due to our close friendship." He gave a little laugh. "Did I ever tell you all about the time we ate *pizza*?" His courtiers were slow to react, and I had a feeling he had probably told that story before, possibly more than once. "Anyway, I'd like to talk to my friend Ruby privately, so..." He flicked his hand.

The group of fae, including a relieved-looking Aster, made a show of bowing—there was much arm-sweeping and skirt-swishing and left through the several arched gates in the other walls around the garden. When we were alone, he sat back in his chair (the only chair in the garden) and folded his arms. The smile he showed his courtiers dropped away.

"They all know if any one of them marched into my presence wearing a scowl like that and failed to address me properly, they'd be exiled to the Fields."

I decided not to be intimidated—at least, not yet. "Lucky for me I'm an invited guest and not one of your minions. Well, I'm here. What's going on? Where's Marly?"

He tossed his hair over his shoulder. It had grown out and was all black again, the gray he'd gotten in my world was gone. "She's fine. You'll see her later. I asked you for two reasons. First, I am holding a fête for Lauren, the one I promised. Some important members of the Seelie Court will attend, and I thought it appropriate you'd be here for that."

"Oh." That was actually a nice thing to do. And the Seelie Court, that seemed like a big deal. "Okay. Thank you. What's the second reason?"

"I have an important job, and I think you're the perfect one to do it."

"Is it bartending?" Other than pouring drinks and making bad decisions, I couldn't think of anything else I was qualified to do.

"Heh, no. My goodness, forgive my rudeness. Here you are with the mud of the road on your...outfit, and me making demands." He raised his hand, and Aster rushed back to my side. He knelt and bowed his head again.

"Please forgive Ruby, I'm entirely to blame. I never suspected she wouldn't know how to address you, lord king."

"What do you think, Ruby? Should I banish this idiot?"

"What? No, of course not." I wondered what exactly was going on, and why Aster was an "idiot."

"I bet he told you how to address his Madame Tournesol, didn't he?"

Madame who? I felt like I'd walked into the middle of a fight during a fancy cocktail party. "Who? Sasha, what is this about?"

"Aster knows. Don't you?"

I heard the other fae take a short breath. Then, barely raising his head, he said, "Madame Tournesol requested that I mind the human brought to court. It is not mine to disregard or disobey her, as my lord king is aware. As was your permission was given to greet the hum—to greet Ruby on your behalf."

"Who is Madame Tor...who are we talking about?"

Aster spoke first. "Madame Tournesol is the hero of the Great War. Without her, all would have been lost."

"*The* hero? Is that so?" Sasha left his seat and stood so close to Aster he was almost standing on his hand and his rich black robes swirled around his head. "Remind me, were you there, at that last battle?"

"I was not, lord king, as I am far younger than you or Madame."

"Then tell me, what did you learn in your history books? Did Madame lead our people into the fight? Did she take grievous injury? Did she lift the sword of glass with her own bloodied hand?" Sasha loomed over the kneeling man, and I got the prickly feeling that happened right before things got out of hand at the bar.

"No, lord." Aster was barely audible.

"Pardon? Did she not?"

"Sasha…" I knew it wasn't a good idea to interrupt, but none of this was Aster's fault.

He ignored me. "Did you not hear my question?"

"No lord." Aster raised his head. "That was you."

Still looking down his nose at Aster, Sasha snapped, "It would serve you well to act like it." To me he said, "Madame Tournesol is a great lady of my court who occasionally insinuates herself where her help is not required. This young man is her…aren't you her nephew?"

"I am related to Madame only through her magnanimity, not by her blood. I am at her lady's service, as I am at yours." Aster now spoke with his head bowed, but I could see the tension in his jaw and neck.

"Well, what's done is done." Sasha, apparently finished with the confrontation, waved his hand and returned to his seat. "Madame will have her way and I'm sure also a full report." Aster took the hint and exited stage left.

When he'd gone, I turned back to Sasha. "A report of what? Why am I here?" This had gone from awkward to scary to frustrating with lightning speed.

"You and Marly will have so much to discuss, and Madame's name will no doubt come up. I know quite well how protective you are of your friend—going after the *kitsune* like that. Don't think I did not notice. I'd like you to show the same resolve in the event Marly once again needs protection."

"From…"

"Madame has a history of making trouble at parties. And other places. It is my wish you stay close to Marly's side."

I stared at him. "When someone's making trouble at my bar, I make them leave. I don't hire a bodyguard."

He stared back, those all-black eyes unreadable. "I'm not speaking of the kind of trouble one simply asks to leave."

"You do understand I'm literally the only one in this joint with no powers. If Madame starts anything, I don't know what you expect me to do except hide under a table."

Sasha gave me his patented why-must-I-endure-the-stupid? look. "Marly has power to spare. That, actually, is the reason you're here. Not to protect her from Madame, but to make sure Marly doesn't do anything…rash."

It slowly dawned on me what he was really asking. "You want me to keep her from…what? Blowing shit up?"

"Not shit. But someone—" he smiled again. "Someone shitty."

I did not laugh. I am not an enabler. He cleared his throat and continued.

"She must not turn her newly gained and still developing

gifts towards Madame. She doesn't truly understand whom she goes against. If she feels either she or myself are under threat, she might act without thinking and come to terrible harm. That I cannot allow."

I cocked my head, wondering exactly what Marly had been up to. "If you're worried that Mar would really go after this Madame person, I think you better tell me why."

He paused. I myself have on occasion taken a few minutes to figure out how to tell a story so that it doesn't make me sound like a dick. Finally, he said, "Simply put, Madame wishes me gone from the throne…and the court… and life itself, if she had her way."

"Why? If you're both heroes? What did you do to her?"

He frowned, obviously irritated. "We have known each other all our lives, and we were once close. She may have made assumptions regarding the throne and her place on it."

"Assumptions? Did you lead that woman on?"

Now, he outright glared at me. "Yes, she had a hand in the battle that won the glass. Yes, we whispered words together. But I spoke no pledge to her in front of the court." He looked at the sky, which had not so much faded to evening as switched off. "I promised her nothing, and that was what she got. I can't help it if she took what we had between us, what was said in haste and under great peril, and…filled in the blanks."

"Um, Sasha, it sure sounds like you were engaged. I don't remember your saying anything about that."

Sasha smirked. "One could write a book about what you don't remember."

"What does that mean?" My stomach twitched, then subsided.

He shrugged airily. "Despite what she puts about town, I have broken no oath. She doesn't see it the same way. And with that in mind, you can imagine what she intends for Marly."

I sighed. "So, she hates both of you, possibly for legit reasons, and you think at the fête she'll try and draw out Marly's fire, which Mar is not ready to deploy. And you want me to be the unlikely voice of reason and stop her? But, why not just, like, enchant Mar into serenity or something? Or just enchant Madame and get it over with?"

"If it were that simple, I would have enchanted Madame thusly, and long ago. But she and I both have wards and guards that are not easily broken. That is the only reason why Madame and myself are not smoking holes in the ground right now. And second, the day will never come when I enchant Marly without her will or knowledge. I would rather hand Madame the crown and turn to dust. So, you see, it must be you."

I leaned in until we were nearly eye to eye. "I do see. But if I'm all that stands between Marly and your pissed off, super powered ex-girlfriend, you might want to give me a weapon."

He sat back, looking surprised. "But you have a weapon. You have the power to move Marly to safety."

I threw up my hands. "Enlighten me."

He smiled. "She trusts you."

I wasn't smiling. "Doesn't she trust you?"

Now he slammed his hands on the armrests, and I

jumped back. I didn't have any wards or guards, or even a can opener to defend myself. "I cannot be the one to whisper in her ear." He took a breath. "I will place myself in front of any danger. But she would not appreciate being told to hold back if our places were reversed. She is strong and getting stronger. But Madame is as old as I am and will not hesitate to strike." He looked at me, and his eyes were shining. "I cannot lose her. I almost did, not long ago." He held up his hand. "She can tell you herself, if she wishes it. But I am asking you, as you love her. Help me keep her safe."

I nodded slowly. "You actually honestly care about her, too. Don't you?" He didn't reply. "Okay. As long as we understand that she has free will. I'll do what I can, though."

Sasha blinked twice and then sagged with relief. If he let me see it, he must have been beside himself with worry. "Thank you. Oh, and of course you must not tell her what I require of you." Before I could agree or argue, he waved his hand, and fuck me if Aster didn't come trotting back in.

"So," I said, "you're somehow related to this Madame person, but you're like my chaperone? And its common knowledge that you all want to murder each other?"

Aster gave me a pitying look like I was a little slow on the uptake.

"Good," said Sasha. "We are in agreement. An excellent start." He raised his hand and the courtiers he had dismissed came streaming back into the garden. "Aster, show Ruby to her room and please find her something appropriate to wear to dinner." To me he said, "Well, this will be fun. You'll see Marly at dinner and meet some of my court. I'll see you then." He turned away to speak to his friends, if that's what they were. We were dismissed.

# 7

*March*

**W**alking into her garden, deep inside the winding pathways of the Unseelie Court, March followed behind a silent young fae servant. He wondered what this Madame Tournesol was expecting, and how he would compare. After all, here he was strolling in on two legs, not four. Not a hoof or horn in sight. Did anything about him say "I am something different?" He did have that tell-tale streak of white in his hair (like Rogue, as Ruby informed him; like Bonnie Raitt.) She must have known he often walked the world as a human-looking man. He wondered if she could tell he hadn't picked these clothes out for himself. (Other than his beloved work boots, of course.)

She sat and smiled and politely waited as he approached. He could feel himself being appraised. She thought he was pretty; she thought his suit was fine. She noticed his dusty boots without any judgment he could sense. So, she approved of the package, he could tell that much. That meant nothing, everyone approved of that. Could she sense his loneliness? His unhappiness? He knew enough about the humans to know they were masters at hiding what was close to their hearts, and that he simply couldn't do the same with any real skill. Maybe she sought them out, those dark impulses, to use his grief for her own purposes—he couldn't know until she told him.

Her maid said, "Master March, as you requested Madame." She crooked her knee and displayed her hands, then left them.

"Well," he said. "Here I am. It wasn't really a request, was it?"

She smiled. She didn't look happy even with that smile, but he thought her unhappiness had to do with something other than heartbreak. Perhaps he'd broken some sort of protocol by speaking first? He knew the human realm was by comparison an informal sort of place. A cat might look at a queen. Or a unicorn might.

"It was so kind of you to visit," she said, rising to her feet, as if he hadn't spoken, as if he hadn't introduced himself with a complaint. "May I offer you refreshments after your long journey? Some tea?"

He didn't really want tea, but he didn't want to insult her (again?), so he agreed that would be fine. Her maid reappeared with a glass tray bearing a slender throated pot—also glass—and two delicate cups. "These have been in my family for generations," she said, although he hadn't specifically admired them. "I hope the tea is to your liking."

He was clever enough at least to wait for her to sit before doing so himself, then quickly realized he was supposed to serve her. He suspected there was a long history behind all this: guests and introductions and food and hospitality. In this, the fae might be similar to humans, who had so much going on around food that it was a relief to eat by himself, when a mouthful of food could be nothing but pleasure.

Once poured, he carefully lifted the fragile cup with finger and thumb of both hands as she watched him intently; he didn't want to risk damaging it. It appeared to be the egg of a bird with the top sliced off, chased in gold. There weren't any birds in this garden. He wondered how old the cups were, how many generations. The effort of being a human-looking creature, of being presentable, of not crushing the cup, of smiling just-so at the flavor of the tea (bitter water) left him exhausted. But, he said, "Excellent." Then, he said, "Your invitation didn't exactly say why you needed to see me." When she didn't reply, he added, "You said it was urgent."

She nodded as if it were the most obvious thing in the world. "It is urgent," she agreed. "The Unseelie Court is in grave danger."

Now they could begin, with information taking the place of pleasantries. "When I last spoke with your...with Sasha, he said as much. He said there aren't enough children." She raised her lace handkerchief to her eye. "Forgive me, Madame, I did not wish to upset you."

"I am not upset, unless rage counts as upset."

"I would say it does, yes. Rage at..."

"Why, at our lord king of course."

He frowned. "I thought Sasha had found someone who might, um, alleviate that problem?" He was desperately trying to figure out how to say it without causing offense, but there was no way at all.

"He did bring home an... individual upon whom he hopes to inflict his person, yes."

He sat up a little straighter. "The person you're talking about is a friend of mine."

"Oh," she replied. "Is our king also? Your friend?"

He looked away. "Hardly. Madame, I answered your call because you said the need was urgent, but also to see Marly. Would that be possible?"

"I don't know why not," she said. "She doesn't need my permission to entertain callers." She paused. "She is only part of the reason I called you here, Master March."

"And the rest?"

"Did you notice, when you came into my garden, that it's in decline?"

He looked around, looked away from the woman and her tea set for the first time. How had he missed this? He who spent his life among the trees? He looked past Madame and noticed a small screen sitting on a low table, painted beautifully with scenes of elegantly dressed fae folk lounging in a garden, and from behind the screen poked out the tips of red flowers—the lotus of her stamp. He wondered if the screen came down when she was by herself. The table was partly in the shade, and the flowers he could see were turning black. Elsewhere, although some of the foliage was strong and vigorous, many of the sunflowers had gone to wilt, drooping on their stems; the roses, which should have been a blaze of red and gold, were yielding to black spot and dropping all their leaves; the yellowing, fading bracts of the heliotrope looked hopeless. And just in the background, the smell of decayed vegetation. The worst of the damage seemed to fall on the plants in the shadows, and he wondered if the shade was to blame.

"I do see. What happened?"

She glanced upward. "That happened."

Above their heads, above all of the Unseelie Court, sat the glittering, fair, and peaceful Seelie Court, like a lid hovering over a pot, except this pot was many miles below the lid of that kingdom. In a great circle around the upper court ran a series of giant glass squares. From this far distance they looked like a series of glowing white handkerchiefs laid end to end—a bright ring in a dark sky. One of them was missing. Most were damaged, flickering on and off, some more off than on.

"Or, I should say," she continued, "That continues to happen. Those glass mirrors are our only source of light. There was a war fought over them many years ago. Ever since our victory, the panes have been going out, one by one."

"Who would do..." he stopped, thinking. If she knew who would do such a thing, she would have asked someone else to visit her garden. An assassin, for instance. He asked the obvious question. "The Seelie Court—what is their position?"

"They will arrive in a few days' time for a fête. You can ask them yourself."

"And you?"

"I suspect everyone."

"Sasha." He was beginning to understand. Maybe it was an assassin she sought after all.

"Until recently, the shatters made a very slow progression. My studies in lambency have been…less than promising. I needed more time. And then he brought *her* home. And what happens next? The greatest shatter since the war ended. Tell me that was a coincidence."

"I still don't know what I have to do—"

"I needed someone very special. In fact, I believe you will play a vital role in the days to come. Because of who and what you are, you need no assistance to speak and understand our language. Any assault on our customs will be considered charming." She sipped her tea. "I understand you owe Sasha a great debt. Your life, even. And yet, when I looked to find someone who would happily see him brought down, one name came up again and again."

"I don't owe him anything. If he told you that, he was lying. Or whatever your version of lying is. I performed a service and he…repaid me. He said it himself at the time, that it wasn't a debt." March felt his expression turn grim; he couldn't stop himself from probing the static and fading places in his memories, the places he once walked by Ruby's side. "It wasn't a gift, though. Far from it." He gathered himself and had another thought. "What if I find that Sasha, by bringing Marly here, is not to blame? What if neither of them have anything to do with it?"

"Let me ask you a question. How much would it cost?"

"What? For me to lie and accuse Sasha even if he was

innocent?"

"Exactly. What is your price?"

He laughed. "The difference between your people and mine is that I *can* lie. I choose not to. There is no price."

She smiled. "That is what I'd hoped you'd say. I wanted you here because you are supposed to be beyond price."

"What if I wasn't? What if I gave a different answer just now, and there was something I wanted that I thought you could give me?" Did she have any such thing? If the cost was Sasha's life, it was too much. It had begun with those men with their hacksaw and that girl on the street, and ended with Marly. He'd taken one life, restored another, and balanced the scales—that was the end of that. But if there was another way...

She simply smiled. Now she was pragmatic. "Then I would have waited for the results, and at the hearing, I would have named you false, rescinded my offer, and possibly had you executed."

He raised his eyebrows. "Ah, I think you'd have a hard time—"

"I did say possibly."

"Well, fortunately, there won't be any need to try." He had another go at the tiny teacup. "May I ask a personal question?"

"I may not answer, but you may ask."

"Why do you dislike Sasha so much?"

She laughed. "Dislike is such a dainty word. What I'd really like is for Sasha to curl up into a ball and fall out of his own ass." Shocked, he laughed, and she joined in. When humans laughed together it bound them. Did this mean they were friends, now? "I know your people have long, long lives. But I also understand you aren't burdened by the weight of memory. This is a gift, I think." That was interesting. So, she didn't know everything about him. About Sasha, and about Ruby. Then he thought about lies, and how "your people" and "you" could mean different things, or the same thing. "You don't remember every slight, every cross word, each indignity... Well. The story is too long and boring to tell, but let me just say that without my influence, the Unseelie Court would not have won that war, and Sasha would not be occupying his precious throne."

"He is in your debt?"

"I *am* his debt. The cost of winning that war was me." There was a tinkling crunch, and he followed her eyes to her own hand. She looked down at the shattered teacup in her palm. Her expression never changed. "I was to be the queen."

# 8

*Ruby*

I followed Aster down a different hallway, this one made of tall, close-planted pencil-thin trees. I thought they were some sort of cypress. My folks had them in the yard back in Palm Beach, and Dad always complained that at least one was always dropping dead. "Looks like a rotten damn tooth," he'd say about the single brown tree, and Mom would remind him not to swear. These trees were a lush blue-green; none were brown. I didn't have a chance to see if they were actually living plants or more glass.

I caught up to Aster. "I feel like I know less than when we walked in there. Are you alright? I thought he was going to hit you."

Aster shrugged. "He's done worse."

"Worse than hitting you?"

"Well, there are those who say he's tossed away the crown."

"Tossed the crown where? Into the moat?" But he just chuckled like I'd made the cutest joke. Since he was clearly at least a little scared of Sasha, I wondered why he was so comfortable talking so casually to me, and how many others felt the same way. But I had an obligation to protect Sasha if I wanted to protect Marly. And yet I found myself also wanting to protect Aster. *You don't even know what you don't know*, I reminded myself. *Don't pick sides quite yet.*

I had picked up the pace to try and keep up with him, but I stopped to take a better look at what appeared to be a giant gilded beehive—if the bees were the size of kittens—growing halfway out of the wall. It looked more like art than anything alive, and if it had ever been occupied, it must have been a long time ago. I touched it—paper, dusted in gold. My finger came away shiny.

"Hey, what's the story with—" I called out, but Aster had moved along without me. I was hurrying down the hall when out of the corner of my eye I noticed something else unusual, though honestly, everything was at least a little unusual. A young fae woman with a heavy looking tray of used plates, cups, and napkins and whatnot made a sharp turn into what I thought was a solid wall. I figured it was the servant's entrance. Here, in this court, I guess even the servants have enchanted doorways.

I caught up with Aster as he turned a corner and we came to another door—the most normal-looking, closed door.

"Here we are," he said. "This room is for our guests from outside the realm. It mainly goes unused, and our king has required it to be refreshed for you. This is where you'll be staying while you are visiting. I think you'll find it comfortable. I'll be back to take you to dinner, but if you need anything, someone will be posted outside."

I looked at the doorknob, and at the keyhole. "I'm a prisoner?"

He looked appalled, and I was instantly sorry I had disappointed him. "Certainly not. If you wish to wander off on your own, you may. The attendant is assigned to you only while I am required elsewhere. They are there solely for your use. The king rarely sees fit to assign someone thus." He paused. "It is considered an honor."

"Sorry, I'm sorry." *Shit*. An apology. I hadn't been here an hour and already I was screwing up. I had to be more careful. "Look, I need your help if I'm going to...navigate this. I didn't mean to insult you."

His expression softened. "I believe you."

"Let's make a deal—I won't leap to assumptions, I'll ask questions. And you've got to promise not to be horrified when the questions are really stupid. Deal?"

"Deal," he agreed.

"Do your people shake hands?"

"We do now." He raised his hands to eye level and shook them vigorously. "Like so?"

I smiled. He was cute, like, on a cellular level. "Not exactly what I meant. When humans reach an agreement, they do this. Put your hand out...the other one." I took his hand and gave it a smart shake. "There. Now we have a deal."

He laughed, delighted. "Shake hands on a deal. I'll have

to show Madame." He practiced shaking his own hand. "Someone will be by with your clothing. Until then, Lady Ruby."

"Lady Ruby, I like the sound of that."

I let myself in and looked around, astonished. Unlike the rococo curls and floral flourishes of every wall and hall in the palace, this room was the dead image of a mid-century, mid-price, off-the-highway motel room. The walls were papered in a slightly textured light brown-and-beige straw print; the carpet was a shade of avocado; a long, low wood veneer desk/dresser combo took up the far wall, and a pair of matching pale green abstract paintings of trees and birds hung over the bed.

"There's a goddamn old timey phone in here," I informed the room. It sat on the bedside table and was tan with a numbered keypad and a row of buttons on the bottom. I picked up the receiver, expecting nothing.

"Yes, Lady Ruby? How may I be of assistance?" The woman's voice was cheerful.

I stifled a yelp. "Um, nothing. Sorry. Mistake, sorry, bye." Again! I hoped I hadn't accidentally signed up for eight million years of servitude.

The closet was empty except for an ironing board. (No iron—maybe even a modern iron had too much iron in it?) The bathroom was bright with white tiles and a shower/tub. The only thing that ruined the illusion of a hotel in Anytown, USA was that all the knobs, fixtures, and faucets were made of glass. I sat on the edge of the tub and read the label on the tiny bottle of shampoo.

*Display only. Do not uncap. Not for use on body. Do not use on hair. If used, put out flames with running water. Seek professional help immediately if inhaled.*

I put it in the otherwise empty medicine cabinet, figuring I'd be unlikely to knock it over and was glad I'd brought my own favorite rosemary-and-lemon scented shampoo.

I cautiously flushed the toilet and heaved a sigh when it simply flushed without flames shooting up or anything leaping out of it.

Back in the main room, I opened the heavy drapes to find a wall in the same brown/beige paper. No windows. Fortunately, there were a couple of lamps. And instead of a tube style TV bolted to the ceiling, there was a good-sized flat screen TV on the dresser, much nicer than the one I had back home. I picked the remote off the side table and sat on the bed.

*Bachelor Island*

*Getting it On*

*Love and Money*

*Losin' It*

And so on. I turned it off. These people need to read a book, or watch Downton Abbey or The Wire, or something.

Instead of playing with the remote, I began to pull open the drawers of the night table. Maybe I was looking for clues. Maybe the last "guest of the king" who'd been in this room had left something behind. At first, nothing. Then I remembered every room shakedown on TV I'd ever seen and felt around the top—bingo. I pulled out a couple of sheets of folded and re-folded paper. I don't know exactly what I was expecting to see, but it was definitely not my name.

*Dear Ruby, I hate it here, come get me, I want to go home.*

*Dear Ruby, This can't be my life!*

*Dear Ruby, Why didn't you just fucking **tell me**?*

I could hear her voice, spiraling up into an agonized wail.

"I did tell you," I whispered. "Just not soon enough for it to help." I still don't know why she got so, so angry when I finally told her Lauren was investigating her. I couldn't even say I was sorry. I had no sorry left.

I folded the wrinkled sheets back up and jammed them back into a drawer.

When the knock on the door came, I was grateful for the interruption.

Since there wasn't a peep hole, and I was under guard (sort of), I just opened the door. The feet almost kicked me in the face.

There was a whole-ass body hanging from above the door frame. For a second, I thought someone had hanged themselves outside my room. But then I noticed they weren't quite people-feet. They were jointed at the ankle like doll parts, the shoes sticking out from the bottom of neatly cuffed men's trousers. When the rest of the body fell to the floor, I bit back a scream. The body—which seemed more like a pile of dark and slightly shabby clothing—quickly rearranged itself into the form of a man, and I nearly screamed again. He had the face of an animated mask of drama, heavily creased in an exaggerated frown, and topped by a wild fright wig of black hair.

"Lady Ruby? A pleasure to meet you." He made an

elaborate bow, his grimace turning to an equally terrifying smile, and I backed away.

"Master Greaves, I think you've startled our guest." What with all the kicking and falling and bowing, I hadn't noticed my guard, a woman in a jade green and pale blue robe. She threw a convivial arm around the ugly man's shoulder. His grin turned to a mask of concern, which somehow made it even worse.

"My apologies, lady. It was not my intention to upset you. I am familiar with the human exercise of 'dropping in' and I thought you might appreciate something from your home."

Now, I was embarrassed. The man seemed harmless, and it was tacky to be rude to him just because he wasn't handsome. "No, I'm so—" I paused." It's fine...Master..."

"Greaves," the fae guard told me.

"Master Greaves. I wasn't expecting any visitors, and you did 'drop in' unexpectedly."

"Literally," the woman added. I reminded myself to get the woman's name, because she seemed sympathetic. "Master Greaves is here about your wardrobe."

"If I might come in," he said, "we can attend to..." he cocked his head at my outfit, "all this."

"Sure. Of course." I stepped aside.

No sooner had I thanked the guard (who told me her name was Marecy) than the strange looking man whipped out a yellow measuring tape and began talking to himself. I assumed it was himself, because the numbers he muttered and the way he waved the tape around didn't seem directed towards me. He then tucked the tape back into one of his many pockets and pulled out a tattered notebook. After scribbling in it for a moment, he looked up. "And we're done!"

"You don't have to, like, measure me or anything?"

He looked confused. "Did you want me to?"

"Not particularly. It's just...we're done?" He gave another bow, this one ending with a dramatic flourish in the direction of the closet. I pulled it open to reveal an explosion of vividly colored robes in lush fabrics. It was somehow both garish and classy.

"Did you just do that? Just now?"

He bowed again, a smaller one this time. "I humbly confess."

"How...how does it work?" I meant the magic, not tailoring.

"Balance," he replied. "To make, we must at the same time unmake somewhere else. It is all balance. Nothing is wasted, and nothing is ever really gone." I nodded. I'd have to chew on that for a while.

"Now," he continued, "to make sure my good work is showcased properly, do we know what we must do when first we meet?"

"We? You mean you and me?"

"No, my dear, for that flower has faded. I mean when you—arrayed in your new finery and such—meet a member of the court."

I thought of Aster's painful prostration. "Do I bow or something?"

"Or something!" He burst into laughter, his face

contorting. "*Ah ah ah.* Yes, quite. Or something. I shall teach you, so the only thing the folk will notice is the extremely elegant cut of your cloth." He took my elbow, and we stood side by side in front of the mirror on the back of the bathroom door. "Now, first is Trade. You must not bow to them, or take much notice beyond a polite nod for a cup of tea delivered."

Trade. That seemed like a "polite" word for maid. Or servant. Or slave, God forbid. "Master Greaves, are you..."

"Correct. No need for blushing or whispers. Trade is honorable. Next. The people you'll meet while promenading on the thoroughfare will be Citizens, all of whom are members of the Court. It was not always so, but these days..." His voice trailed off. Then he brightened and began again. "You yourself, as a guest of our lord king, are an honorary Citizen. And so, bow like this: from the waist, back straight, not too low or you'll make the person you're greeting nervous. A slight tilt of the head so you don't lose eye contact."

I mimicked his bow then asked, "I'm guessing there's a special bow for the king?"

"I might think young Aster has demonstrated, if I know our lord king."

"Yeah, it looked pretty uncomfortable. "Would I have to crouch like that in front of Sasha?

"You won't be quite as oblate, never fear. As so." It appeared all I had to do was curtsey with the addition of one hand on the small of my back and the other palm up in front of my face. It was an awkward position but I'd only have to hold it for a second or two.

"And," he added, "once you've been acknowledged by the

king, you no longer need to bow to anyone for the rest of the evening." He paused. "Even our lady queen, although I hardly think she'd demand a bow from you."

That got my attention. "Wait, there's a queen? Sasha didn't say…" That's when I got caught up on breaking news, and what Aster meant by tossing away the crown. "Queen Marly. Of course."

"Queen Melis, you mean."

"Girl got a new name and everything! Yeah, Sasha left that part out." Maybe he just figured I was smart enough to figure it out on my own.

"I see." Master Greaves looked happy (I think) to be the one to spill the tea. "The reason for this party is twofold: one to honor the life of the Seelie fae Lauren—as you know, and the other is to celebrate the ascension of our new Queen Melis." He paused. "She will, I think, be more than happy to see your face."

I nodded. *Ruby, why didn't you just fucking tell me?* I wasn't so sure.

Queen, though. I knew Sasha's whole idea was to make Marly his queen, it was practically the first thing he said when he met her. How did I feel? Shocked, of course, that it had actually happened—I assumed—with her consent. Happy for her? Maybe? And a little, tiny bit ticked that I hadn't gotten an invitation to the ceremony. But I guess maybe I knew why my invite got lost in the mail.

"Queen…say it again?"

"Melis. Queen Melis. She's still your friend, only her name has changed. Well, that and a bit of biology."

I looked up at him. "Thank you for telling me." This was going to take a minute to process, and I had more questions. I took a leap. "Can you tell me why Madame and the king are, um, at odds?" I felt like there were at least two sides to this particular story, possibly an entire fractal of sides.

According to Master Greaves, it was pretty far beyond a broken engagement. They won a war together, and then he just...walked away from her. No one knew why, although everyone had a theory. There was a price attached to the victory, though. They gained the glass but lost the ability to fix it.

"And every year on the anniversary of our 'great victory', the light fades," he concluded. "Sometimes only a little, sometimes an unimaginable lot. Our last shatter was devastating." He paused. "Devastating for we constructs, I should say."

"Oh, I'm so sor—" *shit* "—um, that's terrible."

He nodded. "Terrible, yes. And one way or another, many of us think the age of shatters is coming to an end, and soon." He looked at me thoughtfully. "You may be here to witness the birth of something new." He chewed his lip. "Or watch as we will all sink into darkness."

I was getting the idea that a straight answer anywhere in this place was going to be a long shot, but it was worth a try. "Does this have to do with the Seelie Court?"

He looked at me quite seriously, his brow even more deeply creased. "It is an old game they play, our king and Madame. Step carefully, Lady Ruby. I will help you where I can, but even I may not always be..."

"Available?"

He gave a crooked grin. "I was going to say reliable, but available has a gentler tone. Don't you think?" He rose to leave, and turned back to add, "I'd consider going with the gray."

"The gray what?"

But he'd already slipped out the door and left me alone, sitting on the bed.

# 9

*March*

**M**arch couldn't help but gape at the woman sitting across the table. "But he said—"

She thinned her lips in a sort of smile and tossed the broken cup to the floor. "He said?"

"Actually, he didn't. He didn't mention that he already had a queen at home when he convinced Marly to join him here."

"He would have been lying if he said I was the queen. I am not." She paused, and he could see the seething frustration barely hidden below the surface. He knew well enough that a face meant nothing, could hide anything, but the face this fae wore seemed designed to fool you into thinking she was a sweet and innocent young woman, as delicate as one of her flowers and just as pretty. Inconsequential. Nothing at all. He would do well to remember she was hundreds of years old and had helped to win a war. "The king is clever, I'll give him that. He is good at words. He arranges them just so." She leaned forward and stroked the petals of a rose, trembling in a vase. "As I said, without me at his side, he would have lost the war to the Seelie Court, and would have found himself a prisoner of war or worse."

"What happened? You were betrothed?" He didn't know much about the fae, but he'd heard they took their promises very seriously.

"It wasn't pledged before the court," she sniffed, "but it was whispered between us. And the war, well, it was hard. All wars are hard, otherwise they'd be more popular. Yes, it was hard. Yes, in fact, I might even say that I turned hard as well. For a while. Because I love my home too much for the softhearted to piffle it away. So, I made the difficult choices. And for what? To see him turn his back on me and put that... person on the throne."

March sat back. "That 'person' is my friend."

"Is she? Do you count many fools among your friends?"

"She was no fool when I saw her last, only much abused by the *kitsune* and in need of care. Are you saying she escaped one monster to fall prey to another?"

She gave the barest hint of a smile. For this lady, that was practically a guffaw. "Monster is a strong word, don't you think?"

"Not if it fits." This was turning into a game of "who hates Sasha more," and he found he didn't object.

"He is still our king. Now, your friend—" *She can't even say Marly's name,* March realized. "Your friend certainly arrived here in pieces. But she's been here long enough to see

77

what he really is."

He frowned. Marly was one of the smartest humans he knew, even if she wasn't quite human anymore. Surely, she could see the truth in front of her. "Have you considered you might have an ally in her and not even know it?"

She laughed and waved her hand dismissively. "Hardly. He has seduced her thoroughly."

He raised his brow. "Like, *thoroughly* thoroughly?"

"I believe I said what I meant. I have no ally there. My question is: do I have one here?"

*She needs me*, he thought. *It's been a while since anyone but Ruby needed me.* The feeling, the look on the lovely fae's face, served to warm him. "An ally in what, exactly?"

She took a moment to compose herself. *She feels things deeply. But she wears a brave and pretty mask. I think she is afraid not to.*

"The king has arranged for our enemies, the Seelie Court, to come here." She looked around at her failing garden, clearly distressed at the prospect. "Here, to walk on our land. To eat and drink and make believe it's all in the past."

"Isn't it?"

The glare she turned his way, he thought, wasn't directed at him. "To me, there is no such thing. Certainly, master unicorn, you understand at least that much."

He nodded, chastened. He wasn't good at the subtlety of court speech, and he knew he shouldn't try to be clever, particularly not with an expert.

"He intends to celebrate the life of the Seelie who was sent to learn about you before her untimely end. An insult, of course, to those we lost in the war. And then to further celebrate *that woman*. But I don't see a celebration. I see only the pair of them dancing on the bones of the life which should have been mine." She dabbed at her eyes again. "I cannot prevent the Seelie Court's arrival, but with your help perhaps we can keep the lights on." She gave him a brave smile. "Isn't that what your humans say?"

"With my help." He cleared his throat. "Help, how?"

"They intend some further humiliation for me. It is their tea and jam. I want you to find out what it might be. After what happened last time…" Her voice snagged in her throat and came out a ragged whisper. "I don't know if I could bear it."

"I'm sorry." But as soon as he'd said it, he knew it was a mistake. This woman didn't want pity. She wanted allies. "May I know what, um, humiliation occurred?"

Her look turned bloodthirsty. "They schemed together to imply he had suddenly seen reason, that they intended to return to the mortal realm, and I would be given the crown. In front…" her jaw clenched; she took a moment. "In front of the court, they laid my hopes out for all to see. It was quite the amusement, everyone said so." She welled up, and he couldn't help but notice the stars glittering in her black eyes and on her lashes. He wondered what stung her more—not getting the throne she so desperately wanted, or being laughed at. He had been denied something important; he knew what that felt like. Had anyone ever mocked him? He couldn't remember.

"I admit this sounds very unlike the Marly I know," he said.

She flashed fire at him. "A woman may change. She certainly has. Dallying with the king has proven corrosive. Spend a few moments in her company and think back on the kind-hearted girl you knew. She is gone." She took a breath and straightened in her seat. "Well, master unicorn, now you know why I've asked you here. To preserve what remains of my home, and protect me from…them. I hope you'll consider my request."

As she spoke, a knife edge of light crossed her face, and the garden faded into twilight. The vigorous sunflowers, the bright roses, the tip of the red lotus flower—they all collapsed and withered as the darkness touched them. The garden was dead, everything touched by shadows was dead, it only had the appearance of life, made possible, he assumed, by Madame's magic.

"There, and this day was shorter than the last. I always enjoyed a long evening, but if this continues, I fear we won't survive the night."

He nodded, thinking about what waited for him back home if he said he wouldn't help her. It looked to him as dark and lifeless as the garden behind her. "Despite what she's done—what you say she's done—I won't allow any harm to come to Marly. Beyond that, I'll watch the king, and listen for your name."

Her smile bloomed with relief. He found that he actually did want to protect her, keep her from harm. She seemed so fragile. He wondered for a fleeting moment if the thing he did to humans might also affect the fae. But the way she looked at him, her cool and alien gaze, told him no.

"Do your people know why you've asked me here?"

She dimpled. "You are a rare and marvelous thing. I am not alone in wanting to see a unicorn. And now that I have, the fair and perfect creature wishes to spend a little time with us, since he has never seen us either."

"I think you'll find me less than perfect. And what about Sasha? Will he be surprised to see me?"

She gave an exasperated snort. "I do not bow and scrape. But I'll make it clear you are my guest, so he'll have to behave himself." She pouted. "He'll probably exclaim I brought you here to antagonize him. Maybe he'll say I wish to disrupt his little party."

He smiled. "In that, he'd most likely be correct."

Her scowl deepened. "He's also brought in a playmate for his 'queen.' Another human. If you're done making jokes at my expense, you might try to find out why."

He leaned forward, ignoring her remark. "What human?"

She gave a little shrug. "I'm sure I don't know. Are they all that different, one from another?"

"Have you ever met one?"

"Certainly not. Travel outside the Realm is bad for one's health, everyone knows that." She looked at him curiously, her anger vanished. "What are they like? Humans?"

He took a moment. "I find them interesting."

"Interesting?" She laughed. "Is that all? Well, I suppose your kind have little use for them beyond momentary diversions."

He couldn't figure out if she was being dismissive of him or of humans. "I count a few among them as my friends. They can be more than diversions, Madame. They might surprise you."

By now the garden was all shadows. The remaining glass panes shone like a necklace around the perfect circular dark underside of the Seelie Court.

"Madame, I think there's something you should know. About me. About my...history with Sasha."

Her smile told him she had been waiting to see if he would tell her this part and that "you" and "your people" didn't mean the same thing at all. "Here we are at last. What really went on between you two there in the human realm?"

"What have you heard?"

"Less than I'd like. Only that you came away bearing—if you were a human or a fae, one might say you were bearing a grudge. What did he do to you?"

"It's more what he did for me. Thanks to him—rather, because of him—I'm not the same as the rest of my kind. You mentioned time and memory. I have that now."

"Explain."

"I'll try. Sometimes, I am still a mystery to myself. But I can count the days. I can tell you where I was two weeks or three years ago. I can feel things...notice things." That man in the truck, he wasn't grateful at all. But the woman in the car, she would have been. "It only seems to be here, among the fae, that I don't..."

She cocked her head. It was so dark that all he could see were the lights swimming in her black eyes. "Don't...?"

"Attract notice." He knew that wasn't quite right, and he wished Bel were here to explain it to this strange and intense woman. "Draw people—human people—to me. But that's not the most important thing. I cannot say Sasha wronged me, although I want to. He gave me back my mind, which had been lost in time and was slipping away. To do so, he removed all memories of me from a human who meant— means a great deal to me."

"Always a price with our lord king." She lifted her hand and the garden was bathed in golden light, although he couldn't make out a source, and rather than restore the garden to life, it seemed to throw a layer of fresh and vibrant life over the limp and wilted stems and flowers, like a pretty blanket covering a corpse. "That said, everything everywhere has a price, doesn't it?" She waved her hand again and her maid reappeared with a fresh tray of tea, new cups and a platter of cookies. His gone-cold cup vanished along with Madame Tournesol's broken one. "Well. Please, eat. I've kept you here long enough, you must be famished." She paused. "Do your kind get famished?"

He nodded, and picked one up. It was a fragile white disc dusted with some sort of pearlescent powder. When he put it in his mouth, it dissolved instantly.

"Sugar and morphine," she said. "An old family recipe."

"Excellent." He took another.

"So, given what you've told me, do you think you'll be able to avoid a confrontation with our king? At least this time you needn't worry, he won't be considering you for his private collection. He will be impossible to avoid, though."

He thought of the last time they came upon each other unaware; the battle fought on the Field of Significant Contact.

Ruby had been dragged along to that dark and frightening place. How much of it would she remember? "I suppose I can act as if it doesn't cause me physical pain to see him."

She smiled. "You must teach me that trick." She rose to her feet. "I'll escort you to your room. And then we must attend a dinner party."

He followed her to the garden gate. "A party? What is the occasion?"

"It is evening, and we are alive. What other occasion do we need?"

# 10

*Ruby*

I spent the next hour or so examining the clothing Master Greaves had created. He seemed partial to silk but had added a few simpler cotton robes—I guessed for days where I only had to take out the garbage and go to the grocery store—and one heavy woolen robe in the back. Did it get cold enough to wear something like that? I wondered again how long I'd be here, and how much time was passing back home.

When Aster got back, I told him about my encounter with Master Greaves.

"Well, now that you understand the stakes, hopefully this dinner will be less confusing." He rose and went to the now-stocked closet. "May I...?" He motioned towards the neat row of outfits.

"I mean, of course." I didn't want to be the one wearing the fae equivalent of sweatpants to dinner with the king. "Thanks. I know looking after me is your job, but I appreciate it anyway."

"Hmmm. It is my job, yes, but in helping you, I'm helping myself." He pulled a pastel pink and hummingbird green robe out, frowned, and murmuring something about "H and C" (was that a drink? Like G and T?), he put it back on the rack. "Being seen with you is a service performed for the king, which is very good for me indeed."

Status. I remembered how much Lauren wanted to do things like host dinner parties, that it was sort of like how they earned money. "Well, happy to help you be upwardly mobile, I guess."

"This one, I think." He handed me a floor length dark charcoal gray silk robe with deep cuffs and a wide belt in persimmon. It was gorgeous. Master Greaves was right about the gray. "It's formal without being pretentious. It says you know that you have no real place here, but are honored to attend and are in a position to learn from whomever you encounter."

"It says all that, huh?" I went into the bathroom and changed, folding my jeans and blouse over the towel rack. I adjusted the belt as best I could and came out so he could give me a once over.

He reached for the belt and retied it so the knot lay flat against my left hip. "This suits you. I think you'll be well received."

"Master Greaves is sort of a genius," I said, admiring the perfect fit. "I was—well, I was surprised by the way he looks. Um, is it rude to ask where he's from?"

Aster shrugged. "He's from here. From the Belly, I

imagine." He noted my blank look. "Below the city. The Belly."

"He's fae?" Other than his all-black eyes, he bore no resemblance to the sleek and pretty fae I'd seen so far. And where was the Belly? Did the Unseelie Court have a downstairs? A rec room maybe?

"Oh, of course not. He's a construct, I think you'd say. Like a clockwork mechanism, you know—with gears and cogs and such. The workshops and so on are down below. He's a made thing."

"He's a robot?"

Aster looked delighted. "I know what that is! It's a dance." And he crooked his arms and began twitching wildly to an imaginary rhythm. "Do doot, do doot, do do do do..."

*Herbie Hancock*, I thought, *has a lot to answer for.* "Oh my God. No, I didn't mean..." but I had to laugh. "No, a robot is a...um, a made thing, like you said. He seems really alive, though."

Mercifully, he stopped dancing. "He is alive. All constructs are alive. They may want less and feel less than we do, but they live, and they serve us."

"They serve you? Then Trade are constructs..."

"It is considered rude to call them constructs, though that is what they are. They prefer Trade."

I wondered who took the poll. "Right, but it's the same thing. But if they're clockwork, how are they alive?"

"Their lives come from magic's breath instead of the seed and the bud. They are as alive as we are. Different, but living. But you asked about Master Greaves. He was one of the first—I believe the very first construct. The workmanship hadn't been quite...perfected, I suppose you could say. But he is a part of the court, and it would be unthinkable to imagine life without him. Sadly, we may have no choice, poor man."

"Poor why?"

"The light—or rather, the lack of light. The rest of us will adapt—get used to darkness, I suppose, or make lights of our own—Madame Tournesol leads the way in the study of lambency. But Master Greaves, as I said, he was a prototype. His life is drawn from light, and he will live only as long as it lasts."

"Well, maybe this thing with the Seelie Court...." I thought of how I'd cringed away—almost screamed—when Master Greaves showed up, and felt awful. Light, lack of light. Broken glass. My immediate thought had been an attack by the losers of the conflict Master Greaves had described, but I reminded myself: *you don't know how much you don't know.* Like, how many constructs were there here in the Unseelie Court? I decided I'd talk to Master Greaves again and ask him what his life was like.

"That is our fondest hope. On that, even Madame and our lord king are of one mind."

I pulled my medallion from inside the neckline. "In or out?"

"Out, I think. Bearing the king's token is no mean thing. Shall we?"

I followed him down yet another corridor, this one lined with simple, graceful urns planted with palm trees, which led to a large, low-lit hall, already mostly filled with several hundred fae. As if on cue, they all turned their dark, glittering eyes in my direction. Conversation ceased.

Aster stepped forward. "It is my honor to introduce Lady Ruby, the human guest of our lord king."

*Oh, clever*, I thought. *He got points for this right off the top and still credited Sasha, so he won't be in trouble.*

As Master Greaves instructed, I gave the most graceful bow I had in me, and—great news!—I didn't fall on my face. There was a smattering of applause, and the fae went back to their drinks and chatter. Aster led me to a table, seemingly chosen at random, where Sasha and his entourage sat. In front of Sasha sat two small glasses and a large bottle. I found it strangely comforting that in this room of shimmering butterfly-hued fae, he wore black. It was hard to imagine him in anything else.

*No, that's not true. When we had dinner, he had on t-shirt and sweatpants.* And he had drunk beer and eaten pizza and looked like he wanted to climb out of his skin. Now, in his home, he looked utterly at ease, leaning back in his seat. I blinked several times—yes, he was really wearing a crown, but it was nothing like I'd ever seen before. It was a handful of lights, like fireflies, hovering several inches above his head. At first, I thought I was seeing things in the strange light of the ballroom, but no. When he moved his head, they followed. For some reason I got the impression they were alive. Beautiful, strange, and sort of off-putting—that was Sasha to a tee. I performed the special bow reserved only for the king, feeling a little like a circus poodle, and he gave an appreciative nod. I was dismissed for the moment.

I followed Aster to our table, where each place was

set with a pair of chopsticks intricately folded into a linen napkin. I watched a young man seated nearby deftly skewer a bite of his meal and slice it into pieces with one hand, all the while gesturing to his tablemates with the other. I figured I'd have that skill under my belt in no less than ten years. The sticks were beautiful little pieces of artwork, though, made of polished ivory chased with silver and set at the top with darkly twinkling stones—rubies, maybe, or garnets— and one stick of each pair did indeed have a knife edge. The young man caught me looking and smiled, raising his glass, and said something that sounded like *"elishy."* I smiled back.

I'd figured the fae would all have the same pale skin and flowing black hair Sasha had been sporting when we met, but I wasn't even close to being right. The man who smiled at me had dark skin and some nice twists in his hair. Aster's was long and dark, and he wore it in what you might call a messy bun. In fact, that seemed to be the prevailing style. But a lot of them had multi-colored hair—pinned up, braided, cut short, shaved off, or long and loose. One young lady seated several tables away from us had a pattern of bright yellow flowers somehow printed on her dark hair, and the tall guard who stood at Sasha's elbow had light blue and brown stripes. A tall and handsome fae holding court in the corner had short dark blond hair which wouldn't have been out of place back home. Trying to figure out if it was paint or dye, I looked over again at the flower girl. That was when she leaned back and I saw the guest sitting at her far side.

It was a human. And not just the only other human in the room, but the most beautiful man I had ever seen. I whistled to myself; where had they found him? He had a silvery stripe in his hair, bright against his glossy dark brown locks, and apparently, he hadn't heard about the dress code. Instead of a colorful robe, he wore an expensive looking dark suit with a purple shirt open at the collar, and, weirdly, boots that looked fresh from a work zone. But despite his gorgeous face and sharp clothes, he looked both angry and deeply unhappy. He said something to the girl sitting next to him, and she smiled to reply, tipping her pretty face up at him.

*Who is that guy? Not a fae, that's for sure. Well, he looks like he's going through some things, better give him a wide berth.* Oddly, even though we were the only humans in the room and he could hardly have missed me, he didn't even glance in my direction. I poked Aster in the side and nodded at the miserable looking man. "Looks like we've got another human. What's his story? He looks like he's going to a funeral."

"The other...you thought he was a human? Oh, that's no human. Can't you tell? Never mind, you'll see soon enough. He is with Madame. Certainly, she'll want to meet you."

It took me a second to put together the fresh-faced girl with the hero of the revolution. "That's Madame? She looks like a teenager!"

"Looks mean nothing here. We look how we wish to be perceived. Madame wishes to look towards the future— hence her youthful appearance. But she is hundreds of years old. She is the last of her line."

"But didn't you say you were her nephew?"

"An informal relationship. I am the progeny of a dear friend of Madame's, long departed." I thought that was kind of a roundabout way to talk about your own family, but maybe it was different here. He continued, still talking about Madame. "Their motto was—is—'The Stage Remains Bright,' which refers to her family's role in maintaining the light from their position behind the scenes."

"Cool. What's your motto?"

"Oh," he laughed, "you are kind to think so. I am not a member of a great family." So, this dear departed friend wasn't quite as fancy as Madame herself; how progressive of her. "There are only four, and of those, two are nearly gone. Our lord king, for instance. His family's crest is 'First and Only,' but if he doesn't produce an heir, it'll have to change to 'Last and Lonely.'"

I laughed. "That is super bitchy! Did you make that up?" He nodded in a way that said "maybe." "Who else is there?"

"Do you see that lady there at the next table? With the green and gold? That is Lady Dahlie. Her family's motto is 'Every Leaf a Story.' They do all the gardens; even though they've mainly moved from living plants to glass, they're nearly as venerated as Madame Tournesol. Lady Noisette is behind you. She's an expert on you." I raised my brow. "I mean, on humans. A 'popumancer.' Smart girl. A little..." He waved his hand next to his ear in the universal symbol for slightly nuts. "And there's Lord Amory—he's quite tall, standing there near the gate, see him? 'The Past is Singing.' They—there's a couple around—they are the archivists. It is said that he was the father of poor Dahlie's child. She's among the youngest of us. I think you—and our new queen of course—must be by far the youngest people currently in the realm, but she is considered quite young as well. When her bud failed to flower, it was a great tragedy."

I took a minute to thank the luck that put the biggest *yente* in the room right next to me. I was about to ask how old Aster himself was, when another hush fell over the room. Everyone turned to one of the arched gates.

Marly—excuse me, Queen Melis—alongside the biggest wolf/hawk combo that ever fell out of a CRISPR had just walked in.

# 11

*March*

**M**arch, once he got the stupid tie off, took a deep, relieved breath. He knew what a human party was like—loud, usually, fun, sometimes—but a party among the fae? He might be breathing easier without the tie, but he could hardly relax.

Madame Tournesol arranged for him to stay in a suite quite near her own, saying she wanted to make certain he came to no harm. *What harm*, he wondered, *did she expect?* Yet he came away from their first meeting prepared to protect her, not the other way around. The room looked more like a garden than a human dwelling to him, although he quickly realized the vines climbing the walls and the mossy ground underfoot were either fabric or colored glass.

"There's not actually any furniture," he remarked.

She looked confused. "Do you require any? I was under the impression you made your home in a forest, far from your beloved humans." That meant she expected him to change back and forth at her whim. The low growl of discontent he'd been feeling grew to something barely audible. "Did you say something?"

"No," he said. "This will be fine."

"Excellent. We are already late for dinner, so you'll have to look around later." She eyed him. "Yes, you will do. Follow me."

He tossed the tie into a pile of leaves—real leaves, he thought, but he wasn't sure—and with a sigh followed her back down the dappled, tree-lined hallway. These trees weren't even pretending to be real. They looked as if they'd died ages ago and had been cast—or at least painted—in silver and bronze. There was a metallic scent in the air which came and went but got stronger when they entered the hall where the dinner would be held. The room was large, open to the sky, and partially lit by the great ring of glass far above them— right now they gave off about as much light as a full moon of summer. He picked out the damaged panes and the gap where one was missing, and wondered again who benefitted. Scores of candles floated above the diners' heads. It reminded him of a place where he had attended a football game one Friday night with a lady who clearly was there to worship him. He recalled how the players were young and beautiful. He wondered briefly if she was still alive, or if the players were. He counted the years in his head and decided it was possible, then wondered at the skills he suddenly possessed.

It looked as if the majority of the fae court was in attendance tonight. There were hundreds of them, all black eyes drifting with interior light. The lights didn't always track towards the person they were speaking to, and he found this disorienting. He momentarily lost sight of Madame in the crowd, and turning to look for her bumped into a tall, golden-haired fae man, who steadied him on his feet.

"She went that way," the man said with a smile. He hesitated; the man's hand lingered on his arm. For the first time since arriving, he felt noticed (as he had come to think of it.) Even with those strange dark and glittering eyes, March could appreciate beauty, and he smiled back. The man nodded and strolled off in the other direction.

He turned to watch Tournesol make her formal bow before Sasha, then go to her chosen table, and she motioned for him to join her. The tables were scattered around in no discernable pattern that he could see—some were set for two, others large enough for a dozen or more, and there wasn't an obvious head table. He had been to banquets before, and the king or empress or sworn protector was generally at one end, a conspicuous table where everyone could see them. Sasha seemed to be at a random table with only a handful of companions. He supposed eventually they'd have to acknowledge each other.

From one of the huge arched entryways, a voice rose above the others.

"It is my honor to introduce Lady Ruby, the human guest of our lord king."

*What a strange coincidence*, he thought, *that there should be another human lady named Ruby*. Along with everyone else, he turned to look. And of course, there she was: the human, Sasha's guest, his Ruby. Of course. She stood close to the fae who had announced her. She was so pretty. She scanned the room with the same suspicious-yet-intrigued look he remembered so well. He felt cold all over. His heart was racing.

"Are you quite alright?" Madame put her hand on his arm. "You looked so interesting just now." She looked past him. "Oh, do you see what I see?"

"Of course I see her," March said to Madame. "How could I not?" He was already angry at being dragged into the contest she and Sasha were playing, and now, looking at Ruby, he had a feeling in his chest, a new one he didn't want to name. He didn't like it. It hurt.

"So," Madame said, leaning close, "that's the woman you care for, the one Sasha did his little mind trick on?" She looked delighted. "What will happen now? Will she suddenly remember you in a blinding flash of passion and lust?" He glanced at her; she was far too invested in this. She didn't seem like a fragile china cup anymore. More like a delicate and intricate weapon. A stiletto, the blade hidden. "Honestly," she said, clapping her hands, "this is exciting."

He was about to ask if this was some sort of game to her, but it obviously was. To her, he and Ruby were no more real than the characters on the television shows all her kind adored. "She won't distract me from watching out for you," he said. "Don't worry."

"What will you say to her? Will you try and seduce her again? Oh, our king was clever to bring her here."

He stared at her. "You people are crazy."

At this point, all he could do was avoid looking in Ruby's direction. He imagined she had seen him by now. All she would know was that there was someone in this strange place who was at least a little like herself. She wouldn't know what he truly was. He had to maintain the fiction that he didn't know her.

He was distracted by the next person to enter the ballroom. All of them—Sasha included—rose to their feet. He was relieved to see Marly make her entrance. By her side was an absolutely enormous dog. No. He looked closer, and saw that the creature looked like a mix of a wolf and a falcon. She'd gotten herself a griffin somewhere—did she, like Madame, also require a bodyguard? She kept one hand on its gleaming flank as she crossed to Sasha's table where she bowed deeply. He acknowledged her with a raised glass—did he call her Elisha? Were there more names to learn? After speaking with Sasha for a moment, Marly headed for his own table. She didn't acknowledge him at first, but waited while Madame and all the fae gathered nearby performed elaborate curtsies. Marly folded her arms and smirked. Her bow complete, Madame gave an icy smile and walked away. With that, Marly's face returned to someone he recognized.

"March, holy shit, is it good to see you. Oh, meet Clover."

He bent just a little—the creature's head was nearly the level of his chest—and offered his hand. It sniffed, and then wrapped itself around his legs the way some huge dogs do, nearly knocking him over. She grinned and reached over the animal to embrace him. "He likes you."

"Are you really the queen?" he asked in a low voice.

"You bet your ass I am. What are you even doing here? I mean, I'm sure happy to see you."

"And I, you. I was called here by Madame. It has to do with Sasha and the Seelie."

"And you're over here with *her*? What's going on? Did you see Ruby? Why is she sitting over there? "

"You need to ask Sasha, but I can tell you she doesn't know who I am."

She drew back. "What? What are you talking about?" Behind them, Sasha loudly cleared his throat. "Look for me later."

"Ask Sasha," he repeated. He watched as Marly, closely followed by Clover, made their way back to Sasha's side. As soon as she was seated, she leaned close to him. March could only imagine what she was saying. Sasha remained impassive, even as Marly became more animated. Finally, he put his mouth near her ear and said something that made her eyes widen. She stared at him in apparent disbelief. Then she folded her arms and sat back, frowning.

"Your friend looks displeased," Madame had returned to her seat.

"She's not the only one." He wished he could talk to Bel about what he was feeling, why his heart ached, how his throat closed up when he thought of what he'd say to Ruby, for there was no way to avoid her. When you have a thousand times a thousand years to learn a new thing by exploring it, turning it over in your hands, holding it up to the light, it had time to make sense. You could learn to live with almost anything. But this avalanche of emotion—everything, all at once—was unbearable.

"I've sent over a bottle of wine," Madame said, either not noticing or not caring about the storm blowing through him. "Humans like wine, I know that much." She peered at him as if seeing him for the first time. She looked surprised at his unease. "You look like you could use a glass yourself."

# 12

*Ruby*

Once we were seated, **Aster** leaned on his elbow and said, "So, tell me about the human world."

His eyes were a little wider than before, and his voice a little louder. I figured he was trying to distract me from my obvious nerves. He also brought his chair closer to mine, and spoke right against my ear.

Once Marly had shown up and done some sort of *Cirque du Soliel* bow in front of Sasha, everyone lost interest in looking at me and started talking to each other all at once. As she headed for the good-looking guy's table, she gave me a little wave, and I returned it. I guess she had royalty related shit to do and I'd just have to wait my turn. That was fine. But the look that Madame gave Marly when she made her bow, well, if she'd put any juice behind it there'd be nothing but a pile of ashes where my friend once stood.

Madame stomped off, and Mar and the young man

embraced like old friends.

Who was this guy?

And what was going on? I knew Madame hated Marly. Was the cute guy Madame's date? And she was jealous of Mar and the cute guy being friends? Or maybe she was angry on behalf of the king, because Marly was paying attention to another man and it was some fae protocol thing? Or—and this was the most likely—I had no fucking idea who was doing what to whom.

Music—I guess it was music—came from somewhere, sounding like a chamber orchestra made of bubbles and car parts. I touched the pendant, trying to imagine what it would sound like in here if I took it off. Probably blow the back of my head off.

"It seems so exciting," Aster continued, "living on the beach, all that arguing and fornicating."

"Wow!" I laugh-snorted. "Wow. Okay, so hang on. First, I don't live on the beach. And there's really much less fornicating than you'd think."

"Oh, well." He furrowed his brow, rewriting his script. "Then in a converted loft downtown, with big windows overlooking the bay and skyline. Or on a ranch. With giant candles and bundles of hay." He frowned. "In retrospect, that seems like a fire hazard. Anyway." He nodded to himself. "Lots of humans live on a ranch." He brightened. "Of course! The ranch people are usually waiting for that special someone. Before the fornication. My mistake."

"Oh my God. Uh, let's back up, like, a lot. Look, you have to remember the shows you watch are all..." He was so proud of being an expert on humans. Suddenly I didn't want to crush his dreams. "Well, they don't show exactly how every human lives. Only a tiny little fraction. Probably because they're the prettiest people, and those are the nicest places."

He tried to hide his disappointment. "I have to confess that you don't look like most of them." He frowned. "Your hair isn't...you're not.... I guess you don't have a job like chicken enthusiast or pet therapist or dental hygienist?"

"No, I don't. And only one of those is a real job. Me, I'm a bartender."

He perked up. "I know what that is. But I would have thought that was Trade." I guess he figured he was basically calling me a working-class robot, and put his hand to his mouth, horrified. "I'm sorry, I didn't mean—-"

I thought of what Master Greaves said, and took his hand and placed it back on the table. "There's no shame in Trade. It's honest." He smiled, relieved, and definitely did not move his hand from mine for a long moment. I reached for a bottle of wine which, while I was looking elsewhere, appeared on the table. Maybe it came with the meal, like at an all-inclusive resort? "Let's have a glass. We can drink to asking questions, even dumb ones."

He poured us each a glass. "Especially dumb ones."

I sipped. "Interesting. Doesn't taste like *wine* wine. It's good, though." I took a deeper drink, and realized despite the utter weirdness of it all, I was enjoying myself. Aster wasn't hurting my good time, either. Those black eyes of his, I was kind of getting used to them. And he had the nicest, shiniest hair. "Okay, it's time." I set down my glass, and had a whack at the one-handed chopstick challenge. On my plate (again, it wasn't there, and then it was) were rectangular bars of something glistening and pink, with a creamy white sauce daubed on them. I wrangled my sticks and tried to slice/stab/retrieve. After one stick landed on the floor and a sizeable piece of whatever I was supposed to be eating followed it, I gave up and speared a bite with the remaining stick and ate it county fair style. "Also weird and good," I said. "Tastes like chicken jello. What is it?"

Aster retrieved my stick from the floor and handed it to a waiter (Trade?) who scuttled past, sweeping up the food and dropping clean sticks on the table in front of me. I did a quick doll-parts scan but no one here had Master Greaves' style detachable feet. "Tonight we are enjoying wrens' brains in crème gallant. The chefs do a fine one."

I slowly set down my stick. "Um."

He took a bite, his single hand in graceful motion with the pair of sticks. "Needs salt." He smiled at me. "As humans like to say."

*Wine for dinner it is,* I thought. *Better find something to soak it up. French fries. A bag of chips. Or even just some bread, that would work.*

"Brains not to your liking?" he asked. "Here, try this." He pushed a basket towards me, which, like everything else, appeared when my eyes were pointed in another direction.

I peeled back the heavy brocade napkin, hoping it wouldn't be a variation on organ meat. Miraculously, it was a loaf of bread. I thought briefly of Persephone, but this wasn't Hell and I wasn't the one taken by the lord king of a dark place.

After tearing off a hunk of perfectly decent crusty white bread, I went back to my wine and took another sip, and then another, trying to pin down exactly what the taste reminded me of. Fruit? Some kind of perfume? It was right on the edge of my mind.

"My investigation requires another round," I announced.

"Investigation?" he asked. "Are you a bartender slash detective? Will you be interrogating the Seelie folk about the Shatter?" The way he pronounced it made me think he'd never said "interrogating" out loud before and felt pretty slick about getting to use it.

"The what? Oh, the glass, right." I took another, longer sip. "This flavor, I can't figure it out. It's this close——" I waved my hand to show Aster just how close the answer was, but instead whacked the person sitting behind me in the back of the head.

"Shit! Oh, sorry, man. Girl. Miss. Lady." And now I was in her debt, too, whoever she was. Damn it!

The fae turned and gave me an uncertain smile, gently fluffing her own short hair. "It's nothing."

"You are so pretty," I told her. "I love your hair. You look just like my friend Lauren. Did I hurt your head?"

"No, of course not," the fae woman assured me. "I'm fine."

"Oh, wait a second. I know who you are." I pointed at her, getting a little too close to her nose. She leaned back in her chair to avoid my finger. "You're that Madame Noisette. Am I right? I'm right, right?"

She laughed and nodded. "Lady, rather. There is only one Madame. But, yes, I'm Noisette." She cocked her head and frowned. "Did you say Lauren? As in Lauren C of the Seelie Court?"

"Yuh." My head was feeling a little swimmy and I wondered how I could get out of this conversation, even though I'd started it. "She was my friend. She was so cool. Have a nice night."

She gave me a penetrating look. "I hope we can continue this another time. Enjoy your evening. Perhaps some more bread." She turned back to her companions.

Aster looked at me curiously. "What was that all about?"

"She looks like my friend Lauren. Hey, do you know her?" Then I remembered Lauren was dead, and it was so, so sad. I felt tears gather in my eyes. "She was so nice to me, and I loved her haircut." *Wow, I am really into hair right now.*

"Lauren...I know several Laurens."

"With a C. For *Seelie*." Shuh, even Nostette knew that.

"No." He shook his head. "I don't know anyone from there. How would I—"

"Rosehips!" Then I burped and covered my mouth. "Noisy was right. Didn't eat enough bread." Sirens were going off in the back of my mind, but I couldn't figure out why. "Is it hot in here?" It was hot in there. I reached for the neatly folded collar of my robe and dragged it away from my neck.

"What are you doing? Leave it." Aster pulled my hand away. Then he looked up at me, wide-eyed with recognition. "Drunkenness! I've seen this part. Humans are so entertaining."

"Nuh uh," I said. "I only had like two glasses of wine. That's not drunkenen. Ness." The alarms got louder. *Oh shit*, I realized. *I am straight up wasted*. I knew the signs from working at The Hare, but typically I was on the other side of the bar. That rosehip (I was sure of it) wine must have been some sort of super potent homebrew, like fae Everclear. I reached for the bread but missed the basket. *Dammit!* It was like when I looked at something, it took another few seconds for my brain and yet a few more for my hand to catch up. "Asher, I'm not feeling..."

"Aster." His pretty dark eyes were wide with excitement. "What would you like to do? Fling furniture? Accuse someone of lechery? Or shall we find a hot tub?"

I closed my eyes for a second and the room lurched. "Bad idea. Bad, bad. Never shut your eyes..." I looked across the table, and sure enough, a glass of water was within reach. Beautiful, crisp, cold...but what if I knocked it over? I'd literally kill myself. I inched my arms along the table, and holding the glass with both hands like a racoon, crouched down to drink it. Taking a sip felt like victory because my mouth tasted like dumpster water in August. Now it was time to go to bed, like, urgently. But when I straightened up and got to my feet, my head spun violently, and my knees went watery. The water glass bounced out of my hands and rolled across the table, mercifully not falling to the floor. I wanted to reach for it, but my arms weren't working. The edges of my vision were going fuzzy and gray. This wasn't just drunk, I realized. Something was wrong. The music stopped.

Aster leapt up and put his arm around my waist, pulling

me upright. "I've got you. Oh, is this the part where you want to dance?"

I laughed weakly, then groaned and leaned my forehead against his shoulder. "Archer, I'm not feeling so..." Another burp, and this time bile burned the back of my throat. "Please take me home, March, please, I don't want to be sick in front of all these people." I couldn't make out faces for all the smears and blurs of light, and closed my eyes again. I was so tired. But as soon as I did, a blast of white light came straight through my lids, and a warm hand touched me on the forehead. For a split second the ballroom was gone, and I was standing on the back porch of a cabin looking out over the mountains. Fireflies hung in the air, and I turned to kiss a man I couldn't see. Then it was gone. *So this is what an aneurysm feels like.* But when I opened my eyes, I was sitting on the floor with Aster by my side, and I was completely clear-headed. Standing over me was a unicorn.

*Holy shit, maybe I did have an aneurysm.*

Wonderstruck, that was the only word for how I felt, looking up at it. It radiated rainbows and gazed at me with anguished forest-colored eyes. *Why does it look so sad?* Hardly daring to breathe, I reached out to touch it. It danced back on slender legs, its silver hooves raising sparks on the slick, dark stone floor. *Aww, I bet it's soft. I bet it feels good.* My eyes watered from the light pouring from the creature's horn, and although I never wanted to stop looking at it, I bent forward and wiped my face with the sleeve of my gown. When I looked up it was gone. The good-looking guy I spotted earlier was standing nearby with Marly, who was holding his jacket as he buttoned his shirt. He looked furious. Was he mad because he missed seeing the unicorn? Sasha had strolled over and stood by with his arms folded. He raised his hand and the music (such as it was) started again.

"Did you guys see that?" I got to my feet. Aster put out a hand to help me up, but I waved it away. "You saw it, right? No one else saw the unicorn?"

"Madame," the cute guy said in a tight, low voice that cut through the chatter and whispers, "please tell me about the wine."

The giant dog thing gave a low growl that also sounded like the word "pet," and Marly put her hand on its head.

Madame Tournesol, who had been in conversation with one of her tablemates, looked up. "Hmm?"

"You sent the human woman a bottle of wine. What was in the wine?"

"Oh," she said. "That. I hope she appreciated it; it was one of my better vintages. It was just roses, is all." She craned in her seat. "Is something the matter with your human?"

"Just roses?" Sasha looked amused. "No special kind of roses?"

"Oh, fine. It was fortified with the blood of black roses."

Sasha and the cute guy exchanged looks. Clearly, they knew each other, and there was something like respect in the look that went between them, even though it sure looked like he was Madame's date, but now he was angry with Madame for...

"Hey, lady, did you just try to poison me?" Aster gasped and looked like he was about to pass out, but I stormed over to Madame's table. "Black rose blood? What the fuck is that?"

She looked up, wide eyed. "Such language!" She was so very lovely, so innocent. "You accuse me?" Was that a tremble in her lower lip? To my astonishment, I was suddenly filled with the desire to apologize for even considering such a... Madame laughed like a fish wife, breaking the spell. "You caught me. Oh, it wouldn't have killed you, that would have been rude. I just wanted to see what would happen. You all should thank me," she said to the onlookers. "Didn't you all want to see a unicorn tonight? You're welcome." She looked at the young man, who had followed me to her table. "Good thing you were here. On *Lookin' for Love* they call this a 'meet cute.' Does that apply in your case, do you think?"

*Do I know this guy? No, I'd remember, wouldn't I?* Remember, remember.

I rubbed my forehead. My brains were clearly still organizing themselves, and my stomach was churning queasily.

The man began to say something, but I cut him off. "We're not doing this here, whoever you are." I turned to Sasha. "If you can't guarantee my safety under your own nose, we've got a problem." I looked at Marly. "You, get your ass over here. We're leaving."

Marly turned to Sasha, who shrugged and said, "You heard her. Get your ass over there." He looked at the cute guy with obvious displeasure. "Welcome to my Court. I'd say this is a surprise..." he glanced at Madame, "but I should have expected no less. Perhaps you'd care to join me for breakfast in the morning. Assuming there are no casualties between now and then." He smiled in a way that was also the opposite of smiling. "I'd love to know all about your plans for your stay."

The guy looked at Madame, who smiled serenely. "I suppose I'll see you then," he replied.

I took a deep breath, forcing myself to calm down. "Aster," I said quietly, "please. Take me back to my room." He also shot a look at Madame, who gave a shrug and pointedly looked away. That seemed to calm him down a bit as well. Sasha may have been wearing the crown, but it looked like this young woman was calling the shots, at least if you were a good-looking dude.

Aster smiled. "I'd be pleased to accompany you." He crooked his elbow and I took it.

"Am I supposed to bow at anyone on the way out?" I whispered.

He covered a smile with his free hand. "After that performance? They all should be bowing to you."

"Seriously, how embarrassed should I be?"

"You? This wasn't about you. Madame Tournesol has just struck a blow at our king, that's all."

"Say what now?" Marly stopped in the doorway, her hands on her hips, the huge dog thing at her side. "Madame struck at me because Ruby's my friend. She fucking hates me because I got the crown." She smiled, not a nice smile. "Among other things."

"Perhaps, but in this case, I don't think you were the target," Aster said. He spoke quietly, many of the fae still watched. "I would say she forced the unicorn to reveal himself to Ruby and the court at her leisure. She manipulated the unicorn, a creature of great power. She wants our king to know she can."

As we turned to leave the hall, I spotted the beautiful man watching me with the same look of despair the unicorn had shown. At his side, Madame Tournesol caught my eye. She smiled at me and turned away, taking him with her.

# 13

*Ruby*

"**So, this is where they** stuck you?" Marly took in the overwhelming beige-ness of my room with her glittering new black eyes. Well, I guess they weren't that new, she'd been here over six months. Her pet, if that's what it was, circled three times and plopped itself down blocking the door, exactly like a dog.

"I've stayed at crappier motels. With you, in fact," I reminded her. "Who's your friend?"

"That is Clover, he is my baby, and you will love him." She ran her finger along the edge of the dresser and gave a nostalgic sigh.

"I stayed here for a while when I first landed. Not the end of the world, even if it is a little…"

"Hideous?"

She laughed, nodding. "'kay, first things first. Help me out of this nightmare outfit." She glanced at Aster, who was obviously trying to stay out of range of Clover's massive beak. He had an eagle head, because of course he did. Clover, that is, not Aster. "Go get us something to eat."

"With no brains in it," I added. "If you don't mind. Thanks." I realized it made me a little uncomfortable to hear Marly bossing Aster around like *he* was Trade. He was the one fae I was starting to think of as my friend. *But you don't know that,* I reminded myself, *no matter how shiny his hair is.* "Oh, and a couple of beers, please." The effects of the wine had completely dissipated, and I was actually kind of thirsty.

"Oh, good call. Ask Ilex to help you. The kitchen will know." Marly waved dismissively at Aster. "Go on." He gingerly stepped over Clover and left.

With Aster gone, I helped Marly undo the lacing up the back of her indigo silk gown, a pair of double spirals. It was way fancier than the simple robe Master Greaves had made me. "You'd be the queen of the Renn Faire in this thing."

"It's so damned pretty, but it smooshes my boobs like a mother." She gave a huge sigh as I loosened the panels of the bodice, and the dark robe slid to the floor. Under it was a cotton slip dress that also somehow had a high, stiff collar. It was in a contrasting shade of rosy pink, designed to show through when she moved. She unhooked the buttons down the front, stripped and tossed it on the floor, then stretched like a cat, clad now in a corset-like device and bikini underwear.

"The bottom half looks human," I observed.

"Yeah, I didn't really have a choice with this eperon thing, but Greaves couldn't get me to part with my drawers." She unlaced the stiff paddles, and pulling them off, gave another contented sigh. "Robes are in the closet."

"They are?" I opened the louvered closet door to find two thick terry cloth bathrobes right up front. Over each left breast, *Hotel Unseelie Resort and Day Spa* was embroidered in curling blue script with our names underneath. "Get the fuck outta here. You've been busy."

"I learned a few things from Sasha. He figured out teaching me magic was the best way to *lure me to his side.*" She laughed and pulled the robe on. "At least, at first. Oh shit, forgot." Like Sasha, she had a mantle of tiny lights. While his hovered above his head, hers were tangled in her curly black hair. "Come on, sweet babies." The lights slowly detached themselves and drifted towards the ceiling. "I mean, I love them and all, but sometimes I can feel them moving."

"Like the time the lizard jumped on your head."

"'...but how did it get in the shower?'" we said in unison.

"Now *that*," Marly said, "was a crappy hotel." She sat on the bed. "Mind if I stay over?"

"Like a sleepover? Yeah, I guess we've got some major catching up to do." The bed, which had been at least a foot away from me, bumped me in the back of the leg like a dog looking for attention. "Oh, come on."

"I have to have room to move. And you're a notorious cover hog."

I sat next to her on the now gigantic bed. "So. A few questions."

Marly's smile faded. Then she held up her hand. "Oh, hang on. This'll help." She retrieved her party dress from the floor and hung it over a chair, then reached into one of the pockets. "One nice thing—loads of pockets. Totally handy. Come to me, friends." She rooted around until she found a finger-sized tightly corked glass tube. She looked up. "Can you get me a glass of water?"

*I guess her legs are broken*, but I fetched her a glass from the bathroom. Marly tapped the contents into the glass. I'd seen this before, from Sasha. Another way of getting her onto his team?

*"Eleshii,"* she said, and drank the water in a gulp. "That means, like, increase, or grow or something."

"Like cheers?"

Marly nodded. "But with flowers. They're obsessed. Flowers and reality shows." She blinked hard a few times and looked up. "Better?" Her eyes were now more or less human in appearance, but honey-gold, not the warm brown I remembered. "I'm still getting the hang of them, so sorry if I start looking up at the trees and into your headlights at the same time."

I smiled at our old joke about cross-eyed squirrels. Maybe Marly hadn't changed so much after all.

A knock at the door brought Clover to full attention on his feet, and when Aster opened the door, the beast only very slowly decided to step aside.

"Nice boy," Aster said, his voice quavery, and rolled in what appeared to be a room service cart. He made a respectful bow towards Marly and then turned to me. "I think you'll enjoy this, Lady Ruby." He smiled at me. Yeah, that was a decent smile. "No brains. But I have a feeling you'll come around—"

"Was there anything else?" Marly asked him. "That you needed?"

"Mar, he was just—"

"Forgive me," Marly said. She didn't even both to smile. "We have so much catching up to do. You understand."

Aster cleared his throat. "There's, um, beer and ice cream on ice. Underneath. I shall see you tomorrow. My Lady." He bowed quickly, and left with his head down, giving Clover as wide a berth as possible

"Rude bitch," I said. "He's been really nice to me."

"He's Madame's. Don't let that pretty face fool you." She pulled the big silver cloche off the tray. "Let's see. Pizza. Oh my God, I'm dying. It's like nothing but hors d'oeuvres at every goddamn meal, not that I'm allowed to eat anything."

I nodded slowly. "Yeah, that sounds like a nightmare." What did that even mean? She wasn't allowed to eat?

Marly set the cover on the floor. "Listen to me, I'm being such an idiot. I'm sorry." She scooched over to sit next to me. "Honest to everything, I am so glad to see you. I missed you like crazy. I'm just not used to talking to normal people."

"You are kind of acting like a weirdo."

"You gotta be one, here. Forgive me?"

After a long hug and a few tears, we both sat back. "Are you seriously, really okay? This place is nuts."

Marly took a long time to answer. "At first I hid in my room and cried. I wrote you a million letters—"

"I was wondering about that."

"But they were all, 'I hate it here, come get me.' Like I was at sleepaway camp or something. I burned all of them."

*Not all of them.* "And I could see myself getting better. Physically, I mean. My hands and everything, it all healed. And after a while I decided to try. Just...try. I began to spend time with Sasha." She held her hand up. "I know some shit went down between you, but he's been good to me." She gave me a worried look. "And don't worry. I'm going to make him fix what he did. Sometimes I think he doesn't understand how emotions work, but other times..."

"Fix? What did he do? Did he do something to hurt you?"

She sighed and nodded, like something had been confirmed. "Right. No, it had nothing to do with me. He would never hurt—" Her eyes widened. "You don't know the whole thing with the *kitsune*, do you?"

"That guy? Um, I know he kicked my entire ass at your apartment. The dragon, Ms. Tha, she's got him now. What about him?"

"It's not a nice story." She told me how the fox man had poisoned her—literally poisoned her thoughts. "He basically planted a cursed fishhook in my throat. At first, I thought I was just sick—after all, I was in pretty bad shape when I got here. But everything else got better, and this got worse. I had...God, this is hard to talk about." She pulled on her hair, and took a breath. "I had terrible intrusive thoughts. I couldn't control it. I thought everyone hated me. But mostly, I hated myself. I—I tried to hurt myself."

I grabbed her hands. "Mar, no. I should have been here."

She squeezed my fingers and let go. "There was no way you could have known."

"I guess we have to kill him?"

She gave a carnivorous smile. "Only a matter of time. Anyway, Sasha figured it out *barely* in time to stop me. He saved my life. He de-cursed me in front of the whole court." If I'm not mistaken, she looked a little starry-eyed. "In retrospect it was incredibly romantic." She shook her head, smiling. "And you don't have to feel bad or worry about me, I am in very good hands, between Sash and my little buddy over there." Clover raised his head with his eyes shut; I've seen cats do that when they know you're talking about them. "Since then, he's taught me some fancy magic."

"And I hear you got some new jewelry? That goes on your head?" I pointed towards the little cloud of lights, hovering near the ceiling.

Her smile was wholly her own. "I did." She got a little unfocused, no doubt recalling the ceremony. I could wait to hear the details, maybe forever. Possibly she knew that because she went right back to business. "It was partially to make sure every-single-fucking-body is at least polite to me."

"Except Madame, I gather."

She nodded. "Yeah. I mean, I'm never going to make any headway there. I don't trust her. And you shouldn't trust your pal Aster either. I know he's cute as hell, but he belongs to her."

I made a face, surprised at the sudden stab of disappointment. "Like, they're doing it?"

"No, gross. He's pretty young, as these folks go, and she thinks of him as an adopted nephew or something. If he's trying to get all up into your business, you can bet she told him he had to. If he had any sense, he'd go after Dahlie, since Amory couldn't get the job done. He should have a go."

"Mar! Come on, the poor thing just lost her baby."

Marly gave me a long look. "Rube, that was over three hundred years ago. There is only one thing that matters here. It isn't about glory, or sitting on the throne, or who marries who. The literal only thing that matters here at the Unseelie Court is having a baby. Everything else is noise. If Aster somehow successfully knocked up Dahlie, the two of them would kick Sasha and Tournesol—and me—into a ditch." She shrugged. "But I doubt he'd try, since it would put him up against his Madame."

"And what about you? Does Sasha mind you telling me all this? Or that you're staying over?"

Marly inhaled half a slice of pizza. "Oh, this is so good. No, it's not like that. I don't have to ask his permission." She looked inside the cart and brought up two bottles. "And he's actually kind of a cover hog, too."

I stared at her. "Give me that beer."

# 14

*Ruby*

I held up one finger while downing half the bottle of beer in a long gulp. "Okay. Now let's go over that again. Because it sure sounded like you said you—"

Marly lifted her chin. "I know you think it's weird—"

"It's not weird, it's gross and... God, Marly. It's Sasha. So yeah, it's weird *and* gross."

Marly's eyes flashed gold in black, the little eye-creatures momentarily overcome. "Okay. You're right. So, tell me what I ought to do, then. Tell me why the man who saved my life, taught me magic, put a fucking crown on my head, married me, and *loves* me—yeah, I said it—is weird and gross. Should I go home with you? Would that be nice and normal? I guess I could live in an iron-free bubble—or wear oven mitts on my hands, that was a good time. Or maybe Tournesol will have her way, and they'll throw me into the moat, or send me into exile on the Fields. Because these people do not play, Ruby.

They're dying and they know it, and they all know—every single one of them who are so, so polite to me—they're all waiting to see if their king's dumbass human is going to do her one job. And since you think it's so weird and gross, I hope you've got a better idea because I sure as fucking don't."

I thought about all the nights we'd stayed up together, grading papers. Me drawing on my extensive knowledge of the eighth grade English curriculum, and her stressing over her kids. Sometimes one of them would be disruptive, and the parents weren't there or didn't care. I remembered how sometimes Marly cried over the ones who were troubled, because sometimes she couldn't help them. Now, that girl was gone. This new one had no tears to cry and only herself to save. Well, herself and the entire Unseelie Court.

"I suck," I said. "I'm dumb. It's the actual reason you came here, and I know that. I'm really sorry, Mar." Outside of feeling stupid, I wondered in a tiny back corner of my brain, if apologizing to Marly was a mistake.

She just sighed; her anger spent. "I know. You are dumb. You're lucky you have nice tits." We laughed, and it was a little better.

"Okay, then," I said, clapping my hands smartly so Marly would know I was serious. "Plan time. If we're gonna do this, we're gonna need, like, a flow chart, post-it notes, some string..."

"Rube." Marly smiled. "I don't really think you can help me with this. Unless you want to get in on it, and *that* would be gross and weird."

"Oooh, point taken. I guess all you really need is a bottle

of tequila and some lube." I was struck by a horrible thought. "That *is* how they..."

"Uh, yeah, in my experience." We drank our beers for a moment. "I mean," Marly added, "it's not like he's hideous or anything."

I burst out laughing. "You like him."

"Sure, once you get past his personality, which is what the tequila is for." She smiled. "Now I'm being dumb. I *do* like him. I more than like him. In fact—"

I bounced off the bed, cutting her off. "Oh, shit, I can't believe I forgot! I have something for you. A couple of things, actually." I dumped my backpack onto the bed and began rooting through it. "Here." I handed over a flat, red leather jewelry case, and she opened it.

"My mom's pearls." She looked up at me, wide-eyed. "How did you—"

"Also this." I passed her a big Ziplock with a bottle inside. "It's your fancy-ass conditioner, still got some in there and somehow not dried out. And here..." At the bottom of my bag, folded over so they fit, a pair of kiwi-green cowboy boots.

She traced the stitching on the boots, her eyes filling with tears. (So, she could cry, even with those eyes.) "How did you know?"

"Sasha. In his invitation, he was pretty clear that if I didn't make a stop and bring all this with me, I shouldn't bother showing up."

She held the boots like they were her babies. "Make a stop? Where?"

"You can thank Dr. Bel. She got you a storage unit. She said if it went south up here and you came home in a hurry, you'd still have all your stuff. Me, Shanti, and Claudio about broke our asses in half hauling boxes."

Marly looked deep in thought. I don't think she even heard me. "I told Sasha I wanted to go home and get this stuff ages ago. He said…he said he had an idea. I figured he'd forgotten all about it. I guess not." She shook her head. "He's full of surprises."

I helped her put the necklace on, and we both admired her. Even in a bathrobe, with her hair snarled, she looked good. Like a queen, even. The Unseelie life seemed to be agreeing with her. She reached over and hugged me.

"Thanks for the delivery. And please send my love to Clo and Shanti. Of course, I'll have to do something nice for Dr. Bel, and I think you can tell her to stop paying for the unit." She sighed. "I wish he was just one way. Like, this was obviously a really sweet gesture. And he's reliably lovely to me. But I'm not the only person in the world, and I can't just blow past what he did to—" Whatever the last word was came out garbled, and my stomach gave a warning twitch.

"To what?"

"To, uh, Madame Tournesol. Can you imagine being engaged for like a thousand years and then your fiancé drags home some fine young piece and tells you to pack?"

I got the distinct impression Marly didn't care if Tournesol set herself on fire, and that she had changed the subject. I wondered what she didn't want to say. "That would suck for her," I agreed. "So, when are you going to…um, you're drifting a little bit, there." I pointed at her face.

"Shit, right or left?"

"Right." With some concentration, her eyes came back into alignment. "Better? Okay, where were we?"

"You and Sasha were, uh, when does this happen?"

She played with the pearls and smiled dreamily. "Oh, it's happening. Like, a lot."

*He is not gross and weird*, I told myself firmly. This girl wouldn't be so smitten if he didn't have *something* going for him.

She came out of being dickmatized long enough to add, "As long as you and March are here, I guess it'll be happening a little less, though."

"Yeah, I need a tour guide—me and who?" I looked up and something struck me. Why hadn't I mentioned this before? "By the way, you did see a big ass fucking unicorn at that party, right? I'm not nuts?"

"No, honey." Marly looked sad for some reason. "We all saw him." She sighed. "Sasha said I should tell you myself... oh." She noticed the empty beers and with a wave, refilled them. "I can't make new things, I can only redo stuff that already exists. I can turn these robes back into those fancy silk ones later if you want."

I rubbed my forehead. "We're talking about a lot of different things right now. Forget the robes, they're fine. Just tell me who...March? Who that is."

"March is a unicorn—the unicorn."

"Really? They have names? That's cool. I guess he touched my head with his horn and de-poisoned me. That was nice of him. But where did he come from?"

"He came from his table. He was sitting next to Tournesol."

I cocked her head, trying to put it together. "No, there was some hot dude sitting there oh my God are you telling me the hot dude is a part-time unicorn?"

Marly smiled. "Got it in one. I think he prefers 'shifter.' His name is March, and since Tournesol brought him here, it has to be for something, like, nefarious. Not him, her." She paused. "I think you'll like him. He's...I think you'll like him."

I wasn't sure why how I felt or didn't feel about some creature I didn't even know was important, but Mar looked pretty intense. "Was that what Sasha wanted you to tell me?" I got another little rumble in my mid-section, like an echo of all the pain and nausea I'd felt for the last six months. But it faded almost immediately.

"That. Just—that's who March is." She looked away, or at least I thought she was looking away. The little creatures that made her eyes human were again drifting around on their own. I pointed at her left eye and she swore and forced it back into alignment. "Sasha says if Madame has any cards to play, it'll be at the party. He thinks she's convinced March to be her bodyguard."

That got my attention. A unicorn was probably a pretty powerful creature to have your back. All Marly had was me, *sans* even a can opener. And Sasha said "don't tell her" so even if I tried, I couldn't. I tried a workaround.

"Madame?" I said, "Who poisoned me for fun? It looks like we need to be protected from her. So, is this March banging her, or is he just an idiot?"

She looked offended and I felt like I'd made a mistake. "Rube! Neither. God. He's just…he doesn't know a lot of people. He can be too trusting." She looked at me warily. "Sasha thinks you might be able to get March to tell you what she's up to."

"Me? Why would he tell me anything?"

She pursed her lips. "Just…just try talking to him. He might even be the one needing help."

I tried to put all the pieces together. "So basically, March will be watching us to see what Sasha's planning, and I'll be doing the same with him, while keeping you both out of trouble."

She looked up at me, quick and fierce, and I realized what I'd said.

"Both?" she asked.

"Come on," I said, playing it cool, "you know Sasha worries about you." I worked up a devil-may-care grin. "Congrats, I'm *your* bodyguard." That was just not true enough for it to slide under the "don't tell her" radar.

She narrowed her eyes. "One *krav maga* class does not make you a bodyguard. But you're right. He does worry. Congrats, you're hired." She drank her beer, and I was relieved to see she let it go. "At any rate, I'm willing to bet no one comes up with anything useful, and this is just the two of them entertaining themselves." She shook her head; her eyes jiggled. "This is what I meant by Sasha being more than just one way. But the Seelie coming here, now, that could be really important." She poked me in the shoulder. "Maybe me and my hired muscle should do a little poking around on our own, see what Madame has in mind."

This was what Sasha warned me about. This is why I was here. I deployed myself. "Promise me," I said, "that we do this together. You're the literal queen, and when I do something wrong, they'll assume I'm just a clueless human. I may even be amusing. Between us we'll figure out Madame's scheme—I know it." And I could make sure she didn't blow shit up while we were at it.

Marly picked at the paper label on her beer. It was plain white and said BEER in block letters. "What about March?"

"I honestly don't have a fucking clue. What does a unicorn do all day? So far all I've seen him do is stand around and look pissed."

"Ruby!" Marly looked surprised. "He cured you—from the wine. He saved you. He..."

"Mar, what? You have that look."

She pushed her dark curls away from her face. "Fine. I'm going to tell you something, and it's going to blow your mind. Are you ready? Fish chair even *bibliothèque* random easy pliers. Backpack." She leaned forward. "Are you okay?"

I laughed, mystified. "Is that code for something? 'Cause my mind isn't blown yet."

Marly frowned. "Squirrel window *debonaire* leafspring, scissors. Scissors maybe stamps, floor."

"That was just a bunch of words. I don't know what you're trying to say."

"Stamps floor! Pliers, stamps. Floor." She'd raised her voice, and Clover lumbered to his feet and came over to lay his head in her lap. He really was cute, once you got over being terrified that he'd rip you in half. "Ruby." She looked really upset. Was she sick? Was the *kitsune's* curse back? "Tell me what happened to me. In the year before I came here. Can you do that?"

I chuckled uneasily. "Um, if *you* don't know, we have bigger problems."

"No," she said, "I think I do. It's just…my memory of the whole thing is a little fuzzy. Can we compare notes?"

"Sure," I agreed. "You know, my memory is also kind of…" My stomach lurched. Too much pizza and BEER, I guess. "Um, let's see. Yeah, it all began when you took that trip to Belize. Some kind of spider bit you and you almost died. We were all so worried. I remember wondering if you'd turn out to be a superhero, and damned if you didn't."

"Right. Belize. Bug bite. I didn't die." She nodded slowly.

"And then Lauren—of course you know who she is— she came from the Seelie Court and started asking questions about you. And I didn't tell you." I paused, wondering if she'd start yelling at me like the last time I made this confession. "And by the time I did, the *kitsune*—that fucking guy again— had taken you hostage. I know, I know—it's on me. I should have warned you. You know how bad I feel about it."

"I surely do." She kept her eyes down. "I understand." Then she looked up. "And Sasha?"

"Well, he showed up after the *kitsune* killed poor Lauren. And then he—the fox man, that is— kicked my ass, and then Sasha scooped you up and brought you here. Does that bring us up to date?" I felt like I was forgetting some important part of it, but Marly was nodding.

"It does," she agreed. "Thanks. It makes a lot more sense now."

I hadn't realized how much I missed just hanging around with my girl. "Here, Aster said there was ice cream...hey, can you turn these empty bottles into spoons?"

"Yeah," Marly replied. "I guess I can do that." She stroked Clover's feathered forehead and looked oddly disappointed, or maybe it was just her eyes.

"You all right? You've got that look again. Oh look! Chocolate chunk, and not a bit of brain in sight. Aster comes through." I smiled. "I know, he's like a spy, but ice cream—that's got to count for something." I paused. "A sexy, sexy spy."

"I'm gonna make him fix this. I promise."

I nodded. "Sure, you are." I wondered if I ought to be worried. After all, Marly had undergone a major physical change, but now she was talking gibberish. Was that part of it? Was she forgetting how to speak English? I waved the ice cream at Marly. "Do you want some of this?"

"Hand it over. And stay away from Aster!"

I snickered. "You're not my mom."

After catching up on Claudio (dating) and on Shanti (pissed that she wasn't invited), Marly yawned hugely and stretched. "My eyes are slamming shut. We should get some sleep; tomorrow's edition of the Bullshit Rodeo starts early."

Listening to my darling girl (and Clover) snore, I was pleased to note that at least some things hadn't changed. But others sure had. Marly hadn't asked about her students, not even once.

# 15

*Ruby*

I cautiously opened my eyes, expecting a headache at least, but to my surprise, I felt fine. I turned to the pile of blankets next to me and gave it a shove.

"Huh? Fuck off," came the muffled response. That at least hadn't changed. Marly had always been hostile in the morning.

I pulled the pillow off her head. "Fuck off yourself. Time to get up." I threw back the covers and padded around the debris strewn room. "Looks like the end of a frat party in here. That was a lot of beer." I handed Marly—who was now awake and blinking sourly at the mess—one of the empties, which we'd apparently tossed onto floor the night before. I delicately picked up the sticky carton of ice cream, which would have melted all over the end table if Clover hadn't daintily lapped up the drippings. "And also we are slobs."

"I'm not sure it *was* beer," Marly said, squinting at the

bottle in her hand. "I mean, it looked like it, but I changed it from an empty bottle to a full one a couple of times. I don't know what it actually was."

Whatever it was had gotten us good and drunk, then evaporated harmlessly while we slept. I figured that at least was a win assuming it didn't give us magical tumors.

"Can you change it from an empty to a coffee?"

Marly thought about it. "Ilex usually makes me coffee…"

"Well, la-ti-da, Queenie."

She gave me one of her new, slightly feral smiles. "First, blow me. Second, I am willing to try. Here we go. Coffee." She passed her hand over the bottle, which was also suddenly a cup of what looked like *cafe con leche*. I took a tentative sip.

"Tastes like beer flavored coffee. I'm going to hit the shower, you practice."

"I could declare you clean. That's what Sasha and the rest of them do. They just…are clean." She waved her hands across her body to demonstrate, fingers fluttering. "Like with the clothes, they're what they say they are."

"Fancy," I observed. I didn't want to be her guinea pig, though. "I'll take a pass. Make me some coffee, please."

I stood in the shower and thought about ordering a coffee from the hands of the queen. Once I was finished, I got back into my bathrobe and wrapped a towel around my wet hair. "What about you? Gonna declare cleanliness? I mean, I'm not saying one of us smells like a brewery at this point…"

"You know, I could have you exiled," Marly reminded me. "How's the water pressure?"

"Excellent." I tried the latest iteration of coffee. "Oh, this is much better. What's the industry standard for breakfast around here?"

"Whatever you want," Marly called from the bathroom. "I mean, if they figured out pizza, they can fry an egg."

When the knock on the door came, I jumped up to answer, pulling off the towel and blotting my wet hair. "That'll be Aster." I stepped over Clover and pulled the door open. "Hey babe, we were just talking about bacon egg and cheese sandwiches—oh. It's you."

March's face fell, and he looked at the floor. I felt slightly bad, but how should I know what kind of a reception he was expecting? Did people usually throw a parade when he came over? He had traded his good suit for a dark ochre robe with forest green at the collar and cuff but kept his dusty work boots. Tilting his head, he looked at me through that odd streak of white hair. "I could go for a slice of tres leches cake."

"For breakfast? Too sweet for my tastes, but you do you."

Clover muscled past me, and March dropped to one knee so Clover could wrap his massive front legs around his neck. March grinned at him, ruffling his crest. "Hi, boy, good morning, yes, you're very handsome."

Clover said, "Pet."

"And he talks now," I said. "You did hear him say 'pet,' right?"

March had his face buried in the soft fluffy feathers under Clover's wickedly sharp beak. "Of course he can talk, he's a smart boy."

I cleared my throat. "What's up?" I asked.

"Sasha asked me—-well, told me—to tell you he'd like

to have breakfast with you. And Marly, of course." He took in my still-damp hair, robe, and bare feet. "Are you close to being ready?"

"There is a legend among my people that Marly will one day get out of the shower."

"I'M ALMOST DONE."

"Noted," March called. Then he dislodged Clover from around his neck and got back to his feet. "Are you...feeling better? After last night?" He looked genuinely worried, and for a second, I thought he was talking about the beer party Marly and I put on. "Yeah, I'm fine." Then I swatted my forehead. "The wine. I'm a jerk—I never thanked you. I mean, I didn't realize what you are...were...I mean...You know, we were never actually introduced. I'm Ruby."

"I'm very pleased to meet you, Ruby." He took my hand and it must have been the dry air of the Unseelie Court because there was an actual spark. We both jumped back. I laughed a little, but his face fell again. "I'm March. Well, I'll see you at breakfast, then." He turned away.

I wondered about that little jolt, and the way he'd been so friendly with Clover. It was odd. I swear we'd had that same introduction before. *Déjà vu* is so weird. Anyway, it was nice to know he had other modes than morose. As good as he looked when he was annoyed, he looked even better when he was...if not happy, at least not in a rage. I watched him make his way down the corridor; I supposed in the direction of Sasha's breakfast nook. I smiled, watching the fae in the hallway draw back to let him pass and then turn to watch him go by. They seemed a lot more impressed with him than they'd been with me. I mean, obviously—I'm not a unicorn. For some reason, it was hard to keep it straight in my head. I'd seen him in both forms—like this, and in his other, magical body, but I kept...forgetting he was also this unhappy, beautiful young man.

"What did March want?" Marly was ready to go, wrapped in a white gown with deep bell sleeves. The reverse of the fabric was black. It was what my grandmother would have called a *schmatta* compared to last night's dress. I guessed Marly had re-made it into this new one. I thought about Master Greaves and balance, and wondered if I understood exactly how it worked. I had a strong suspicion I did not. She did a pirouette for me, then pulled on her beloved green boots with a happy sigh.

"Striking," I said. "I have to get dressed, then we're off to see the king for breakfast." I couldn't bring myself to say "your husband." I just couldn't.

Marly reached for me, gripping my wrist. Her not-quite-right eyes drifted away from me, but her voice was intense. "We do this together. Right?"

I nodded. "Together. Me and you, like always."

"And March," she reminded me. Clover hauled himself to his feet, hearing the name of his new bestie.

"Pet," he said enthusiastically.

"Oh, right." Marly stroked the animal's head. "He can only say one thing but he's very expressive. Aren't you?"

"Pet," he agreed.

"Sure. March, too." I agreed. "Since it's important to you."

She sighed. "For now, I'll take it. Let's go."

# 16

*Ruby*

"Thank you for attending. I trust we all had a peaceful, casualty-free evening." Sasha was back in the garden where he had welcomed me to the Unseelie Court, but this time it was set with a long table and chairs for everyone. The light, while not what you'd call bright, did make me feel like it was morning. It was still a little like stage lighting—cheerful and fake. The glass panes high above us looked like they had shifted a little—maybe it was the angle that changed the quality of the light as the day went on.

I spotted Aster and waved him over. Marly was just a little too late to stop him sliding into the chair next to me. She tried to glare, but her eyes were now pointing in two completely different directions.

"Girl, just take them out." She did and looked both happier and more alien without them. I watched the maids and waiters as they set our meal—looking for doll joints or wig hair, but they all looked like normal fae, which is to say sleek and gorgeous. The only difference was the Trade folk actually lifted a finger. I smiled at the woman who put a cup in front of me. She was Marly's maid; I think her name was Ilex. Instead of smiling back, she stared as if I had done something wrong. Master Greaves did say a word of thanks was appropriate. I'd wondered what I'd screwed up this time. I caught myself in time to not apologize, when she leaned over me, and as she poured the coffee said, "You are here to help my mistress?"

Surprised, I looked up then turned back to my plate. If she wanted to tell me something, I'd need to be more discrete. "I am."

"Make sure you understand not all of us agreed." At that, she called Clover to her side and they vanished down one of the hallways.

No one noticed, and she was gone before I could ask her—agreed to what and who? I drank my coffee (Marly's version was better) and thought about it. Were there factions or divisions within the Trade community? And if this had something to do with Marly, then it also had to do with Madame. Maybe Marly's idea about investigating was a good one. It sure sounded like the constructs were more than just Rosie the Robots—they seemed to have at least as much interior life as any of the fae I'd met. And if I took point on this mission, I could make sure Marly stayed safely out of trouble. The only thing I needed to do was figure out where they hung out. Trade lounge? Trade after hours bar? A dog park for Clover? Then I remembered the hidden door near the beehive. That had to lead to the underground network of labs and workshops: the Belly.

Marly, who for some reason did not have a plate in front of her, watched me struggle with the sharp chopsticks to pick up my scrambled eggs (I hope that's what they were, and not like, snake eyeballs in bearnaise or something). She finally snatched them away, held them between her palms and, after a moment of concentration, handed me a fork; ivory and silver, and with the red stones now polished smooth and part of the handle. "You probably should keep this with you," she advised.

Aster looked crestfallen. "I should have realized."

"Yeah, well, you're not her friend," Marly said.

"Mar, dial it down. Aster, it's fine, you didn't know."

Sasha watched us with a small smile. I'm sure this was the sort of thing he was hoping for. March, at the far side of the table, was scowling at his plate. I hoped if we had to spend time together, he'd cheer up. He might be a unicorn, but so far, he was sort of a drag. Okay, I know that's unfair; I mean he did de-poison me, and I didn't know what was going on in his life. Maybe he missed running through the woods? Isn't that what they do?

When we'd all eaten our (probably) eyeballs, Sasha clapped his hands smartly.

"You will be delighted to attend a fête tomorrow evening," he informed us. "Ruby, I promised you I'd memorialize your friend Lauren C, and we will do just that. There will be dignitaries from the Seelie Court attending." He paused to give us all time to ooh and aah at his diplomatic swagger, which we politely did. "There's more. As most of you know, in the days before the Light War, the Seelie Court maintained the glass. It may be that they still have the ability to repair the damage." We all started talking at once. He put his hand up. "I will try to convince them to help us."

"Out of the goodness of their heart?" I asked.

"I did not say that." He had a plan, which was good news, even if he wasn't ready to share it.

Marly looked dubious. "Do you think they'll go for it?"

"I don't know," he admitted. "But it's time to try." He paused. "It's not outside the realm of reason that they are indeed behind the increasing violence of the shatters, intending to force my hand."

March was watching us...watching me. Wasn't this the sort of thing he was supposed to be doing surreptitiously? Gathering intel on Sasha's plans? Either he was the world's worst spy, or didn't actually understand the concept. He leaned forward. "We should talk about this."

"We? You mean you and me?" I looked up and down the table. "Is no one going to ask this guy why he's even here? Aren't you Madame's personal escort or something?" I looked at Aster. "And that goes for you, too." Everyone looked pointedly not at each other and I felt like I'd farted at the dinner table. "I withdraw the question since I clearly do not understand how 'sides' work."

Sasha set down his sticks with a loud *click*.

"They are here at my invitation. Nothing has been said that isn't already common knowledge. Isn't that correct,

Aster?"

He lowered his eyes to his plate and said, "That is true, lord king. Madame has spoken of this theory, as have many at court. And all understand that help from the Seelie Court may be a way out of the darkness." He paused. "At what cost, of course, remains unknown."

Sasha nodded and looked back at me. "As far as Master March's presence, one might wonder why someone would refuse the company of a unicorn."

"Fine," I said. "We'll go have lunch. We can get pedicures together and braid each other's hair, whatever." Why did everyone—March included—want us to be friends? And why was I so annoyed by him? I'd have to watch it, as Marly obviously liked him. I didn't want to alienate any possible allies while I was here.

"Meet us at my house later today," Marly suggested. "We can talk then." March shrugged and looked away.

"So, Sasha, at your party..." I said.

"Hmm?" He had that same infuriating, slightly amused look he always had, like he had no idea what I might bring up. If I was Marly, I'd be tempted to hold a pillow over his face after the deed was done.

"Can I cling to the hope that Madame won't try and poison me, or drop a safe on my head, or release the hounds on me?"

Aster perked up. "The hounds? The ones that shoot bees?"

We all turned to stare at him. Then Marly and I burst out laughing. "Yeah, those. What about it, Sasha? Am I safe?"

He scowled at Aster. "You're her boy, please remind your patron that this occasion is too solemn to disrupt. I would be highly displeased."

Aster smiled. "I already reminded Madame that since I am in charge of Lady Ruby's well-being during her stay, it would reflect poorly on me, and so on her as well if Ruby should come to harm." He touched my sleeve. "I think you'll be safe, now."

I put my hand over his. "Thank you. That was very smart of you." I'm not ashamed to say the way he beamed at me made me a little tingly in my lady parts. For some reason, Marly and March were shooting meaningful looks back and forth.

"Hey," I said, "how do you two know each other?"

Marly went wide eyed. "We, um..." she cleared her throat. "It's actually a funny story. March, you tell it."

"Oh, yes March." Sasha looked delighted. "Please do."

March looked like he wanted to re-unicorn himself and leave town on the next bus. He opened his mouth, closed it, and then finally said, "I've been here before. To see Marly. Before now."

"Oh," I said to Sasha, "so, that's how you two also know each other?"

Sasha gulped back a laugh. "He has indeed been here before."

March narrowed his eyes at Marly. "I was called to help her because once she got here, she didn't know how to act. I was to instruct her in simple, common behavior, since no one here might serve as an example. I see my efforts were wasted."

Now they were glaring at each other, not even pretending nothing was up.

"You gave her etiquette lessons?" I asked. "Because, yes, that sounds like something that actually happened."

"Fine!" Marly was a little pink in the face. "Book parade cheese face!"

I laughed. "Sure, Mar. Never mind." I burped into my napkin like a lady. "Where were we? Oh, we were talking about the Seelie fae. Who are they bringing?" I was just hoping they were more like the lovely Lauren C. and less like this dog park full of high-strung bitches.

"I know the Spire will attend," Sasha said.

"The what?" I asked.

"The Spire is like the Seelie king, except they don't have a king," Aster said. Well, that cleared it up. "It is said that the Spire took the place of the court's departed royals."

Marly turned to Sasha. "You have to fix this."

When he looked at her, I could see his expression soften. How about that? He did have feelings. "It's as fixed as I can make it. I can't change it."

She shot a worried look in my direction. "We'll see. This isn't over, Sash."

"Did you just call him Sash? You guys are adorable."

March stood. "You'll excuse me." He didn't even finish his scrambled eyeballs. Well, I hoped he removed whatever climbed up his butt before we all got together later at Marly's. Aster also excused himself. I'm guessing he had to go tell Madame that I was now using a fork.

"Can you find your way to my house?" Marly asked. "I

could send Ilex."

"I bet Aster knows where it is."

She made a face. "Leave him home." She hugged me hard. "I'll see you later."

I finally pulled away from her embrace. "God, Mar. Are you okay?" I swear she was trying not to cry. I'd really have to get to the bottom of what was bothering her. That left me and Sasha at the table.

"I'd like to apologize for last evening," he said. "Madame oversteps." He sipped his...I want to say coffee but honestly, it could have been lighter fluid for all I know.

"Yeah," I agreed, "Poisoning me in front of a room full of witnesses, you could call it an overstep. Tomorrow looks like it's been taken care of, but can you promise she won't get 'curious' again?"

"No." I waited for the rest of the sentence, but he just sat there. Finally, he said, "That promise would be a lie, after all. And once a promise is made, it may not be broken."

"Then why should I stay?" I actually did want to stay—mostly to help Marly, but there was a sliver of 'get some Aster' in there as well. I also was curious to see what Sasha had in mind.

"Because Marly needs you. And so do I. And so does March, for that matter." March? What would he need me for? Polishing his horn? Oh my God, I take that back, it sounded filthy. Sasha continued. "I'll do what I can to protect you while you watch over Marly, but you must be vigilant on your own. Must I warn you again about Aster?"

"No, Marly took care of that." She tried, bless her.

"Hmm. You feel pity for him because he is not well-regarded by myself or by Marly. As he is Madame's creature, she will use your kindness against you."

More vague bullshit, and it wasn't even true. It wasn't pity. At least, not all of it. But I asked, "How? As what?"

"If I knew, I'd say. All I ask is that you recall who poisoned you out of curiosity. I won't mention this again because I know you are at least as clever as any other human, and humans don't like to be...what is it? Nogged?"

"No, nog is the good one. I think you mean nagged. Maybe negged." I sighed. "Sasha, I'm here. I said I'd help. But I feel like I only know part of what's going on. I mean, you said I'm needed. By you. What does that mean?"

He thought about it for a moment. "I'll give you an example. I need your advice."

You do? About...?"

"Marly. I want to make sure this event is as much for her as it is for the memory of the Seelie woman. I have given her many gifts, but you have years of friendship and know her better than I. I wish to do something she'll appreciate. What should I do?"

*The Unseelie king is asking me for advice about his love life. This is a day of firsts.* "As a matter of fact, I know just what you should do. See, Marly needs some help with her eyes." And I gave him some spectacularly good advice. Maybe this wouldn't be so hard, after all.

# 17

*March*

**U**nable to continue to sit and watch Ruby and that boy Aster make eyes at each other, March decided to do something he'd been putting off—a chat with Madame. After the disaster at the dinner the night before, he'd made excuses and hidden in his room, letting the (fake) leaves run through his hands and wondering what he was doing there. It was Madame's intention he observe Sasha, and he was becoming more convinced she was correct in thinking the king intended her harm. But if Ruby knew anything about Sasha's plans for the Seelie's visit, which he doubted, she had made it clear she had no inclination to tell him. He thought about the way she looked at him, at her impatience and indifference, and lowered his head. No, she wasn't likely to share anything with him, not anymore.

He found Madame sitting in her garden, almost as if she hadn't moved since their first meeting. This time, he looked more carefully at the plants and flowers. Had some of them—many of them—been replaced by glass replicas? Because today in the soft light of the unseen sun, they all appeared lush and hearty. The dead foliage scent was gone as well, replaced by the faint fragrance of fresh flowers. That was strange in and of itself, because the sheer volume—masses of roses in shades of crimson and orange and butter yellow climbing on the mossy stone walls, a low hedge of pomegranates, vivid with scarlet blooms, and of course her namesake sunflowers, golden and russet and butter yellow, all lining the path to her nearly hidden house. The roses alone should have made the air thick with perfume. It was just one more thing he'd never know.

Madame received him as before, with a sweet smile and the offer of tea, which he accepted. He understood now it was a mere formality and he wasn't expected to do more than touch the cup to his lips.

"Master March. I do hope you'll forgive the incident with the wine. It was not my intention to create such a scene."

He nodded slowly. The way these folk phrased things was deadly important. What she'd just said could mean she intended a different outcome, but a "scene" all the same. "I'm just glad I was able to help Ruby." Then he looked up at her, meeting her eye. "Did you know the wine would make her ill?"

"I know you wanted to interact with her, you'd made that clear." She smiled kindly. "You looked rather sad. I was only trying to…facilitate." Her smile faded. "And now you have spent some time with her. Perhaps you can tell me why you think she's come?"

"The king wishes her to be present at the fete. Since she was a friend of the Seelie fae woman he intends to honor, it seems reasonable. Beyond that…"

"Beyond that he wishes her to hold hands with *that woman,* yes, I know all of that. Everyone knows that." She leaned forward. "In his pandering to the Seelie Court, the king will bring this place to ruin, and your friends along with it. Look around, you know I'm right." She waved her hand, and as the golden light faded, her garden, glorious and flourishing, collapsed into heaps of broken glass; the crimsons and golds turned to ash and dust. The cloying reek of dead vegetation was strong in the air. "If you don't help me, the whole of the kingdom will look like this. Master March, there must be something else. What has he said about the glass?"

He drew back. "Nothing—"

"Has he mentioned the constructs?"

*The constructs?*

"Madame." He took a breath. "Since my arrival, I've spent the length of one meal with the king, and that was just now, before I came to see you. He said nothing beyond hoping the meeting with the Seelie Court goes well. Obviously, he has a plan to deal with them. Obviously, he knows I am here at your request. Why would he share his plans with me?"

She frowned at him. "I did not expect him to. I expected him to share them with *that woman,* who will tell her little human friend, who will in turn tell you. Surely that was clear. All I had to do was bring the two of you together."

*If Ruby were here, she'd say "Don't call me Shirley."*

He thought of her (he always thought of her) as she'd

been the previous evening; sprawled on the floor of the fae ballroom, her face dead white, her eyes rolling back. And of Aster comforting her. Of the pair just now at breakfast, with his hand over hers. He saw the way Madame watched him now, how her fragile mask had been cast aside. This woman needed protection from no one, except maybe her own impulses, and he certainly wasn't the one for that job. He knew he'd been duped, but even so, it didn't matter. He'd made his promise and was bound to protect her no matter how he felt or what she did. But that didn't mean he had to linger here another second.

"Tell me, Madame. Are you in need of protection at the moment?"

She looked a bit surprised. "In my own garden? I should hope not, unless..." and here she smiled slyly. "Unless the threat comes from you."

Was that an invitation? "That would be unlikely," he said firmly. "Well, you brought us together, Ruby and me. As you intended." He shifted forward and set down his teacup. "If you will permit me, I am expected at the house of Queen Melis." He took a mean little satisfaction in the way Madame stiffened when he said it. "Perhaps some great truths will be revealed to me." *That,* he thought with some wonder, *was malice, followed by sarcasm.*

"Don't forget," she said. "You are bound to tell me what you've learned."

"I accepted your invitation. I accepted your hospitality. I agreed to help you *if* I learned anything I thought you needed to know."

She coiled herself in her seat and smiled. "I see you've also learned how to turn a phrase so that it may be used as a weapon."

"You're correct." He paused, feeling light headed. "I have never had need for a weapon before." *Or malice. Or sarcasm.*

Madame regarded him, and apparently liking the confusion she no doubt could see on his face, raised her hand, restoring her lovely garden and the glowing mid-day light. "Well, consider this when you go. Your friend the human, she is charmed against her knowledge of you. But here, in this place, our magic is fading along with the light." She gestured at her glinting flowers, kept from ruin by the sheer force of her will. "As you can see. Perhaps some pressure, artfully applied, will jog her memory." She nodded thoughtfully. "Yes. You might start by drawing her into the shadows."

He frowned. "That sounds suspiciously helpful."

She laughed her sweet and tinkling laugh. "Why should I not help you? I intend for you to help me, you ought to have something for your trouble. And," she added cheerfully, "it would no doubt put a blade in the back of whatever our lord king has in mind." She rose to her feet; this audience was over. "You have your assignment. Remind your human of who you are. Find out what she knows. And, or. I'll accept either one today. But," she added, "unlike you, I don't have all the time in the world." She waved her hand. "So get to work."

# 18

*Ruby*

I did a slow one-eighty. "Goddamn, Mar."

"I know, it's nice, right?"

"Nice?" Marly's house was bright and airy, big enough to hold a well-attended dance contest, and every single thing in it looked like it had just been snatched up from the most darling flea market in all of Paris. The front door opened onto a sitting room with overstuffed, cozy furniture arranged on the bleached pine plank floor in front of a marble-mantled fireplace, with a tiny kitchen off to the side. The shelves and tabletops were littered with antique globes (of what worlds?) stacks of gilded leather-bound books, what looked to be a miniature dragon skull mounted on a brass stand, a group of tiny terrariums hung like Christmas tree ornaments from the ceiling, and stuck in a coffee cup next to the sink, a small Pride flag. In the second room, a huge bed, resting on a shimmering teal rug, had elaborate feet and headboards of antiqued white wrought iron (although it definitely wasn't iron, of course) and the mountain of quilts were stitched from creamy white silk. On the floor, I counted at least three beds that could only belong to Clover. Next to the window stood a tall, elaborate Victorian birdcage. The little flock of lights that made Marly's crown drifted around inside it. That there was a window was made more interesting by the fact that there was no roof—like so much of the palace, the whole place was completely open to the sky. I could see the bottom of the Seelie kingdom like the bottom of a pot—a darker circle in a bright sky—and the remaining rectangular glass lights twinkling and flickering above, filling the room with daylight. One side of the room was devoted to a wall of floor to ceiling white chiffon curtains, which moved gently in the non-existent breeze.

"It's based on something I once saw in an Anthropologie catalogue," Marly said.

I burst out laughing. "You may be a queen, but nice to know you're still an aspirational college girl from the 'aughts in your heart."

Marly grinned, showing her teeth. "You don't have to call me that. Want a beer?" She went to one of the perfectly scuffed and faded dressers and swung the front open.

"Okay, Queen Melis." There, her new name, out loud. "Is that a dorm fridge in there?"

"Except this one won't leak all over the rug. I may get my security deposit back." She rooted around in it and pulled out a pitcher.

"Seriously, this is all so cute I am going to die. No beer

for me, thanks."

"You're probably right. We have an event to prepare for. Schemes to perfect. Let's see. We already went over Aster."

I rolled my eyes. "Consider me warned."

She handed me a slender blue wine glass with seltzer in it. "Amory is kind of an interesting dude."

"Amory. He's the big blond one, right?

"That's him."

"If by 'interesting' you mean 'stone fox.' Team Marly or Team Madame?"

She laughed. "Team Amory, one hundred percent all day every day. He's fun but I wouldn't necessarily trust him to drive me to my kidney transplant. Who else? Oh, did I see you talking to Noisette last night?"

I had a vague memory of a short haired woman, but in my state at the time, her face had been replaced by Lauren's. "Sort of?"

"Watch out for her. She isn't a fan. We had a…" she swallowed. "Sasha gave her…"

"Jeez Louise, out with it!"

She sat quite still for a second. "Noisette stole a book from the library, which is all Sasha's property. He punished her, and it was so crazy I made him take it back, and he did."

"I'm guessing a hefty fine?"

"Heh, no." She looked at the floor.

"Stern talking to? Slap on the wrist?"

"In a way. He took her eyes and hands." Before I could scream, she added, "But he gave them back like an hour later. He understands it was too much."

I laughed right at her. "You think?"

She reached out and laid her hand on my arm. "The fae are not like you. They look kind of like you, but they aren't."

"What about you?"

She stared at me. "Look at me, Ruby. Do you really have to ask me that?"

I'd insulted her by wondering if she still felt human. "I'm…I'm sorry. I just think of the old Marly and—"

She squeezed me arm, then let go. "I am still me. Except where I'm not. But Rubes, this is my home. It doesn't mean I'm tossing human Marly or anyone she loved in the trash, but it's important that you understand what my life is now, and that I don't hate it."

I didn't reply. I don't know why I wanted her to hate it.

She sighed and shook her head. "Anyway. She'll want to talk to you, Noisette. She's obsessed with humans. She loves music. I…we were almost friends. Just…be careful." She smiled sadly. "That seems like overall good advice."

She stood up and I followed her through the gorgeous house, still thinking of hands and eyes. Careful, yeah.

Advice given, she went back into tour-guide mode. "Oh, you haven't seen the best part."

"There's a best part?"

With a smug smile, Marly raised her hands, giving it a little more theater than was probably necessary. The white curtains evaporated in a drift of mist, revealing a gigantic garden—it actually looked more like a public park, minus the pigeons and people.

"First, nice trick." Make, unmake. She was good at this.

"Second, holy shit times two. This is all yours?"

" As I've been telling you, Sasha did not come to play."

"Are you blushing, bitch? Okay, never mind. Show me around the rest of Versailles, here."

Marly met Clover right outside, and once the great beast had informed us about "pet" and gotten a good head rub, the pair led me down the gravel path past heaps of tiny cream-colored roses and crisscrossed with silvery creeping thyme, which released a delicious fragrance as we crushed it underfoot. The path led to an ornamental fountain in the center of a raised, stone pond. It was bigger than my bedroom back home, and it was stocked with silver and white koi which came to the surface to look at Marly. A few birds—something like miniature herons with lacey white tail feathers—stalked among the irises. Looking around, I realized almost everything was in shades of white, silver, cream or black.

"Sasha says it's a Night Garden. He says its very traditional." She trailed her fingers in the water and the fish swam over to examine her hand. "They're all constructs, of course, and the plants aren't real, but isn't it cool?" An enormous silver moth that was easily the size of a sparrow darted past on its way to the moonflowers. I'd never been so jealous in my life. "Well, he wasn't going to stash me in a Motel 6! And don't worry, if your trip goes long, I'll get you an upgrade. I'd invite you to stay here but I don't know how you feel about me and Sash in the next room." She paused, then laughed. "Oh my God, your face. Never mind, Hotel Unseelie it is. Okay, you're going to love this." Past the fountain was a free-standing door in an elaborately carved wooden frame. "It's the Lookout. Go on," said Marly. "And take your time. I'll go inside and make tea for when you come in."

"Just...go through?"

"You look dubious, but it'll be worth it." She was grinning in a way I recognized—when there was a treat waiting in the refrigerator; when she found a Groupon for our favorite day spa; when there was an unexpected Queer Eye marathon. I turned the doorknob, and walked through.

The garden was gone. Not gone, but far away. Far below. Instead of the gravel path, I was on a small balcony.

"Hollleeey...." I got a blast of vertigo and clung to the rail, then my brains acclimated and I took a deep breath and a look around.

It was a lookout, all right. I had to have been a mile at least above the Unseelie Court. I could see all of it, the whole city, the churning grey clouds of the moat—laced here and there with violet lightning. And I could see the dark and featureless plains beyond the moat, and the mountains at the edge of the world which were mercifully not moving at the moment. I gripped the railing with both hands and looked up. This high, I could see the places where the glass was damaged, where the light sparked and flickered, and I could even make out the fragmented remains of the pane which had just exploded; the thing everyone called the Great Shatter. They looked like someone had gone at them with the world's biggest shovel. I looked down and could just about make out Marly's Night Garden. I squinted...someone was at the front door. Should I have been able to make out such a tiny figure at such a distance? I had no idea.

I leaned on the rail and looked out over the city. It was easy to see where people still lived, as there were lights in their homes, a glowing patchwork of gardens and walkways. But only a small fraction were lit up. *Sasha was right, this place won't last much longer*, I thought. *How long did it take to get this bad?*

As I watched, I noticed in the "dead zone" here and there would be a little spark of light, and then it would vanish. Kids, I thought right away. Kids like Ray and Sheena, skipping school and hanging out in abandoned houses. Then I realized—there was something moving around out there, but it wasn't a bunch of kids. Because there were no kids. I hadn't seen a single one. I mean, Aster had told me Marly and I were "by far" the youngest person in the kingdom, but I guess it hadn't really dawned on me until that moment.

*This is my home*, Marly said. This is what she is now, and this is her home. If it dies, so does she. I couldn't lose her a second time. I wouldn't.

Whether she was still "us" or fully "them," it didn't matter at all. I had to help Marly, whatever it took.

# 19

*March*

I t was the way the place ignored geometry, March thought. He knew about angles and planes and gravity from a high school textbook he'd found in his woods, and while it hadn't been current since the 1960s, there were things that ought to be true, but weren't. Like the way Marly's house was both inside and outside, the way the wall of the building next to her place seemed to curve and drop away, until he was standing on her doorstep. It made him uneasy but there was no point in dwelling on it, because different things were true, here in the Unseelie Court. *Shadows*, he thought, *there's something wrong with the shadows. Draw Ruby into the shadows.*

Even from the outside, March could tell Sasha was indulging Marly's whims. Her door was painted cornflower blue with white trim, and there were pots of caladiums on either side of the steps leading inside, their crumpled-silk-looking leaves pale green and cream and rose pink. The outside of their homes wasn't something the other fae thought about, as far as he could tell. He couldn't recall anyone else he'd passed with a shiny black mailbox. Did Marly expect to get a letter? He wondered, and rang the doorbell. Inside he heard chimes, and footsteps. The door opened and Clover burst out like he was shot out of a cannon. March held his hand up and the animal sat back on his haunches.

"Pet!" Clover said happily.

"No jumping!" Marly put a warning hand on Clover's head, although March figured it would be like a butterfly trying to take down an elk. "Hey," she said. "Good timing. I was just making tea." He followed her in, both charmed and alarmed by the elaborate recreation of a mortal urban paradise. Or maybe he was wrong, and every fae decorated like this, like the reality TV they all loved so much. "You should know that Ruby is here." He looked around; was she was hiding in a cabinet or under a chair? "I sent her to the Lookout, she won't be down for a few minutes."

He followed the pair into the house, where Clover turned three times and curled up in a huge dog bed under the front window. He himself slumped in an overstuffed armchair and watched as Marly heated water on her doll-house sized stove. He thought it was interesting that she didn't simply magic the tea into existence. There was a part of her that clung to and relished those little human rituals. "This isn't a real stove, of course," she said, as if she'd heard his thoughts. "I mean, it gets hot when I turn the knob, and the water boils like a real stove, but it's not hooked up to anything—there's no gas, or even electric, God forbid. It took me like a million tries to get it right. No one could help me; no one has stoves, or any sort of kitchen. Sasha thought I was nuts." She handed him a steaming mug; it smelled like chamomile and mint. Here, in Marly's house, the tea wasn't a formality. He took an actual sip with pleasure and even began to relax.

"So, how are you hanging in there?"

His good mood evaporated. "I don't know if I can do this," he said. "I don't know if I believe what Tournesol told me. She said she brought me here to learn what Sasha's plans are, because she thinks I can't be corrupted." He paused, then made a decision. "She says proximity to the king has turned you cruel and sour, and she said she's afraid of what you two might do to her."

Marly paused at the stove, and turned to him. "She said that?" He was surprised to see that she looked…pleased? Was that right? "Well, she's not completely wrong," she continued, pouring her own tea. "If she tries anything, it's on. But I'm not, like, sneaking up behind her with a knife or anything." Yes, he thought she looked pleased. "That's not how we do it here, anyway. So, what did you say?"

"I agreed to at least listen for trouble. But I don't know how that happens, or what to ask, or who, and she must know that. Is there another reason she brought me here? I wonder if she needs one, other than to make trouble for you and Sasha. And yet I also know it can't be a lie."

Clover, perhaps hearing the anxiety in his voice, came over and pushed his head into March's hand. He stroked the animal's soft feathered head.

Marly sat across from him on the matching loveseat and reached across to give Clover a pet as well. Then she sat back. "Nothing is ever a lie, exactly, but that's not the same as a straight answer, not by a mile. I mean, Sasha brought Ruby here for the party and as a gift for me, but also to make trouble for Madame. And you, I guess. It's an endless parade of bullshit with these people. Madame and Sasha are engaged in something heavy, and they have been since forever. I'm just sorry you and Ruby got caught up in it. Right now, I have a little influence, and I'm trying to think of how I can help, so let me sit on that for a minute. As far as Sasha and his plans go, I felt the same way when I got here. How do you ask a question when no one says what they mean, like, ever? It's never a lie, but it's all in code."

"Yet you seem to have figured out how to speak to Sasha."

She glanced around her lovely home. He thought she looked guilty, but with her new eyes, who could tell? "I don't know his mind, and it would be dangerous of me to think I did. But the thing is, I feel like I know his heart."

"Then this is a true marriage?" He was surprised, and pushed away his disappointment.

"It is. I'm sorry. He told me what he did to you. And Ruby."

"Then he must also have told you why." He rubbed his eyes. "He gave me back my life but…"

"But took Ruby away from you. I…it's possible he didn't understand what you meant to each other. Interior life is kind of a new concept to the fae. I'm doing my best to teach him. It's even possible that he brought her here to make it up to you." He raised his brow and she smiled. "Yeah, that's a long shot. But I have to say, he's working overtime to take care of me. I mean, I know why he's doing it, or why he was doing it at first, but…He bet everything on me." She swallowed hard. "He loves me."

"And you?"

She met his gaze, now bold. "I feel the same way."

"So, I can't hate him." He let her see him smile, and as he hoped, she looked relieved. His issues with Sasha were not hers, after all. "How about Tournesol? Do we hate her?"

Marly chewed her lip. "I'm obviously not a fan, but I don't know if I can hate her, either. Don't get me wrong, I don't trust her and I know she's actively working against us. But I get where she's coming from. That's one of the things I've learned here. Just because someone is your bitter enemy, it doesn't mean you can't appreciate the skill and finesse of their strike against you. You don't pout. You give them their moment and even applaud if they left you hands to clap with, and then you strike back, harder. If I was her, I'd be plotting my ass off against us, too." She paused. "When I say plotting against 'us', am I including you? You are part of her retinue."

He'd been dreading this question and managed to avoid thinking about it until now. That, and Madame's advice about Ruby, which would almost certainly work against him in some way he couldn't see, even if he did manage to jog loose a memory. "You are my friend."

"But Sasha isn't your friend. And he and I count as one."

He leaned forward. "I must abide by the laws of hosting in this place. But I would never, never see you come to harm."

He sighed. "I don't know what this will look like. I can't disregard her wishes even if they go against yours." He ran his hands through his hair. "I can't even hate her."

"Wait, I know. What about Aster?"

Aster. Young and handsome and a new friend in an unfriendly place. The way Ruby looked at him. Yes, this was an easy one. "Oh, that guy? Him, I hate."

Marly laughed. "I knew we could do it. Maybe we can pin the Shatter on him."

"Certainly, if he had something to do—you're joking."

"Probably." She smiled. "Anyway, here we are."

"And the question remains the same. What am I doing here?"

"Same thing I am. We're saving this big dumb place."

He had to smile. "Okay."

"I'm the damned queen of the fairies, and you're a real live unicorn. If we can't help these jerks, who can? Am I right?"

"I suppose if anyone could do it..."

She frowned, thoughtful. "I just wish I could ride you."

He leaned back, surprised. "Well, I guess you could...I mean, we'll probably want to be discreet. If Sasha found out he'd—"

She burst out laughing. "Ride on your *back*, March. When you have four legs. I'm over here trying to bust out a fae baby, but thanks anyway."

"Oh. Oh! Uh, sorry. Wow, terrible idea."

"Completely."

But for just a second, it seemed like a terrific idea. He pushed that firmly away. "You know, it's funny but I think of all the humans I met, you were the only one who wasn't interested in sex with me."

"Well, let's not go crazy. I mean, remember the night we met? At The Hare? You were hot as hell and totally disoriented. That's *so* my type. But I knew Ruby would slit my throat, so I was cool. You know what they say: Sisters before Shifters."

March frowned. "Do they actually say that?"

"Yes?" Her dark eyes gleamed. "So, could I? Ride you into battle?"

"No, I don't think so." He shuddered. The idea made him dizzy. "No."

"But could I touch you? I know humans can't, but I'm out of that club."

He wondered. "I really don't know."

"Is it true about virgins?" He turned in his seat—Ruby was standing behind him. "They can touch you, right?"

He took a breath.

"Yes. When I am in my body, as you saw me, only a virgin can touch me. I don't know why. It just is." He reminded himself: *it's not her fault, she doesn't know me, she doesn't remember Margaret.* But it didn't make it any easier to see the annoyance she was trying to hide.

"So, kind of weird. Okay. Anyway." She sat across from him, closer to Marly, and he let her words settle on his skin. He wanted to leave—this room, this realm. Instead, he said, " I am bound to serve Madame's interests, and so my purpose is to find out what Sasha intends. He glanced at Marly. "Unless you already know and can save me the effort."

She pursed her lips and looked thoughtful. It took her a while to answer. "He's funny about sharing. He only tells me what he thinks I need to know. So you and I—" she looked at Ruby—"We'll do the same thing but with Madame and see if we can pry anything loose."

"Will Sasha be ticked that you're in on this?" Ruby asked Marly. He couldn't help but notice the way Ruby looked at her friend. He thought she was more than just idly curious, and wondered why.

Marly stretched her arms along the back of the sofa. "He can be whatever he wants, I'm involved."

"I am not ticked." They all swiveled their heads and turned towards the door. The voice came from outside. It was Sasha, leaning on the window sill. "Tell me, what is 'ticked?'"

# 20

*Ruby*

nstead of being irritated at the intrusion, Marly covered her pleased smile with an eye-roll. I was suddenly a little more in favor of these two weirdos making it work. She got up to let Sasha in.

"Rude," she told him

"Ticked is rude?" he asked.

"No, rude is eavesdropping, which you were just then. Ticked is annoyed, which I am right now."

I am here to tell you she was not annoyed. And she might consider explaining to Sasha how a door works.

He gave her a short bow. "I am enlightened."

"Well," she said. "You're also here. Why? What's wrong?"

His eyes widened with what I'm certain was mock confusion. "Why must something be wrong?"

"Because," she said, "we had breakfast not two hours ago and you didn't tell me you were coming over."

"And yet here I am."

Honest to God, they already sounded like my parents. March, Clover, and I watched the two of them like we were at a tennis match.

I said, "So what brings you around, then? Because we're working on our strategy."

He glanced at me. "I'm sure." Then, turning back to Marly, he smiled. "I made you something. It's outside."

Well, outside and inside were pretty much the same thing, but we exchanged looks and she shrugged, I guess deciding to humor him. We all filed out onto the neat little porch, and since it was only big enough for two—plus Clover, who I kept wanting to call a dog—March and I stood in the "street."

"What...wow, what is that?" she asked with a wide smile. It was good to see her light up like that.

"You like it?" He looked pretty pleased with himself.

"I love it. Thank you." While the fake morning light was now fake afternoon light, the air was different—soft and damp, a little cool. It felt like the first nice day of spring after a hard winter. It felt alive.

"It's called 'petrichor,'" March said. "What it smells like after the rain. I saw it in a book once."

"Correct." I think Sasha was annoyed that he didn't get to announce it, but Marly was delighted so he let it slide. "You told me you missed human things, and this is a human thing, enjoying this smell." I wondered if he'd taken my advice about the eye situation. Even if he didn't, this was a pretty nice entry in Operation Happy Queen.

She was beaming at him, deeply inhaling the sweet air. She grinned and said, "Show me how, and next time let's do the beach." She clapped her hands. "Or maybe a moonlit pine forest!"

"Pet," Clover agreed. He was such a suck-up.

They smiled at each other in a way that shouted "inside joke." I caught March's eye, figuring we were third and fourth wheels at this point, and he nodded and followed me. We left them there in the cloud of good smell and walked back in the direction of the palace. I only knew that because I could see it—otherwise it was all odd angles and streets that looked like they dead ended that didn't. If you asked me to draw you a map, I'd be sunk. March followed, silent.

After a while, he said, "She cares for him. He is fortunate."

Was it that simple? He was jealous of their relationship? "Must be kind of hard for you to watch, huh?"

"I have a long time to recover. I'll be fine." So it wasn't me at all. I couldn't believe it—Marly had a crown, a palatial mansion, and a griffin, plus a unicorn and a fae king both were hot for her. I mean, she was the best and all, but it seemed a little unfair since all I got was a chronic stomach ache and a gig hustling drinks. I felt sorry for March, and even worse that I made him confess.

"Um, I don't know what happened between you guys, but it looks like Marly's in a good place right now. I'm sure there's someone—"

"What?"

"You and Marly. I mean, Sasha is a tough sell but you have to admit they have a lot in common." Then I clapped my hand over my mouth, figuring I'd missed the obvious. "I'm sorry—if it was you and Sasha…"

He stared at me. "No, I think you misunderstand. I know you do." He shook his head with a short laugh. "It's nothing like that at all."

Back to square one, and I didn't think I could stand five more minutes of pouting and glaring. "Okay then, tell me. March, what's the problem? I mean, you seem like a decent guy." I struggled with all the parts of him. "Who is also, um, a unicorn. What is going on with you?"

He looked at me with the same anguished expression I'd seen from his other self. "Oh, Ruby."

"Look, if I said something wrong, I'm sorry. I just feel like you maybe have a problem. With me."

"A problem…no." He looked at the ground, at the distant towers of the palace, anywhere but at me. "I recently lost someone. Someone I loved. Love. And I never got the chance to tell them how I felt. And I miss them very much."

Maybe I reminded him of his missing person. No, that wasn't likely—I was just an ordinary human. Probably my company didn't measure up. "Oh, yeah. That sucks."

"It does," he agreed. "It sucks."

"Well, are they dead?"

He smiled, not looking even a little happy. "No. They're very much alive."

"Then maybe you'll get the chance to fix things, one day."

"You're right," he said. "Maybe I will." He smiled a sad and beautiful smile, and for a second my heart ached with sudden urge to reach for him, to comfort him. Of course, I didn't do anything of the sort. That would have been nuts—I mean, can you imagine? Me, comforting him?

Magic, it had to be. I kept hearing the magic here in the kingdom was fading away with the light, so maybe it was acting on me in strange and unpredictable ways, too. What else could it be?

I still felt bad for March, but at least I knew for sure I wasn't the reason he acted the way he did. I wondered who it was, and exactly how you'd go about breaking a unicorn's heart.

# 21

*Ruby*

After we wrapped the most awkward conversation of the day, (I shouldn't assume, the day wasn't over) I finally got around to telling him my theory about how the constructs were up to something. True, my evidence was based on Ilex's fairly vague remark, but in this kingdom, vague remarks were currency. Plus, it was all I had to go on.

Originally, I was going to try and take Marly with me, both to keep an eye on her and because I was a huge giant sore thumb in these parts, but it looked like her afternoon was booked. And when I thought about it, I wondered if the constructs would be less likely to spill anything interesting in front of their queen. If Ilex was talking to me and not to Marly, well, there had to be a reason other than she thought I had a trustworthy face—she knew my job was to protect her boss. She was the one I really needed to track down, and this seemed like the perfect time to look for her.

It also looked like I was saddled with March, so I told him I wanted to talk to one on their home turf, and I even knew where that was. He looked at me, expectant. "I guess you might as well come with me," I said, then silently cursed myself—why did every exchange between us always turn so uncomfortable? He did his patented stare at the ground and then followed me.

After a while he said, "I think you're right about the constructs."

I nodded. "I mean, why else would Ilex say they weren't all in on it? In on what?"

March looked thoughtful. "When I spoke with Madame earlier, she asked if the king had mentioned constructs. Why would she ask that, specifically?"

I nodded. "And why would Sasha talk about them at all? He's like everyone else and kind of ignores them."

"If the constructs have aligned themselves with Madame against Sasha, he may be in more trouble than he knows."

"Well, I mean, we don't know that's what's happening here. I can't believe they'd just go along with that nightmare woman. They must know their home is at risk."

"Maybe if you're a slave, this doesn't feel like a home."

I didn't have a good answer for that.

I followed the map I'd made in my head—starting at my room, make a left, pace pace pace, make a right pace pace pace, another left at the giant golden beehive, and there it was; the door that led to the Belly. And no one bothered us, after all we had the blessings (or something) of Sasha and of Madame, so we could wander around to our heart's content.

"Here. You can even see the seam in the wall." No doorknob, though.

"Maybe you just push?" March peered at the wall. "Or magic it open?"

"'Speak, friend, and enter,' you mean?" He stared at me, confused. "Never mind." I said to the wall: "Open, please." It did not open. Or maybe my accent was wrong.

"Are you sure this is the place?" March looked dubious. "Let me try." He placed his hand flat against the wall and closed his eyes. Nothing.

"Oh, wait a second. I have an idea." I pulled the king's medallion from inside my robe and touched the door, which instantly swung open. "I think this is a sort of get out of—or into—jail free card," I said, although I was pretty sure March wouldn't get the reference there either. He pushed it the rest of the way open and we started down the stairs, because of course it would be a long, twisty, dark stairway. You'd think if it was for the constructs to bring up food and whatnot, they might have put an elevator in, or at least made it brighter. But maybe the constructs didn't care. Maybe March was right and they didn't care about the realm or glass or light at all, they only wanted revenge on their master the king. Maybe this was a revolution. Maybe we were on the wrong side of it. This little vacation I'd taken to visit my old pal Marly had gotten extremely heavy.

The lights that they did have down there were set into recesses cut into the walls, and turned themselves off as soon as you looked at them. Sort of reverse motion detectors. And the stairs went on and on. No one saw us, and I didn't hear anyone in the stairwell.

Finally, we reached the bottom of the staircase and came to a small antechamber and a big doorway. The door stood partially open and I squinted through the gap at the hinge. I could see a medium sized room with chairs and tables along the wall, like once upon a time it had been a classroom. It wasn't empty.

"Fuck—shit—back up." I backpedaled and crashed into March. "I think it's the constructs—it looks like they're having a meeting." As if that wasn't enough, we heard footsteps above, coming our way.

"Be still." He pushed me into the alcove under the light—which promptly went out—and hidden by the shadows, he leaned against me. Like, all of him was pressed against all of me. "Don't move."

"Are we invisible?" I whispered.

"Sort of?" That wasn't the confidence I was looking for. "Maybe more like transparent."

He was so close I could feel the warmth radiating off his body, and smell the clean, foresty scent of his hair, and a wave of desire I didn't even know was inside me said *go for it*.

I was so startled I did the opposite—shoved him away. He looked at me with such confusion, and I probably looked the same way. I know it wasn't me he was missing— but I wasn't thinking with my brain at this point, and I didn't care. I shook my head wildly, took him by the arms and pulled him close, hating my behavior. This wasn't like me at all. What was I doing? But when I put my arms around him, he let out a little gasp. That small sound, it was just his surprise, I guess.

But in that moment, it sounded like desire and pleasure and sex and joy. We fit together in a way I couldn't explain or deny. In that moment we were perfect.

I reached up and wound a handful of that silky dark hair around my hand and pulled his head down and kissed him so hard I think I chipped a tooth. I kissed him so hard I could feel his heart pounding, stronger and faster than my own. He pushed me back against the wall and I let go of his hair and plunged my hands inside his robe to stroke his long, smooth back, and then reached down to grab his ass. And yes; it, too, was perfect. My head filled with light, gloriously pulsing to our bodies shared rhythm

Finally, he let me go, and the light between us went with him. Before he pulled away, he pressed his forehead to mine, and I heard him sigh. Then he took a deep, shaky breath and a half step back. "They're gone. We're safe."

Remember when you first started getting your period? (For non-period getters, you'll just have to trust me.) Everything is so damned intense. Everything, all the happiness, the anger, the things you don't have a name for yet—they're all dialed up to a thousand. That's what it felt like, standing in that dark alcove looking up at him. A tsunami of emotion broke over me, a wall of things I couldn't name. I didn't try to stop my tears.

"How did you do that?" I asked. I guess he knew I meant the magic and the light, not the kiss.

He smiled down at me, looking at me with the same wonder I felt looking at the unicorn, and he gently touched my face, wiping away my tears. I could feel his breath on my cheek; sweet and warm. "Come on. You know this one."

"Because you're a unicorn," I answered my own question. "You can do lots of things." It felt so familiar—he felt familiar. It was the weirdest *déjà vu* ever, again. I mean, if I'd been hiding from mechanical fae-built rebels with a hot unicorn before, I feel like I'd remember it. The wave of emotion receded as quickly as it came over me, and I straightened my robe and took a step away from him. It was this place, I reminded myself. It had to be. The fae and their magic can't be trusted; they do things to people. So disintegrating Unseelie fae magic has to be an order of magnitude worse. It felt like a dangerous mistake to lead on a powerful magical creature like March, even if he was beautiful and sweet and sad. No. I couldn't let it happen again. No, Ruby.

I pulled myself together and we peeped through the hinge, and there she was.

"Thank you, friends, for helping me to change the course of our world, our court and our lives."

We stared wide eyed at each other. It wasn't just constructs here in the Belly. It was Madame.

"Can you make us invisible again?" I squeaked. March shushed me.

"You are making a mistake." It was Master Greaves. I *knew* he was a good guy. "This will earn you nothing but pain. Not right away—I have no doubt you'll be happy with your results in the short term. But it will come back to you. It always does."

She gave him a withering look. "Why do you oppose me? Because one of us was nice to you that one time?"

"No, Madame. My wishes are the same as your own. It's your method I can't condone."

"It's worth it," said one of the constructs. It looked to me like there were representatives of different groups I'd seen on the edges and fringes of court—cleanup, cooking, trash. They really ought to consider unionizing. Maybe that's what they were doing.

Another agreed, "It's for all of us, even you. You'll see, Master."

"As old as you are, one would think you'd be tired of...all this," Madame said. "Don't you long for something else?" She cocked her head. "Surely you worry about the light? In my work in lambency, I've had some interesting results. Nothing, yet, that will restore the glass, but interesting none the less. What if I told you I could...retrofit, I suppose you'd call it... rewrite your charms to protect you against the darkness?" That was quite a bribe, and he took a while to answer.

"What indeed. I will not stand against you," he said. "I only wish there was another way."

I guess she took that for 'you've got my vote' and nodded graciously. "Even if there were, my path is fixed, I would not change it. We all have a role to play. When next we meet, a new world will be waiting for us." She smiled as her construct friends left—fortunately there was another exit on the far side. Eventually only Madame and Master Greaves were left, along with Marly's maid, who had one foot out the door. "Ilex, a word?"

Ilex, who whispered to me that 'not everyone agreed.' Looked like someone overheard and ratted her out. She returned to stand in front of Madame, bowed gracefully and stood with her eyes fixed demurely on the floor.

"I notice you look less than enthused about what is to come."

"I am sorry about the condition of my face, Madame. Please tell me what you would prefer and I'll fix it for you."

March and I exchanged admiring glances; Ilex had balls.

Madame gritted her teeth. "Did you honestly think you could keep your indiscretion from me?"

"Nothing I said or did was in error," Ilex replied, but I could see her hands shaking where she clasped them behind her back.

"Why do you remain loyal to *that woman*?" Madame wasn't even pretending to do that sweet-faced look at me among the flowers tra la bullshit. Now that she was alone, she looked turbo pissed and ready to take poor Ilex's head off. "Tell me, what do you hope to gain, taking her side? What have you gotten so far? No, don't bother speaking. Nothing. You remain invisible. You carry and fetch for her, and *she* not even one of us. That's all you'll ever do, though you may mistake her desperation for company to be some sort of friendship. Ha, you're like a little pet, aren't you? That woman likes her pets. Well, please recall that I made you, and I can just as easily unmake you."

Ilex lifted her gaze and stared Madame down. "You did not make me. You don't own me."

Madame's eyes widened and she took a step back. "I never..." her fingertips went to her trembling lips. "I never realized...I didn't think you felt..." Ilex actually started to look hopeful when Madame dissolved into laughter. "Stupid girl. I wrote the charm that gave you breath, and so by my logic, I own that much of you. And now I want it back. "And she poked Ilex in the chest.

Ilex gave a strangled gasp and put her hands to her throat, her knees buckled, but she remained standing. I could see the lights in her eyes dimming.

"I'm going in there," March said.

"The fuck you are." I hissed at him, and held him back. "She's not going to kill Ilex. *Think*. Marly would literally flip her shit, and Madame doesn't want that kind of attention right now." And then I prayed I was right.

After eight million years, or about ten seconds, Madame rolled her eyes in irritation and poked Ilex again, and she fell to her hands and knees. We could hear her gasping as air rushed back into her lungs and see her back heaving; she was alive. When she could get to her feet, she swayed and righted herself. Madame took Ilex's chin in her hand, leaned forward and whispered in her ear…a word. Something. For an instant I greyed out, like a headrush from standing up too fast. If March hadn't been so close behind me, I might have fallen over. The feeling went as quickly as it came, and I watched as Madame released Ilex and they exchanged a long stare. After a bit Ilex nodded and walked out of the room and past us, back up the stairs.

"Thank you, Master Greaves, for coming to me with this. I trust this is the last of this kind of foolishness?"

He didn't look happy, but he nodded. So, excellent tailor but not such a good guy. My track record of knowing who did what to whom remained intact at 'no idea.'

Before he left, Greaves said, "There will come a reckoning, Madame, of that you may be certain. I rather hope I'm alive to see it."

# 22

*Ruby*

After everyone was gone, I followed March back up to the main hallway, past the beehive and into my room. I was shaking like a leaf, and as soon as the door shut, I began pretty much babbling at him.

"Okay. Okay, let's think. They didn't mention the Seelie. Did they mention the Seelie?" I didn't wait for him to answer. "No. They didn't. But they're planning something, Madame and the constructs. And Ilex got ratted out by fucking Master Greaves, of all people." I paused. "He actually did tell me he'd be untrustworthy. Still gonna kill him, or Marly will for sure. What was that at the end? What did Madame say to Ilex?"

He shook his head. "I felt it, too. A charm, I think, of great power."

I pulled on my hair and paced. "We have to go to Marly and Sasha. Like, this is what he wanted us to do."

"You," March corrected me. "He wanted you to find out

what Madame had in mind. My job is still undone."

"Are you gonna sit there and tell me you're still working for that woman? Seriously?"

"The laws of this place don't change just because you don't like the players. I am bound by the rules of hospitality to at least make an attempt to find out what Sasha has in mind. Of course, I might fail." He rubbed his chin. "She's offered something to the constructs, something that will hurt Sasha. And it seems like she has them all on her side." He got a concerned look. "You understand that even if I do fail her and I find out nothing, she could still win this and take the throne back. That would impact you and Marly. And Sasha."

I nodded. "Unless whatever Sasha's planning is something the Seelie can't resist or refuse. I don't know what he'd have to offer them, though. Marly thinks—"

"Her faith in him is remarkable." He smiled sadly and repeated what he'd said earlier; "He is fortunate."

"Yeah." I didn't want to get back into the respective love lives of every single fucking body in the kingdom. Okay, that's not true—there was one person whose body I was interested in, and that had been a mistake. A beautiful, intense, hot mistake. I cleared my throat. "So, I'm guessing Ilex didn't tell Mar what she knows, she probably thinks she's protecting her boss. That makes tracking down Ilex my next job. She already came to me once, so later I'll try and find more, and see if she's okay. As far as your mission—"

"Failure is within my reach, I just know it." That was the closest thing to a joke I'd heard him make, and I even got one of those heart stopping smiles to go along with it.

*It's too dangerous, leading on a magical creature. Remember? Mistake?* I reminded myself. *But I want to,* I cleverly countered. Both sides of the aisle agreed to keep talking while also hoping the rising tide of desire would somehow evaporate.

I resumed pacing, the other option being sitting next to him. "Good, great. I know you can't do it; I don't believe in you." I chuckled weakly, reached the bathroom, and turned to head the other way.

"Could you not?" March took my hand and gently tugged me down onto the bed next to him, which only made me think—unhelpfully—of grabbing him by the hair. "Let's try and think of what Madame said."

I sat next to him and wracked my brains trying to remember her speech. But all I could think of was how I felt in his arms. This was nuts. Oh, he was talking again. I tried to tune out my lady parts and tune into his voice.

"We should be more careful, if all the constructs are indeed with Madame. My options are limited. I must take care not to learn anything useful."

"I have to get ready for tonight. You should get moving," I said, which was better than 'you should take off your pants,' which is what I wanted to say.

He looked surprised. "Are we finished with this conversation? Because something happened..."

"Yeah, sorry about that whole... I think it must be this place, right? Crazy making things happening." Yeah, Rube, that was a masterful thesis statement. I took a breath. "What happened...I'm sorry. I don't know...I mean, I usually don't climb on top of guys I barely know." He looked at me like I'd slapped him. "I don't know what to say to you. Now you look upset. Are you angry that I kissed you?"

Thinking back on it, he hadn't been angry at the time—maybe more confused than anything. Maybe a little conflicted. He sure hadn't pushed me away, though.

"Of course, I'm not angry." He leaned back and looked at me, like he was trying to decide something. "You're starting to remember. Aren't you." Not a question. "A little. I know you are."

"When this is over, we should get Chinese food. I know you like it." As soon as I spoke, my stomach did a slow roll.

"Ruby...?" He looked at me with such hope and such longing, and it was like every light in the universe came on at once. And somehow I recognized that look, and I wanted it to last forever. God, but he was beautiful.

How was any of this possible?

"Why are you looking at me like...I...I don't know why I said that." I gave a little laugh. "What a weird thing to say. Sorry."

I watched him deflate, and my stomach settled down. Not the rest of me, though. I could actually hear my heart. I wanted him to look at me that way again. "I'm sorry I'm not making sense. I'm just, um, shook up, I guess. I keep feeling like I'm forgetting something, but whenever I try to remember I start to feel—well, you don't want to hear about that."

"I want to hear whatever you have to say," he replied.

"Why?" I looked up at him. "Who *are* you?"

He replied in a soft voice, but I couldn't understand what

he said. It didn't matter, anyway.

I could feel the heat coming off his skin, and I wanted to touch him. And then I did remember something—while he was in this body—this beautiful body—I could. I didn't want him to leave anymore. I didn't want to talk, either. But I said, "Maybe you should stay and I'll see if anything else comes back to me," because it seemed like that was what he wanted me to say.

He looked at me closely. "Anything else? Then you do remember?"

I smiled and felt my nausea recede. "I honestly don't know what you mean." In that moment I didn't care about his past or mine, or what he thought I'd forgotten. For the first time in ages, I knew what I wanted, and my whole body felt fine.

I leaned forward and sort of closed my eyes, and then I *fell* forward, face first onto the bed, because he'd jumped out of the way. I sat back up to see him scrambling to his feet. "What the actual fuck...?"

He looked horrified. "Not like this, Ruby." He backed away, and it felt like a slap. "I can't, not with you like this. It would be wrong, worse than wrong. I'm sorry."

"You're sorry? That you kissed me? You know what, that's fine. I was right about you. I didn't like you when I met you, I should have stuck with that. You're right. This was a mistake." I beat him to the punch by turning away. Let him leave, I got the last word. Wow, good for me.

I heard the door shut.

I didn't feel so well.

"Fuck. March, don't—"
But he was gone.

# 23

*Ruby*

Still swearing at my own stupid heart, I followed March out into the corridor, but he already vanished. Fled, I should say. My heart was still pounding, but the desire had been replaced by a looming grey weight, one I knew very well.

It was back, like it'd been waiting at my shoulder for me to relax for one second, like I'd been attacked by vampires not years ago, but now. I could feel their damp, cool hands. I could smell them rotting inside their rags. And I could feel their teeth.

The weight settling on my shoulders; I was garbage. I was dirty. I stank.

*I'm alive, I'm in my body...* I tried Dr. Bel's mantra to try and climb on top of this wave of despair, but it was too heavy and I just sank to the floor. I could handle a civil war, even if I wasn't sure what side I was on. I could take my best friend's transformation. I could even take Sasha. But March, this man I didn't even know—he brought all my hard-earned peace of mind crashing down.

*Ruby,* I reminded myself, *something's been wrong with you for months. Don't blame March. Blame yourself.*

I leaned against the wall, lowered my head onto my knees, and blamed myself.

He doesn't want me this way. It isn't right. He can't. He's perfect, and I'm—I'm garbage. He can tell, he can smell it on me, he knows what I really am.

I would be this way forever.

"Who did this? I'll pop a cap in their punk ass."

I jerked my head up, and to my astonishment Amory was sitting on the floor next to me. "Pop a cap means explode, right?" He stretched out his long legs; they reached halfway across the corridor. He looked at me expectantly. "Right?"

"Um, sort of."

He grinned lazily. "Knew it." God, this was the day of weird interactions with gorgeous men. "We don't get many weeping humans around here, so I thought I'd investigate. Who was the punk ass attached to?"

I sighed and wiped my face. "It was just a misunderstanding, I guess. See, March and I—"

He gasped and slapped his hand to his chest. "My March?"

"You...your March?" My face got hot and then cold, and my heart sank, and I didn't know why. "You two are..."

"Well, not precisely. Informal introductions were made, and I did touch him on the shoulder. But I have plans in motion. What happened?"

"Nothing." Even though it made me feel more stupid, it kind of made sense. Why would he want someone like me when Amory was also on the menu? And I did grab him and kiss him, not the other way around. "I thought…I didn't respect his boundaries."

He put it together in about two seconds. "He didn't go for it?"

"Swing and a miss."

"It happens." He got to his feet and held out his hand. "Let's go get drunk."

I hesitated. "I have to go talk to Marly."

"Aw, come on. Marly can wait." His eyes sparked and shimmered like late-summer heat lightning over Biscayne Bay. Marly said he was fun. What else did she say? Something about…dialysis?

I heard myself saying, "Yeah, I guess she can wait a little while."

"She's been busy, our lady queen. What with usurping the throne and all." He laughed at my expression. "Gotcha." He shook his head. "The look on your face just now, it was so interesting." He stuck his hand out again. "Ready?"

I took his hand and he hauled me up, my black cloud partially dispersed, although I couldn't help but feel like I'd forgotten something. "Can I ask you a question?" He looked at me curiously. "What do I smell like to you?"

He stopped. "Did you say *smell*?" To his immense credit, he didn't laugh. He leaned towards me. "Salt and honey. Women smell like that to me, mostly. Oh, and rosemary, maybe lemon, but I think that's coming from your hair."

"Salt, honey, lemon, and rosemary. So, I smell like the chicken roasting for Shabbat dinner." I laughed, probably sounding a touch hysterical. "What was that about a drink?"

"Right this way." Still holding my hand, he took a step, and I followed—and were no longer in the palace, no longer anywhere I'd been in the kingdom. We were in a charming, crowded country pub complete with a packed earth floor, little round windows looking out onto a Disney-perfect pastoral landscape, raw timber beams overhead, a long, battered oak bar, and not one single woman.

"This is the cutest gay bar in the Shire," I said wonderingly. I didn't know if the patrons—mostly field hand looking dudes, a couple of guys in robes that might have been bards or wizards, and the shirtless staff—were real, or constructs, or cosplayers, but they were all crazy cute, and I couldn't help notice that quite a few of them closely resembled Amory himself.

"It's nice, isn't it?" He led me to a table and an adorable dark-haired kid came over, kissed his cheek and put a couple of beers down in front of us. "I keep this place around for when I want to be alone, but not *alone* alone."

"I actually completely understand." I drank the beer and felt my heart slowly go back to normal. "So, your March, huh? He's...I honestly just met him." Talking about what happened like it meant nothing at all would eventually make me feel less mortified. Eventually. I hoped. I took another sip. "I thought he was into me for a minute, and I guess I...extrapolated."

He looked at me with pity. "You know everyone gets

vibes from unicorns. That's how they're built. Add the vibes to his overall…Marchness, and well, he's a lot to take in. Don't be mad at him, he can't help it."

Was that all it was? That March put out some sort of magical pheromone, some kind of weird effect, and it made me act like a dumbass horny teenager? I looked at Amory archly. "But you and your plan don't rely on vibes."

"Nope. The fae are immune. That's why he likes it here."

Well, now I felt worse, like I'd gone to his vacation spot and foisted myself on him. "I'll leave him to you, I guess."

"We just need to find you someone else. The kingdom isn't huge, but there's plenty of lights in the trees."

That made me smile. "You know who's kind of cute? Aster."

"Yeah…I mean, he is. Sweet kid. But…" he looked uneasy.

"What?"

"Just…don't get too attached. In the next few days, things are going to change." He gave a short laugh. "Change hands, even. I mean, you know that—yes, of course we'll honor the venerated, faultless, lamented Lauren C—"

"Hey, now—she was really nice—"

"…but everyone knows the king invited the Seelie Court here for something dramatic. And some of us have a part to play. I'm just being honest."

A part to play. I thought about Madame, and how Aster was "Madame's boy," and wondered what part she had in mind for him.

"Okay, so Aster is off the table. Who else you got?"

He frowned, looking thoughtful. "Are you absolutely wedded to human appearing folk? Like, what are your thoughts on trolls?"

I chuckled. "I guess that would depend on how they feel about chicken."

He folded his arms. "Oh look, a callback to a joke you told an hour ago that still doesn't make any sense."

I drew myself up. "It makes sense to me."

He rested his chin on his hands and gave me a sideways grin. "I believe that you've uncovered the secret of comedy."

I lifted my glass. "I already know that one. The more you drink, the funnier I get."

# 24

*Ruby*

After another beer and a conversation regarding the dateability of trolls, Amory dropped me back off outside my room. We'd decided to hold off on getting completely faced for another time, because it suddenly came back to me that I had to go find Marly and let her know what I'd overheard. We'd overheard. March and me. In that shadowy, warm little alcove.

*Oh my God, snap out of it!*

Yet even though he was out of my league, didn't play for my team, and Amory had called dibs, how could I possibly stop thinking about him? No, just concentrate on the assignment. Yeah, that's it. Concentrate on Marly, on Sasha, and maybe even on getting Ilex to talk to me about Madame, and on anything other than March's delicious mouth...

Sitting around my room wasn't going to cut it. I rummaged through my closet and decided on a cobalt blue robe with pale gray accents. I thought it was the chicest thing ever, but what do I know? In my closet back home, I have going-out-to-dinner jeans (white tablecloth), going-out-to-dinner jeans (no tablecloth, table optional), housework jeans, and work jeans. Oh, and sweatpants. I am truly whatever the opposite of fashion is. Anyway, I tied the belt as best I could, trying to remember how Aster made the knot nice and flat. My version was a little lumpy, and I think that's what they'll put on my tombstone:

Ruby Black
*She was a little lumpy*

Once I was pulled together, I got Marecy, who had discreetly been out of sight during my little hallway meltdown, to point me in the direction of Marly's house.

"One more thing," she said. I turned back, expectantly. "Let me fix this for you." She retied the damned sash and got rid of my lumps. Trying to sound casual, she asked, "Are you feeling better?" I said I was. "Unicorns, huh?"

Everyone knew the human girl had a meltdown! That was definitely excellent news. But I couldn't even be mad about it. He was what he was—it was like a peanut allergy. You can't be mad at Planters. Anyway, I nodded ruefully and thanked her. I was going to have to send her flowers when this was over.

I was most of the way to Marly's house when I managed to get kissing March out of my mind for long enough to remember what she was doing when I left, and I had a hideous thought; what if Sasha was still there? Like, still there? I decided to take a chance. If they were 'busy' I would slink off into the night. Maybe look for Aster. Even if what Amory said was true—and why wouldn't it be—he'd be a good distraction. I mean, Aster had a nice mouth too, right? Right?

When I got to her place, the coast was clear—I mean, the front window was wide open, and you could see all the way through the house. "Hey," I shouted, "let me in." When Marly swanned her way to the front door, I could see by the look on her face just what kind of an afternoon she'd had. "Oh my God," I said, "you absolute tart."

She grinned. "Jealous."

"Okay," I said, "We are definitely going to circle back around to this, but a lot just happened and we need to talk."

"Hmm," Marly said, sounding extremely just-got-laid. "Sure." She flopped on the couch and patted the cushion next to her. "Let's talk. What's up?"

"First of all, Madame is building a coalition among the constructs."

She frowned, but didn't look particularly surprised. "That actually makes sense."

"Because...."

"Well, we did something to Madame a while ago, and in retrospect it may not have been the smartest thing in the world."

"Why do I feel like you're burying the lede, here? What did you do to her?"

"When Sasha gave me my crown, the night it happened? We made her think he was going to give it to her, instead. She was hella humiliated in front of the whole court. It was fantastic...for about twenty-four hours. Then she got right to work, and it looks like she got some traction among the constructs."

I sat forward. "You publicly humiliated her? The same Madame whose super powerful and knows all the magic? That Madame?"

She blushed. "It seemed like a good idea? I mean, I wanted to straight up murder her. Sasha thought—"

"Well, there's your problem."

Her eyes flashed. "Enough."

I guess we were done joking about Sasha. "Have you seen Ilex today?"

That got her attention. "No. What happened?"

I told her how March and I—intending to maybe talk to Master Greaves or even Ilex on their home turf—had stumbled on something unexpected. "And after she told them how they'd live in the light or some shit, Master Greaves stood up and said it would rain back down on her, but he wouldn't stop whatever she was up to. Then she called out Ilex for being loyal to you, and..."

"What?"

"She put her finger on Ilex's chest and it looked like she stopped breathing for a few seconds."

Marly's eyes went wide and she grabbed my arm. "You better tell me she's okay."

I yanked my arm away. "She's fine." I paused. "Honestly,

I don't know if she's fine. Before Madame let her go, she said something, some kind of charm. I don't know what it did to her. But Ilex definitely walked out of there under her own power." I straightened my robe. "When we had breakfast, she told me, 'We don't all agree' like it was a big secret. What does that mean?"

Now Marly looked pissed. "I have no idea. She didn't say a word to me, or else we'd be on top of this whole construct situation. She was trying to protect me. She got in trouble because she's loyal to me. Fucking Madame again and as usual." She sighed. "Sasha and I were going to address the construct situation *after* the party. Looks like we missed our window."

"And it was our dear old friend Master Greaves who ratted her out."

"Aw, shit. Madame, the constructs and Master Greaves? Yeah, we'd better go see Sash and ruin his afternoon."

"There's actually something else."

She gave me an appraising look. "You've had a day."

"Maybe it's nothing…"

"That is not a nothing face. Let me have it."

"I kissed March."

She almost tumbled off the couch. "You whaaaaaat?"

"Geez, no need to yell. You heard me. I don't know what made me—"

"Oh my god, you fish scissors. Backyard face tree cat, honey."

I ground the heels of my hands against my eyes. "Knock it off! Stop saying stuff like that. I can't understand you." I figured the medallion wasn't translating right. Maybe it was disintegrating along with everything else in this place. "Anyway, it was a mistake and from the way he reacted, it won't happen again. Amory says he's not into women, anyway."

"Amory? He said that, huh?" She frowned. "What else did your friend Amory say?"

"He said not to get too attached to Aster, either." I rubbed my head. "That he had some sort of part to play in whatever the fuck Madame is planning." I stopped, thinking about what else he'd said. "And something will change hands. Or was it someone? No, I think he said 'thing.' What does that mean?" I know what it meant back home, but based on what I'd been hearing it could be a literal swap of appendages, how would I know?

She frowned. "A trade. She's going to make a trade." Her eyebrows pinched together. "Okay, you know how I told you and March I didn't know what Sasha had in mind?"

"It turns out you actually do?"

"I do. I didn't want to tell March, in case he was…I don't know…compelled to tell Madame." I didn't think he'd willingly do that, but I agreed it was good policy. "Sasha has something he wants to give them. A trade of our own."

"Yeah? Don't keep me hanging."

"Sasha's sword. That's the trade. It was made from glass that was, ah, broken during the Light War." I looked confused, I'm sure. Why would they want that? "It's partially symbolic—that we're giving up our rights to the glass. It may not be popular, but Sasha thinks it's our only chance to get the glass re-lit and save the kingdom."

"Yeah. Speaking of chances, March thinks there's a chance you and Sasha might, um, lose." I added quickly, "He's not going to do anything to help Madame, but you have to admit, she's been busy." I took a breath; she wasn't going to like this. "Have you given any thought at all to what might happen if things go south? Like, about having to leave?" She began to argue and I held up my hand. "I know, iron and all that back home. But you may have no choice."

"If anyone does leave—and no one is leaving—it would have to be me. I brought a lot of this down on him, even though he'd never admit it."

I tried to picture Marly leaving Sasha behind and came up empty. "But if you had to go? What would happen?"

Marly frowned. "Nothing good." She paused for a minute, thinking. "Do you remember that time we drove to the club in Fort Lauderdale?"

I went through the mental rolodex. "Which one?" My college years—at least, pre-vamp attack—had been a blur of trashy bars and even trashier boys. "Oh, you mean the one off of State Road 84?"

"Yeah. The one we thought was going to be some retro punk new wave thing?"

I laughed. I did remember that night. "And when we got there it turned out to be a country bar. What was it called? Hot Pants? Or was it Boot Cut? I can't remember."

"But we were tricked out in black lipstick and torn fishnets." Truly, we were glorious.

"And we went in anyway, and we were the belles of the fucking ball." Marly leaned forward and poked my arm. "And you danced with a real cowboy!"

I smiled. "I was on the dance floor and got felt-up by a guy wearing a hat. Granted, the difference can be hard to spot."

Marly cocked her head. "The last thing I remember is his hand on your ass. After that…"

"After that you decided to finish off a pitcher of Alabama Slammers. I believe your rationale was that the color was so pretty, and you could barely taste the alcohol. And you also reminded me that I am not the boss of you." I steepled my fingers. "A bitter lesson."

Marly giggled and clapped her hands to her head. "Just thinking about the taste is giving me a headache. I woke up next to the bed, but at least I was in the house. And then…"

The next part, I remembered very well. "And then the barfing. All the bright pink barfing. If you listen hard, you can still hear your barfing echoing in the wind. Man, you were sick for three days."

"That exact feeling," Marly said, suddenly deadly serious, "is what I think of, when I think of leaving. Come on. Sasha better hear about this. Walk over with me, and I'll tell you about my day. That'll cheer us both up."

By the time we got back to the palace, I'd learned more than I ever wanted to know about fae mating habits. Suffice to say that once they make a decision, they do not hold back.

"I know you two have, um, a history and you think he's a snob, but he's honestly kind of an animal," I was informed. "I'm three inches taller and can see the ultraviolet spectrum." She paused. "This is TMI, but he can kind of…shape shift?"

That brought me to a halt. "Like turn into other people?"

She nodded. "Anyone. Like, Wesley Snipes, or Kurt Vonnegut, or a young Jane Goodall."

"Jane was pretty dishy," I agreed.

She laughed. "He's never actually turned into any of them, specifically. But he has turned into…other people."

"No wonder you like it here. Hey, if he can turn into two of himself, well, you'd be living the dream."

"To be honest I don't think I'd survive it. But I'd die doing what I loved."

"*Mazel tov?*"

She grinned, the lights in her eyes dancing. "I can't tell if you're happy for me or if your face is frozen like that."

"Is it sort of a rictus?" She slapped my arm. "I'm kidding. I am happy for you. I know you're stuck here—"

"I am not stuck—"

"…and it wasn't your idea, and it was a tough road."

She cocked her head. "I am grudgingly agreeing with you." We turned a corner, and the palace gates opened in front of us, despite the fact that they should have been behind us.

I squeezed Marly's hand. "It doesn't matter what I think of him. You deserve to be happy."

"So do you," Marly replied. "So do you."

"…and then it turns out that Master Greaves informed on Ilex." I tried to read Sasha's expression, but he had been king much longer than I had been a spy, and I didn't know if what we learned was helpful or useless.

"It makes sense, unfortunately. Greaves was her first creation," Marly said. They sat side by side in his (their?)

reception room, not touching, and I have to admit they looked like the perfect Unseelie royal couple; he with his flowing hair and shiny armor, and her with dark silk and chiffon, and both of them with their crowns of light. Like a cake topper at the gothest wedding ever. "Ilex is undercover. We even have a code phrase if shit really goes down—Aunt Harriet." She frowned. "I think getting your breath stolen counts as 'goes down', and she still hasn't come to me. Time for us to have a conversation."

"You may find that difficult," he said. "From what you described, I fear she has stolen Ilex's spirit."

"Spirit?" I asked. "You mean like her soul?"

He shrugged. "There is some debate as to whether the fae possess souls at all, much less constructs."

The look on Marly's face told me she'd heard the collective *gasp* from every one of her abuelas from the last three hundred years, but she decided to be more upset (for the moment) about Ilex. Sasha must have known she'd lose her shit, because he took her hand and quickly added, "Madame has temporarily taken that which makes Ilex her own unique self. She wants Ilex silenced; I imagine until after the fete. How long after, I can't know."

Marly ground her teeth. "I'll kill her for this." She folded her arms. "And I definitely have a fucking soul."

He sighed. "Of course you do. And you'll have your friend back, my queen. Please don't try anything with Madame. We have discussed this." He gave me a pointed look and I gave him one back. Marly sure as shit didn't look convinced. I could see the 'plotting revenge' wheels turning. I had to figure out how to defuse her, on top of everything else. Speaking of which…

"There's something else," I said. "Something I don't think you know. It sounds like Madame is going to make some sort of exchange, offer something to the Seelie Court. But what that means, I have no idea." I repeated carefully edited parts of my conversation with Amory, and how he thought Aster was somehow involved.

He swore full-blast in Unseelie, and even with the medallion it made my ears ring. Then he grilled me on what I thought it meant, and whether March knew anything about it.

"After all," Sasha said, "he is here at her invitation, and technically is bound to her. But I rather doubt he'd keep faith with her if it meant harming either one of you."

"Unless he had no choice," said Marly.

"Well, what do we do?" I asked.

"Perhaps Aster might prove useful after all. Of course, take care lest he figure out what you're doing."

"Well, he knows what I'm doing. Sort of." I rubbed my forehead. "He just seems so nice, it's hard to imagine him signing off on all of this."

"'Seems' is the key word," Marly reminded me. "Other than me, March is the only one you can absolutely count on." She patted Sasha's hand. "No offense, sweetie."

He smiled at her. "None taken. Marly is correct." He nodded. "Get what you can out of Aster and leave the bargaining to me." He looked at the sky, at the ring of glass. "Well, it's time. May I accompany you both to dinner?

Tonight should be interesting."

I looked at Marly curiously. "Pre-party-party," she said. "Maybe avoid the wine."

# 25

*March*

She is starting to remember me. I know she is. Isn't she?* Why else would she have touched him, held him close, kissed him? She even mentioned the food in the cartons he liked. It wasn't this place affecting her. Was it?

It had to be something. Perhaps Madame was correct and the shadows—and his presence, his carefully applied pressure—brought her back to him. Or, of course, it could be what he was, the thing that humans responded to. It could be like the woman in the car. It could be nothing more than that.

He hoped it was something more than that.

He didn't like how he had left her, but he couldn't see any other choice. It wouldn't be right to do what he wanted and take her, right then and there, even if she thought she wanted it, too. It wouldn't be honest. It wasn't consent. If she ever did remember him—and he lived in hope that somehow, she would—it would be an outrage. It would have been one more thing he got without deserving. Had he ever deserved anything?

He paused, recognizing this feeling, one of the new ones. He put a name to it: guilt.

He walked on without seeing the walls and halls of the palace around him, remembering her touch, the rosemary scent of her hair, the warmth of her skin. He walked and thought about her and came to a halt when he realized he had no idea where he was. The hallways stretched away from him in all directions, and they all looked the same: gleaming wood paneling; urns and vases and plants and glass made to look like plants; the black and red marble tiles on the floor becoming black and dark green and then black and cream; the ceiling, which was nothing but sky... the shadows, where something was wrong. He tried to regroup and figure out which way to go by the light of the glass panels—the broken one should stay in the same place, but did it? Or did they rotate? He couldn't remember.

He walked and again his thoughts drifted and wandered, from the stolen moments with Ruby, to a long-ago midnight thunderstorm on a broken hillside and him watching the lightning set fires to the distant prairie. When he blinked back to reality, it was dark, and he knew he had taken a wrong turn.

He stood on a street in the carcass of a city that had once been thriving, but any residents were dead or had fled. The tattered veils of low and fast-blowing smoke burned his nose; his eyes watered. All around him he could see the past in the glinting shapes of lives flitting about, moving in and out of the faint chalk outlines of houses; in the lit windows and flowers on the path, which had long since collapsed. He could hear dreams and hopes like the tinkling of bells muffled by dust. The things that had replaced the former residents noticed him, and lifted their…well, it wasn't strictly "heads" that pointed in his direction. Something was in front of him, quite close but draped in shadows. Something was right behind him. Something breathed wetly against his neck.

He changed.

He took a tentative step forward, then looked down, feeling something move under his hoof. It was a huge beetle, iridescent as an oil spill, and he'd stepped on it.

"Wait, friend," he called, but it vibrated its hand-sized wing carapaces with a sound like teeth rattling in a jar and then raced under a pile of stones before he could reach down and heal it. He wondered if he could reach down and heal everything, this whole place, and why not at least try? He poked his horn through the piles of ash to touch the dead earth.

For a moment, nothing. He held his breath. Slowly, the ash began to twitch and shiver. More quickly now—and his heart leapt to see it—grass; living, growing, grass, frail and tender at first, but gaining strength and coming up through the cracked and broken ground. He could smell it (petrichor) and could feel the new growth, and he laughed in his own true voice, and the creatures who called this dead place home shuddered and moved further into the gloom. The grass grew under his feet in a soft fragrant carpet, and for a moment he felt awe and joy. Creation and life, this was what he was for, not secrets and ties, and shoes and polite conversation.

But the grass kept growing, and as it grew it changed from grass to something else—something that hungered. It sent tendrils up and around his legs, and the tendrils grew fat and began to tighten. It wasn't pain, exactly, it was more like a numbness that spread from where the pale green shoots touched him, and when he realized he couldn't lift his feet he began to panic. The grass on the stony ground around him kept growing, even if it wasn't grass anymore, crawling over itself to join the choking vines around his legs and chest, wrapping itself around his long and slender neck, and coiling quickly over his head, smothering him. The numbness spread through his body, and he realized it had been several moments since he'd taken a breath. Even though he could no longer see the grass, he could hear it, shrieking joyous victory as it strangled him.

*I'm going to die*, he realized, and felt surprise and regret.

But when the vine reached his horn, it touched the dimming, silvery light and screamed like a burned animal, and withered, and was gone. Whatever had befallen this place was worse than just the dark—it was a sort of anti-light, which corrupted his magic and turned it against him. Like *malice*, like *sarcasm*, like *guilt*, it had never happened to him before.

This was the future Madame feared, and what the whole of the kingdom would fall to, once the lights went out and the gardens were dead. Were the things who retreated from his light some fae folk who had somehow been transformed? Or consumed?

If he had wandered here accidentally, it must be close.

It must practically be on their doorstep. He didn't know whether Madame or Sasha had a better chance of convincing the Seelie Court to come to their aid, or if they could put aside their games and squabbles long enough to see it through, but he vowed as he stood in the burned street with the faint fragrance of spring dying in the air, he'd do whatever he could to save them all.

# 26

*March*

After putting his human form back on, March took a moment to brush off the dust, and with some disgust picked the dead vines out of his hair. He thought about the shower in Ruby's house back in the mortal realm with longing. It (and she) felt very far away.

He gave a last look around for the beetle, wished it luck, and moved on.

This time he paid much closer attention, and soon came across a hall of roses (which made him think of Madame) and he thought perhaps the roses were real, although he didn't stop to inspect them. They smelled alive, and he didn't want to be disappointed. As he walked on, the roses stopped blooming but the thorns remained, and although the thought of vines grasping him and thorns piercing filled him with fear, he forced himself to continue. Fresh, cool water ran across the floor in places, and sometimes the walls vanished when you looked at them (like the lights in the alcove, and then he had to pause and remember what they had done there, he and Ruby in the alcove), and sometimes the walls rushed towards him, like they wanted an embrace.

He turned a corner and stepped into nothing. Midnight darkness all around him, not a star above or a bit of gleaming glass. Unlike the dirty darkness of the ruined town, this was nothing but peaceful. He took another tentative step into it, feeling a sort of pull in his belly and legs. He was afraid to look down; what if there was nothing left of him? He closed his eyes. It felt fine, this nothingness. He took another step—

"Hey friend, I don't think you want to go any further." A strong hand on his shoulder pulled him away from the velvety darkness. Returning to himself was like a blast of cold water; he shivered. "You alright? You were starting to look a little discorporeal, there."

"I'm fine, I think. What is that place?"

The man who had pulled him away (saved him?) regarded him with the all-black eyes that were starting to look normal by now. He ran his hand through his cropped dark gold hair. "It's called the Eye. It's a place of reflection and return. But I don't think it would be a good idea for you." He smiled. "You're not exactly from around here, are you?"

March smiled back. "Is it that obvious?"

"Other than your..." he pointed at March's face; his eyes. "Not obvious at all. I'm Amory, by the way."

He had seen this fae before, he was the one who pointed him in the right direction in the dining hall. "I believe this is the second time you've rescued me. I'm March."

"I merely did what any friend would do. That was quite a performance at dinner, by the way." March ducked his head. "No, it was kind of you to rescue that poor human girl. Tournesol will have her fun, even when it's not very funny." The two contemplated each other for a moment. "Were you going somewhere?"

"Um, yes. I was trying to find my way back to my room, and I'm afraid I took a wrong turn." He glanced back at the Eye, and thought of the vines around his throat, and shuddered. "A couple of wrong turns."

"Well, allow me to escort you back to civilization." March followed Amory away from the Eye, even as it pulled him, like a persistent little hand on his sleeve, and tried to lure him back. "So, you and the little human, huh?"

March blanched. "We were seen?"

Amory narrowed his brow. "Was it your intention not to be seen?"

March sighed. "That was the idea. Was it you?"

"Oh no. My man, Rue. He was on his way down to the Belly and passed you. He said it appeared you two were... busy, so he elected not to interrupt. And he told me what he'd seen." Another pause. "Forgive my being so forward, but judging by your behavior—and hers—last night, I wouldn't have guessed you two were...involved, is the right word? Or perhaps *Make-Out Island* is truer than I thought and humans are extraordinarily quick to decide whom they favor."

He ran his hands through his hair. "It's complicated. It's a long story."

Amory stopped walking and leaned against a silver

filigreed panel separating the corridor from some large hall or other. He touched March lightly on the sleeve, his fingers tracing the subtle pattern in the weave. "In case you hadn't noticed, I have both plenty of time and a sudden keen interest."

March couldn't think of a reason not to tell him. Even if he was one of Madame's agents, she wouldn't learn anything new. "The short version is that we were once involved, as you said. Very involved. But now she is under an enchantment which has caused her to forget who I am or that we'd ever met."

"Hmm." Amory thought about it. "She's fallen in love with you twice. Nicely done."

"No," March said. "In fact, she told me to leave, and that she doesn't care for me at all. It was a mistake. What your man saw—it should never have happened. She doesn't know her own mind, and so I would be taking advantage. That's why I almost fell into the Eye—I was a little distracted."

"I've definitely seen that strategy before on *Make-Out Island,* but let's set that aside for the moment. Give me a bit of the longer version. Who enchanted your human? And why? I know you are here as a guest of Madame. Is she somehow involved?"

"Indirectly." He chewed the inside of his cheek. Amory seemed sympathetic, curious, helpful. And he felt a sort of pull, much like the way the Eye had drawn him in. But would he endanger his new friend by telling him the truth? He decided, as he almost always did, to accept the help that had been put in his path. "She was enchanted by Sasha, your king." Amory raised his brow. "He did it to prevent me from coming un-stuck in time. As I said, it's complicated."

"Unstuck...this is a unicorn thing, I gather?"

He found he didn't mind explaining how his mind worked. "...and so it's everything, all at once. Except, not her. I mean, I remember her, but I can't re-experience my time with her." He was surprised at how his usual frustration at not being able to describe how he felt or how he saw things seemed to vanish. This tall and interesting fae seemed to understand him.

"Our Lord king, he's always got one eye on the horizon. It may have been offered as a gift—"

"It was not. And as you know, it was Madame who brought me here. I don't think Sasha was happy to see me."

Amory nodded slowly. "Madame has eyes and allies everywhere. You must take great care with your words and your trust, and then take greater care again. And you may be sure she had a reason to bring you here, one that benefits herself first."

March realized that while they talked, they had been making their way back to his room. It had been too long since he'd had a conversation this interesting, this pleasant; certainly not while he'd been in the Unseelie Court. Perhaps he ought to continue it?

"This is where I am staying. I'd invite you to come in but there's nowhere to sit."

Amory looked confused. "Madame didn't provide you with furniture? She's a lot of things, but I've never heard her called a poor host."

March smiled. "She provided perfectly well for someone who lives in the deep of the forest. With four legs."

"And a horn? I'm afraid I was at a distance last night."

*He wants something*, March thought, and remembered a time when such a realization would never have occurred to him. The humans taught him what to listen for. But he, March, wanted something too. He said, "I am told it is quite a sight to see up close."

Amory gave him a long look. "You tempt me to stay. But..." He slipped his hand inside March's robe and placed his palm over his heart. "When I hear you say 'yes,' I'd much rather be the only one on your mind." He withdrew his hand and took a step back. "I'll see you this evening."

Once inside, March cast about at the piles of (fake) leaves on the floor, the two hooks on the wall for his two robes, the water which ran down the wall into a pool, as if this was a forest glade, a place like home, a place a million billion miles away. He didn't know what to do with himself, and finally he threw the robe on the floor and changed into his real, other self for the second time that day. Lightness lifted his heart and his spirit, and lasted for a long, sweet moment, until he was filled with the desire to run.

There was nowhere to go.

He changed back and lay down on the bed of soft leaves, and folded his arms behind his head. Was it better, his life before? When he had never lived a week of life as a mortal man, or loved a human woman, or known about things like loss or regret, or confusion or guilt? Before he had felt time's touch? It had been a simple way to live, moment-to-moment, tree to cloud to mountainside. Winter to summer. But was it better?

He was still trying to decide when his eyes closed, and he slept.

# 27

*Ruby*

**M**arly, Sasha, and I came back to the big room—the scene of my drunken glory—which I was starting to think of as the ballroom. The crowd gathered for dinner was significantly smaller and somehow more relaxed. We followed Sasha as he decided where to sit. Before I grabbed a chair, I started my fancy curtsey. He flapped his arms at me.

"No need for that. Now sit, and let us begin."

"What are we beginning?" I asked Marly, who settled in next to Sasha. Aster showed up with Madame, and March arrived late and sat with them, looking mighty thoughtful. Since they hadn't arrived together, and she hadn't taken anyone's head off, I thought he probably was sticking with "failing" and hadn't told her what we'd seen. With some effort, I tore my gaze from him and put everything that happened between us in a box, then sealed it with duct tape.

"Some kind of rhyming contest, I think."

"Rhyming—are you telling me we're having a rap battle?"

Sasha stood and said, "My friends, tomorrow our cousins from the Seelie Court will join us for the first time since the Light War." He waited for the polite applause to simmer down. "It will be an event of great solemnity and import as we celebrate the life of a brave fae soul who was taken too soon. One you may one day tell your children about it." He paused again, as this remark set off a bunch of heated whispers among the crowd. "As is our custom," he said to me and to March, "before a fete, we have a more informal gathering. After we dine, the versette. As usual, I will participate, but must not be considered. After all," and he lifted Marly's hand, "I have already claimed my prize."

She looked so happy and so pleased with herself, that shape-shifting D must have been wild.

Dinner was fine, since I had my human fork at the ready and managed to eat whatever kishkes they put in front of me. March and I spent the meal trying not to look at each other, so we were kind of back to where we started. He didn't look angry, though, just more lost in his own thoughts. Aster, after getting Madame's permission, joined us and sat close enough to me so that he could accidentally bump my leg with his, and I let him. It was a nice leg, after all, and, I reminded myself, he was still first in line.

*Liar. As usual, you only want what you can't have.*

"What am I eating?" I asked Aster quickly, trying to drown out the voice in my head. "If it's eyeballs, please make something up."

He laughed. "Lady Ruby, I cannot lie to you, as you know. It isn't eyes, or any organs at all. You see, the chef here has taken the shell of the turtle and made a fine foam, and it's been garnished with that very turtle's—"

"Got it," I said. I mean, turtle soup is a thing, isn't it? (I wasn't entirely sure if it was made with turtles or just called that, and even so, I was almost positive it had zero percent shell in it.) Still, after last time, I soldiered on. I concentrated on another bread basket appearing (no dice) and worked on resisting the temptation to peel that duct tape off the box in the back of my brain. I cast a sideways look at Aster. *Just because March doesn't want me, that doesn't mean I'm unwantable. There. Dr. Bel would call that growth.*

After a small army of Trade folks cleared the plates, Madame got to her feet. I guess she was going to kick things off.

She smoothed the front of her robe—stiff white satin, with an explosion of embroidered poppies from hem to waist—cool, she invented Marimekko! —and waited for everyone to quiet down.

"For new friends and those who haven't attended," she said, "the versette is a battle made of poetry. Pick your target with care, and put a fine point on your words. I'm looking at you, Noisette—watch your meter."

"I consider it my métier," Noisette replied.

"Oh, it's that kind of party," I said to Marly. "Word nerds." She snickered.

Madame continued. "I'll begin, if no one objects?" Obviously, no one did. She moved to the center of the floor and clasped her hands.

"The lion and the unicorn/ Went fighting for the crown/ A story so exciting / That to us it's handed down/ How sad to learn in our case/ we've no lion, but a clown."

I elbowed Marly. "I'm the clown, aren't I?" I began listing words in my head: bitch, ditch, punk-ass, dead grass, hard pass.

After that, my old pal Amory stood up. Who would he single out? Hmmm, who could it be? Wait, no, let me guess. It'll be March. That's who he'll single out. His March.

"The unicorn is fair, though shy/ And lives among the trees/ How fine a thing to lure him out/ How sad to watch him flee/ Perhaps if I were drunk enough/ He'd show his horn to me."

Oh my.

There was appreciative applause and laughter. Across the room, March ducked his head and blushed until he was the color of Madame's gown. But he was grinning like a fool. Marly shot me a look.

"Hmm," Marly said, "The rare burn slash come on." Then she leaned towards me and whispered, "Was Amory actually telling you the truth? Is March into guys now?"

I cleared my throat. "He sure seems to think so." I didn't know about guys in general, but he sure seemed to be into Amory in particular, who looked pretty stoked at both the audience and March's reaction. So far, he seemed to be in the lead in more ways than one. "What's the prize for this thing?"

She shrugged. "This is my first versette."

Aster leaned over from my other side. "The victor may

claim their own prize. Amory has already told us what he wants, don't you think?" *His March*. Well, good for him, I guess. I was both happy for Amory and wanted to crawl off and die. Both things can be true, right?

Noisette was on her feet. "Sit down, pretty boy, and let an expert demonstrate." With a graceful bow Amory let her have the floor. She cleared her throat. "Now Ruby, you're a friend to all/ And your options daily grow/ But what the court can't wait to learn/ Is who will get your rose?"

Oh, shit.

Amory laughed. "Grow doesn't rhyme with rose."

"Well, yours didn't scan properly, but you don't see me complaining."

Aster looked at me curiously. "What options? What did she mean?"

It meant someone saw March and me. Or March squawked. Or Marly did. I turned and gave her the Death Stare. She threw her hands up. "It wasn't me, I swear!"

Fuck this. I stood up. "The Unseelie Court is new to me/ With your ideas of fun/But I shouldn't be surprised at what I see/After all, you're not the nice ones." I hadn't worked in "nasty horse-faced twat," but I felt pretty good about it. I waited for the reaction.

Nothing. Dead silence, blank looks, no reaction at all. Then Madame of all fucking people stood up and applauded. "Good for you, dear. You see? The humans aren't completely inept at verse." She smiled, that sweet smile. "Of course, 'fun' and 'ones' don't quite...well, it was a lovely first try."

Having been the opposite of complimented, I sat down

and grabbed Marly's wrist. "Is someone going to assassinate me now?"

She was trying not to laugh. "That was soooo rude. I love you."

Sasha was next up. "My garden's flowers bloom by day/ The petals pink and white/ But far more sweet is the blush on the cheek/Of my lady every night."

There was a fraction of a second pause when all eyes turned first to Madame, who rolled her eyes and gave a sarcastic clap. After that I guess everyone figured it was safe to applaud their king, which they did enthusiastically (whether they liked the poem or not, I'm sure.)

I whispered to Marly, "I thought they were supposed to be sort of insulting?"

She smirked. "Not if he knows what's good for him." She poked my arm. "Quit making that face."

Aster stood up to have a go, and I braced myself.

"My days were spent just thinking/How Unseelie are the best/ We live without a care/And never need to rest/But the lady and the unicorn/Are now our treasured guests."

Well, no one could be mad about that, even though it didn't seem to make sense—they had plenty of cares, and I knew they slept. Poetic license, I guess? I applauded along with the rest and gave him a smile and a thumbs up, which he happily returned.

After a few more fae took the floor with jokes so inside they came with wall-to-wall carpeting, it was time to announce the winner, and it turned out to be that hot bitch Amory. He sauntered (accurate, look it up) over and eyed

March up and down. "I wouldn't presume to ask you to shift here and now, friend, much as I'd like to see that horn of yours. That would be rude."

March was smiling up at Amory in a way that made me feel things. "Then what do you claim as your prize?"

"A kiss." He leaned over and said more quietly. "Of course, you may refuse."

"To refuse would seem just as rude."

And that was it. Amory bent over and put his hand on the back of March's neck, where my own hand had been only a couple of hours ago, and I sat there and watched them kiss. It looked like a really good kiss. It went on for a while. Their lips looked soft and skin looked smooth, with maybe a trace of a beard over on March's side. He made a kind of purring noise in the back of his throat. At that point my brain melted, so I can't really report back on further details.

Marly handed me a glass of cold water. "Unless you want me to pour this over your head?"

My ability to speak had left the building. I glared at her but drank the water.

Amory raised his head, smiling. He let his hand rest on March's neck for a long moment. "I've changed my mind. I'll take your 'yes' however it is offered." Then he looked right at me. "Do you think I'll get it?" And off he sauntered AGAIN.

"What the fuuu..." I muttered.

"Dear Penthouse," said Marly, "I never thought this would happen to me..."

"Looks like it's not only Lady Ruby with options," said Madame cheerfully. "This has been a most illuminating

223

evening! I take my leave." At that, the crowd began to disperse. March stood up so fast he knocked his chair over. He looked at me, looked like he wanted to say something, but shook his head and took off. I wondered if he was going to look for Amory, and why it mattered so much to me if he did.

# 28

*Ruby*

**M**arecy woke me the next morning with a knock and an invitation. "Lady Noisette would like to have breakfast with you," she said, handing me the calling card. "Just follow the glowing arrow on the card and it will show you the way. See?" She took two paces to the left, and the card displayed a bright green U-turn with updated directions.

The fact that I wouldn't get lost on the way there wasn't much comfort. I knew it was coming, but I still got the idea I might have to fight my way out. I couldn't stop thinking of suddenly having no hands or eyes, for the crime of stealing a book. And as far as Noisette knew, Sasha and I were old pals. Careful, Marly said. Be careful.

I got dressed (pale blue, sort of a robin's egg, with espresso accents—take that, H&C!) and presented myself for inspection. Marecy re-tied my sash, and off I went. I vaguely remembered saying Noisette had nice hair…then it all came flooding back to that magical night I'd arrived and talked to her in the period between taking the first sip and falling on the floor. She wanted to talk about Lauren C. It had been a lifetime since the Light War, and as far as I knew there had been no contact between the two courts. How could they possibly know each other? And know each other well enough to have matching haircuts? I guess I'd find out.

Her house—really more of an apartment, since it was part of the palace complex—was way nicer than my dowdy "motel room," but it sure wasn't a Marly-level mansion with a walled garden. It did have a roof, though. Noisette herself showed me in.

"You," I said, looking around, "live in a library, and I love it." I did, and there was no reason to start off with hostility on my part. Maybe she wasn't going to hold Sasha's torture against me with the hands he let her keep?

She laughed (whew) and moved a stack of well-thumbed leather-bound books off a chair so I could sit. She perched on the edge of her couch. "It's just some of my collection. I can't seem to part with any of them."

She did well enough to have a maid, despite the small digs, and the woman did the by-now familiar ritual of bowing to us, setting down the tray, and pouring tea before disappearing.

"The versette," she said, "Did you enjoy it?" She smiled. "You and Master March were quite the center of attention. You might imagine how tired we all are of writing about each other."

I took a good long time to answer. "Your verse was very clever. It was…interesting."

Interesting was what you said when your third grader asked how you liked their band concert, or your conceptual artist pal wanted your opinion on their most recent installation. So yeah, it had been interesting.

There was a pause. Noisette stared at me with those glittering black eyes. Finally, she said, "I just can't believe you knew her. In person." She pressed her hand to her lips, composing herself. "I was hoping you could tell me about her."

I did, happy to move off the subject of March and Amory while avoiding Sasha completely, and towards a person I had genuinely loved. Even more, I was glad to have someone who appreciated just how special Lauren C. had been, how brave, and how fucking unlucky to have run into the *kitsune*.

"And you really do resemble her, a bit. Your haircut." I smiled. "I apologize for my drunken behavior the other night. I'm normally a better guest." I was really leaning into apologizing to these people, although in this case I think she deserved it.

She shrugged, unconcerned. Maybe she wouldn't call it in as a debt? "Sorry seems to be the hardest word. We are normally better hosts."

"Anyway," I hurried on, "Lauren and I had lunch together a lot, and she was super interested in human behavior. It made me look at my own actions a little differently. She was…well, she was just a cool person. The last time I saw her, she was happy. And I know this won't be easy to hear, but you should know she died fighting back." I hoped it would make Noisette feel better.

I was mistaken.

She set down her teacup hard enough to slosh. "If our new lady queen had done anything at all but hide and cry, my friend might still be alive."

Hide and cry? From whom? She hadn't hidden from the *kitsune*, he'd kidnapped her. What was she talking about? "Um, you know Mar—Queen Melis is also my friend, right?"

She pursed her lips. "Perhaps this court isn't the right place for her. She's been in the right place, but it must have been the wrong time. Dr. John," she added, "known as the Night Tripper."

I was expecting her to go after Sasha, but it looked like she had pinned her troubles on Marly. "Oookay."

"Certainly, you miss having your friend home and by your side. One might say that even with the atmospheric corruption of iron, she might be safer there. It would appear that unlike my Lauren, she is no fighter."

This was a million miles from the woman I knew. "You are so wrong about her. But let me see if I get you. What you're telling me is you want Mar—Queen Melis to give up the crown and leave the kingdom because she didn't defend Lauren while she was still a human, before she even met Sasha? And months before she somehow transformed into one of you fae?"

"In a nutshell." She frowned and looked at me with curiosity. "Wait. 'Somehow transformed?' You know how my dear Lauren died…"

"The *kitsune* killed her." My stomach did one of its slow rolls.

"But what else do you know? About our lady queen's transformation, for instance. 'Somehow transformed,'" she repeated. "There are some missing pieces, it would appear?"

Her words came through an angry buzz, like she had a mouthful of wasps. I leaned forward, pushing away the nausea. "If I tell you she got bitten by a tropical spider and almost died in a resort's clinic, will that fill in the gaps?"

She looked confused. "She was attacked and turned by a...spider? Is that what humans call them now?"

"No, she was just bitten. Spiders don't attack people. And 'turned' is a word only used for making vampires." I got a wave of lightheadedness and gripped the edge of the table.

"How interesting. Then I've heard true. Tell me more about vampires, please."

I tried taking deep, even breaths through my nose. "No. They're gross and I'd rather not. But you should know this: If Marly leaves? The throne is completely empty. Because Sasha goes, too. Is that what you want?" Then it struck me—maybe it was. "Is your whole thing to get rid of Sasha? Because of what he did to you?" It made sense—Marly was a much softer target.

She just stared. "What he did was first, none of your concern, and second, quite appropriate according to our customs. Of course, you wouldn't know that." She sipped her remaining tea. "But since you brought it up, our lord king was kind enough to let me keep her writing after that unpleasantness—along with a few other things that belonged to me."

I gave it one last shot. "It was only a book, Noisette. What he did to you was wrong."

"Only a book?" she snarled. My last shot obviously went wide. "I would have gladly given my eyes, my hands and my heart to keep it. *Only a book*. You know nothing about it, and you probably don't care."

"Then explain it to me because I *do* care. Lauren was my friend, and that means maybe, just maybe you and I could be friends."

Her face, like all of the fae, was unreadable. "You and I..." she mused. "You think Lauren and I were merely friends. She—an academic, an adventurer, a poet. Tell me again, what are you?"

*I'm just a bartender with a stomach ache.* "I'm a mortal person who liked her a lot. I would never presume," I backtracked. "Just...please. Tell me about the book."

"Her book. Our book. The book that bound us together just as surely as its own pages. The one in which Lauren wrote about our queen before she was our queen, and about you, and your...." Whatever the last word was, it came out like a bark. I flicked the medallion with my fingernail, hoping it wouldn't completely crap out. She continued. "Would you defend the king, I wonder, if you really knew? She knows, our queen. I think she's tried to tell you. But she likes the throne and her pretty new life here, so she wouldn't dare dream of going against him."

I was right; the grudge Noisette was carrying had Marly's name in big red letters on it. My shiny new idea of making friends was going down in flames. I bailed out. "Do you want to talk about Lauren, or do you want to rag on Marly? Because I have things to do."

"Ah, yes. So very busy doing busy things. Has our lord king told you to follow around the unicorn?" She smiled. "He didn't have to, of course. You do it despite yourself. But does the king wish to atone? No, that's not his way. Sport, perhaps? Are you the bait or the quarry, I wonder? Just walk away, Renee. But you won't, will you?"

"Atone for what? And who's Renee?" Was she high? "If you have something to say, I am begging you. Out with it."

"Whose side are you on," she sang. "Basia. Great jazz album." Then she thought for a moment. "Consider the players on the board, and which side you'd rather be a pawn for. That's all. Thank you for talking with me about Lauren. I know she liked you despite your human flaws."

I walked back to my little room, following the glowing arrows on the calling card, and trying to figure out what the hell happened. What did Noisette want from me? She didn't seem to be holding a grudge against Sasha, and it wasn't just reminiscing about our dead acquaintance. No, she was looking for revenge on Marly, but why? How could she possibly have defended Lauren against the kitsune when she was still a mortal? I barely fought him off, and if it hadn't been for... if it hadn't....

*Knives, all the knives*

I staggered and leaned against the wall while my head spun, and for a second I thought I was going to pass out. I bent forward and caught my breath. When I first arrived, I hadn't felt so bad, and I was starting to think I was safe from being sick, but that clearly wasn't true. And it was definitely getting worse. Maybe I'd go to Sasha and see if he had any idea what was wrong with me. Maybe have him look at the medallion, too—after all, sometimes the internet goes down, and it sure seemed like my necklace was on the fritz. I figured I had a fifty-fifty shot of getting an answer that made sense.

I straightened my robe, pushed back my hair and looked around—at least no one had seen me.

Even though the encounter had been borderline gibberish, I did come away with another person for our no-fly list: Madame, Master Greaves, and now, Noisette…and maybe all the other constructs…and who knows how many of the fae themselves? Marly herself had said the only ones I could trust were her and March, and the less I thought about him—like where he had spent the night and with whom—the better. I began to wonder if somehow smuggling Marly out of here might not be the right move. But she seemed dead set against it, and I was willing to bet she'd never leave Sasha. What to do next? I still had to find out what Madame was going to do with her new construct friends, and there was one person who just might know the answer.

# 29

*Ruby*

Once "home," I asked **Marecy** to track down Aster. "Tell him I'm in need of an escort."

I barely had time to run a comb through my hair when he knocked. He was slightly breathless, just like the day we'd met in the parking lot. He seemed pleased to be of use.

"Hey, " I said, "Looks like we have a day to ourselves. So, remember when you asked me about interrogating?" I'd been half in the bag on poisoned wine when he brought it up, but I did recall how excited he'd sounded.

Sure enough, he looked thrilled at the prospect. "Are we putting someone in the box? Will they lawyer up?"

I laughed. "I hope not. But I do want to talk to some folks. What would you wear to an interrogation?" I held up two robes—one black, the other dark blue. I figured low-key was the way to go.

He smiled, nodding at the blue outfit. "Is that why you called me? Fashion is more Master Greaves purview."

"Yeah, but I wanted your company. And someone your people would actually talk to. I'm not so sure they'd be happy to chat with me."

"Who wouldn't want to spend some time with you? I can't picture such a thing," he said with a sweet smile. Aw, he was flirting! Maybe the investigation could wait...*Liar. Name what you want.* God, when did my internal monologue get so pushy? And horny?

Then he cocked his head, still processing what I'd said. "Who are we interrogating, exactly?"

"Waiters. Cooks. Garbagemen, although I haven't seen any garbage. Maids."

"Trade." He tried not to make a face. "And you think they'd talk to me?"

"Not with that attitude." I thought about his poem, and how he was trying so hard to be welcoming, and decided to see if he would flip on Madame. "I overheard one of them— they must have been on someone's household staff, I guess? And they said 'not all of us agree.' I think they were talking about the Seelie coming here. Of course, that's just a guess." I threw in a little misdirection, since I was both bad and good cop. "Agree to what? Any idea?"

"Who knows? It was just a construct. You can't take what they say seriously."

First, "it?" And second, kind of racist, Aster. "What does that mean? Why not?"

He gave a disinterested shrug. "They don't think and feel

like we do. I mean, they're really just tools, aren't they?"

Tools—that was pretty harsh. I bit back disappointment. He clearly wasn't the right person to help me figure out what Ilex meant.

"I have a better idea, anyway." He grinned. "How would you like to go on a hunt with me?"

"A hunt? For what? Is it dangerous?"

"Nah. Done it hundreds of times. It'll be a new thing for you to see, what we do here at court." I agreed to go. I mean, hundreds of times, right? And maybe I'd learn something important—just not what I was intending. He took one of the outfits I'd pulled out, and did the hand wave thing over it. "You'll need this. Here, put this on." My blue robe was now mottled black and dark brown, and the long sleeves ended in gloves. I slipped it over my head. "The main thing is to be invisible." He did the same trick on his own robe, so we matched, then adjusted the robe around my shoulders. "And this." He pulled a half-dollar-sized piece of glass in a delicate, curly silver frame out of his pocket, and clipped it to my medallion's chain. The fact that this trip involved jewelry instantly made it more interesting. I held it up to my eye like a monocle. It was just glass.

"What does it do?"

"You'll see. When we cross over, I'll also show you how the hood works. Are you ready?"

Not even a little, but I wasn't going to tell him that. He held out his hand. I took it. My comfortable, safe room faded away.

We were in a ragged grove of trees, and it was dark—

like, the air itself felt dark. The trees weren't trees at all; they looked like giant strands of carpet fiber, twisting up and away out of sight into the black air above us. They moved and writhed in the chilly breeze.

"We are now on the Field of Significant Contact," he told me. "We're going to be quiet and move slowly. Follow me."

The Field of Significant Contact? Who came up with that one? I trailed after him, picking my way through the "trees." As we passed by, I brushed against one of them.

"Oh, is that how it is?" it asked. It gave a deep sigh and began to disintegrate. "I was ready to leave this hideous place anyway. I should thank you," it said in a fading voice as the fibers floated past us, buffeted about by the wind.

Aster leaned close to my ear. "Don't do that."

"Sorry," I squeaked without thinking, both at him and the quickly dissolving tree.

"No need to apologize," it said as it vanished. "I'm off to a better place. I hope."

Aster stopped and took me by the arm. "Do not talk to the trees."

I nodded, gulping, and followed him, shoving my gloved hands deep into my pockets and pulling my elbows tight against my body. Eventually, the trees thinned out. It was so dark I could only see about twenty feet in front of me, but it didn't really look like a football field, which was what I had been expecting, though I wasn't sure why. Aster knelt down on the cold ground, and I did the same. We were behind a low hump, ready-made for cover. Every now and then the clouds would tear apart and I recognized the mountains in the far distance from the Scenic Overlook—fortunately none of them were moving. The moat must be between us and the kingdom, then. Thanks to the heavy, low clouds, I couldn't see the glass plates above us for the first time since arriving. But I could hear something—squeaking, like wet balloons rubbing together.

"Pull up your hood," Aster whispered. "Like this." He adjusted it so it came over his forehead, like a regular hoodie. But of course, this being the Unseelie Court, it was a magic hoodie, and a shadow completely hid his face. With his hood up and his hands covered by his gloves, it was hard to see him even though he was only a foot away. I followed his example, and then I was invisible too. He reached forward and tied a set of straps in a bow under my chin, taking his time. I noticed his own hood didn't have any straps. "Madame made the hood for me," he said, "so I am well-protected. I have several but this is my favorite."

"Cool," I said. "I sure hope she made mine, too."

I could barely see his smile. "Your is—as the humans say—off the rack. Don't worry, it's quite sturdy."

That was a relief. "What happens now?" I asked.

"Look through the glass."

I hitched myself up so I could see over the edge and held the glass to my eye. I gasped—hopefully quietly. About fifty yards away from us was a herd of monsters...or something. They looked like octopi—only the size of elephants—and were floating twenty or so feet above the ground. Their flanks were a muddy mix of grey, white, and bruise-blue with dripping tentacles that trailed down to gently brush along the dead grass. The sound I had been hearing was their huge, sac-shaped bodies brushing against each other as the wind moved them around. There were at least twenty of them.

"Not sure what they eat, but they always hang around in herds like this. They're called pulpo. Aren't they fabulous?"

Gross, definitely. Terrifying, absolutely. "Yeah, amazing." I looked closer. "Hey, look at that." I could see a bunch of short tentacles in between the huge ones, and a minute later a group of what I guess were octo-children came into sight. These were more like cow-sized compared to the massive adults. They kicked up clods of dirt and grass, tossing them at each other, and I gasped again. "I can hear them—they're playing." I could hear them—faintly, but clearly. They were speaking to each other—yelling and laughing about whose turn it was. "They're kids," I hissed. "We can't hunt them, they're just kids playing around!"

"No, they're not."

"How do they speak English?" I demanded. Then I paused and added, "And how did the tree?"

"It didn't. They aren't speaking."

"But listen, can't you hear them?" I insisted.

"It's not them. It's this place. It's one of the things the Field does. It provides dialogue."

"It does what now?"

"There are some who believe that the Field is not a place at all, but an entity. It makes up stories, and talks to itself to relieve its boredom."

"You're saying the baby squids are just messing around,

and the Field is dubbing in dialogue? To amuse itself?"

"Pulpo. Yes, exactly. They are not intelligent, not as we are." He paused. "Neither is the Field, I suppose. But in a different way."

"And we're inside this thing?" The kingdom just kept coming up with new ways to horrify me.

"No, more like sitting on its back. You've already added to the plot."

That meant I hadn't really helped the tree commit suicide. I guess that made me feel better? As I watched, one of the baby squids separated itself from the herd and moved in our direction. "Hey, that one only has six legs. I mean arms. I wonder what happened to it." I felt curiously relieved—no, maybe satisfied? —on seeing it. I only know I felt like I'd been looking for it. It continued to wander closer to where we hid. "Can it see us?" I was starting to get nervous. "It's getting close."

Aster shook his head. "We're good. Just stay low. They have poor hearing and almost no sense of smell." And sure enough, it seemed to get tired of poking around on our side of the clearing and headed back to the herd. It went to what must have been its mother, and she enveloped it in her tentacles, making a rumbling, cooing noise. It would have been charming if it wasn't so slimy. The mother creature pushed the lamed baby behind herself, and then sort of extruded her eyes in our direction. They were manhole cover sized, golden as owl eyes, with sharply defined rectangular pupils. She was looking right at us.

"She can see us." I put my hand on Aster's sleeve. "We

should get out of here."

"I'm telling you, we're fine. She doesn't know we're h—" The wind caught Aster's hood and blew it back. His face shone like a star, the mid-day sun, a searchlight. Anyone could see him. The mother creature sure did.

The "tree" behind us giggled and whispered, "Uh oh, someone's been spotted."

The mama-monster rose higher off the ground, her eyestalks bulging. She gave a roar like a freight train and came at us. Aster, muttering curses, reached for me, but she was so fast. She was too fast. In between one breath and the next, she shot her tentacles towards him, looped one around his face and neck, and dragged him from behind our little hill. He screamed and tried to bat at her, but he was face down and couldn't reach her. Once she had him snared, she threw her huge bulk onto her side, squelching wetly into the dirt, and raised her tentacles. Now I could see she was dragging him in toward the middle of her body, and a wide ring of twitching and contracting muscle, wet and gray, and knotted with blue-black veins. Set in the center was her beak which was the size of a car hood and razor sharp. She'd cut him in half. He'd stopped screaming and his arms dragged limply in the dirt as she pulled him closer.

*Run at it! Go, run!*

I stumbled to my feet, took a big, whooping breath, and put down my shoulder. I charged that tentacle gripping Aster like I was on the 1972 Dolphins defensive line, and blew right through it. It was as thick as my waist and yet it parted like rotten meat. She screamed; it was so loud I could almost taste the sound, and I fell down and covered my ears—I think I screamed, too. She heaved herself back into the air and charged back to the herd, spraying black blood that stank like fish guts, low tide, and motor oil. I was covered in it. I grabbed Aster and turned him so he was face-up.

"Babe, we gotta go, now." No response. The lights in his eyes were out. My hands were shaking so much that I dropped the glass twice, but when I got it to my eye, I could see the herd caressing and comforting the mother creature. Some of them had their eye stalks out, looking our way. We only had seconds. I reared back and slapped Aster across the face. "Wake up! Aster, we have to go." He took a deep, shuddering breath, and lights pinwheeled in his eyes. I looked up again, and they were coming for us. I screamed and threw myself across him. He took hold of my wrist just as something damp and cold touched the back of my neck. I squeezed my eyes shut.

# 30

*Ruby*

**I** **opened my eyes.**

It was light and dry. The dark and stinking Fields were gone. The squid monsters were gone. We might never have left my room at all, except we were covered in goo and still reeked like low-tide and burned oil. But the smell was the least of my worries. I gave my head a good shake to clear it, and looked down at Aster's face.

"Aster? Babe?" His poor face was covered with a sort of shiny slime, and there were rows of livid round welts from those tentacle suckers running across his face and around his neck. He coughed weakly and groaned and although I'm sure it hurt like hell, he was alive.

"Marecy!" I rolled off of him and raced to throw open the door. Thank God she was stationed outside. "Aster's been hurt." And thank God again that she didn't stop to question me or hesitate—she barged right in and took charge. I loved that girl.

"Let me move him," she said, and she just fucking picked him up and set him gently onto my bed. I filled her in as quickly as I could.

"One of the...the things that live there saw him, and it attacked before he could get us out."

"Spotted by a pulpo just as his equipment failed," she said, lifting the edge of his slime-soaked hood. "Bad timing. You two were lucky." She straightened up. "I have to go and fetch Madame Tournesol."

"Yes. Of course." Madame was definitely going to murder me.

She called over her shoulder, "I'll return soon. Watch him."

For what, and what to do if anything happened, she didn't say. I made sure he was still breathing, then went to the bathroom and pulled off the slimy black outfit. I tossed it in the tub, hoping I could get someone to disappear it for me later. I took a second to wipe off my face and hands, and the towel came away covered in black slime and gold glitter. That was kind of weird, but they were already at the door, so I left the towel on the sink. I pulled on my day-spa bathrobe, and let them in.

I knew that in the Unseelie Court, people only let you see what they wanted you to see. I thought Madame would either show me nothing—after all, he was alive, or pull what my mom used to call my Sarah Heartburn (named after some long-ago actress, I guess?) which involved an over-the-top dramatic performance usually featuring the back of my hand pressed to my forehead. To my surprise, from Madame I got neither. She stood for a quick second in the doorway. Then she walked over to the bed, her eyes filling with tears.

"My poor boy." She took his hand, then used the edge of her gorgeous butter yellow sleeve to wipe his face. "I assume this happened because he was protecting you?" You could've melted glass to slag with that voice, but she never looked up.

"No, no. It was an accident." She leaned down to get a closer look at his wounds. "He just wanted to show me the things you all do around here. He said he'd been to the Fields hundreds of times."

"Aster?" She gently shook his shoulder. "Darling, can you hear me?"

The lights in eyes slowly resurfaced. They were still dim, but he blinked several times and turned to face her. "Sorry..." he whispered.

"Well, you ought to be." She looked extremely relieved, even if she still sounded pissed. "Do you have any idea of what he'd do to me, if harm came to her?"

*He who?* I wondered. I figured "her" was me, but "he"? Sasha? Really?

She sighed and said, "I'm afraid we have no choice." She turned to Marecy. "Please fetch Master March. Quickly." Marecy gave a short bow and bolted. To me she said, "They use poison to immobilize their prey. It's working on him now. Unless we convince the unicorn to help us, he will die."

"Madame, he can hear you." I was shocked at her words, and the cool way she announced them. But I realized I was wrong, and that Aster hadn't heard her at all. His eyes were lightless again, black and glassy. His head rolled to one side.

We sat together there for a while, watching him take increasingly shallow breaths. "This young fool," she said, "he should know what he's done." She gripped his hand tighter. I recognized the look of someone who was trying hard not to cry.

I said, "Don't be angry with him. I wanted to see the Fields." That wasn't entirely true, but maybe it would help.

"He took you to the Fields?" I swung around to see March in the doorway. He was absolutely shaking with anger. "And you went? Are you mad?"

"Am I what now?" I was frankly not expecting this.

He took me by the shoulders, sort of roughly, I thought. "Are you hurt? Tell me. What was he thinking, bringing you there?"

I shook him off. "Hey, go easy, pal. I'm fine. He's the one who's hurt. And I had no reason not to go. It would have been okay but he lost his hood, and one of those things saw him." Oh! *He*, I thought. Madame wasn't talking about Sasha— she meant March. March, and me. I figured our make-out session in the stairwell was common knowledge by now, but that didn't explain why she was afraid of what he would do to her if I got hurt. It wasn't like he had any special reason to want to protect me.

March gave a disgusted snort, and went to the other side of the bed, and looked carefully at the welts, which were slowly trickling blood. It caught the light in a strange way, it didn't look like any blood I've ever seen. "Did you know about this?" he asked Madame.

She made a face. "I certainly did not. He was tasked with her safety; he wasn't supposed to be dragging her off on some ridiculous adventure. I'd say there would be repercussions but it appears he's already met them."

March took a deep breath. He was obviously trying to get his shit together. "Ruby, what happened? How did he come to be so hurt?"

"Really, it wasn't his fault. We were watching the...squid things—"

"Pulpos," Madame said.

"Right. Pulpos. And we were being super careful and keeping out of sight, but it was windy, and his hood blew off. One of them saw him, and she attacked."

"She?" March looked at me, curious.

Damn. I hadn't meant to go into detail. I don't know why not, what difference it would have made. I only know I didn't want to talk about the children. "There was a smaller one, and it was missing two of its legs. Arms. Tentacles. It looked like the one that attacked us was its...mother."

"Then it told on you after all," March said quietly.

"Told...on me?"

"Never mind. Go on."

"Well, she had him, she had Aster by the neck, and I just, I ran through the tentacle holding him. It fell apart and the mother creature—the pulpo—flew off. Aster woke up long enough to bring us home."

"Interesting," Madame said. "How did you know to do that?" I stared at her. "How did you know it would break apart? The tentacle? That you wouldn't simply bounce off? Or that she wouldn't grab you with one of her other arms?"

I felt bone-tired and I wanted to lie down. "I... don't know. I just did. Maybe...I read it in a book?" I was more queasy than usual but at least this time I had a good reason.

March and Madame gave each other a look, and I was starting to get mightily tired of being out of the loop.

Madame nodded. "You are brave, human girl, I'll give you that." To March she said, "You know what will happen if you don't help him."

March looked at Aster's injuries more closely, touched one of the welts, then lifted his bloodied hand into the light. He squinted at the moisture on his fingertips, and nodded slowly. To my surprise, he gently brushed Aster's long hair out of his face. His whole demeanor changed. He held out his hand so Madame could see it, and she stiffened. "He doesn't know, does he?"

"No." She was rigid. "Please. Don't speak it."

March got to his feet. "Very well. I'd urge you to remember, though. My folk are not well versed at keeping secrets." He looked around the room, sizing it up, then he sighed and reached for the sash on his robe. "Cover your eyes. Or, turn around. Please."

We did. Madame turned just far enough to catch my eye. "You saved his life." It wasn't a question.

I nodded. "I'm sorry he got hurt." I knew I was breaking the rules with yet another apology, but I didn't care. I really was sorry.

"As am I." She frowned. "You've put me in a difficult position. I was perfectly content counting you as a minor actor, and here you are at the front of the stage."

"I don't...what does that mean?" The stage? I thought of what Aster told me, about her family's crest. That had a stage in it, didn't it?

"It means, young human, that you have put me in your debt. I don't care to carry debt." She sighed. "Very well. It'll complicate my plans, but there's nothing for it." She pulled a flower—it looked like a daisy—out of her sleeve. "Here."

I looked at it. "A flower?"

"A marker for a debt to be repaid. I have no doubt you'll be asking for something, sooner or later."

*Answers, she can give me answers.* Then I thought *No, don't waste it on something you can find out another way.* So, instead, I laughed. "What would I want from you?"

She smiled. "Let us say you don't know what you don't know. But soon enough, you will."

I found myself longing for the pure sincerity of being flipped off in traffic, or insulted by a rude customer, or Claudio's 100 proof verbal shots. At least with those, I knew where I stood. However, I tucked the flower away, although considering the source I figured it had some Monkey's Paw-style asterisk.

"You really don't have to do anything for me, honestly," I said.

"Honestly? It isn't up to you. This conversation is over." As she spoke, the room filled with light. When we turned, the unicorn stood next to the bed, looking around, like he was getting his bearings. Just like at dinner, I wanted to throw my arms around his long, gleaming neck. It was a different sort of feeling than the one that came over me in the alcove, but the longing to touch him was just as strong. I had to physically stop myself from reaching for him. It was starting to be a habit, wanting to climb all over him. I reminded myself I had to check that in a hurry. Anyway, I knew I wasn't allowed, and forced my hands into my pockets.

"March," I said, "you're so beautiful." Wow, that was not what I was planning on saying. Thanks, mouth. He looked over at me with those sad, soulful, eyes, and for the first time since I got here, I knew I was about to vomit. I didn't want to do it with an audience, so I clapped my hand over my mouth and barely made it to the bathroom. By the time I was finished and re-washed my face, I found Aster awake, and blinking at Madame and March, who was tying his belt.

"How do you get in and out of your clothes so fast?" I asked.

He laughed. "That's your main takeaway?" Then he turned to Aster. "How are you feeling?"

"What...where did you come from?" The way the lights in his eyes were darting in all different directions made me think he wasn't quite back.

"What's the last thing you remember, dearest?" Madame wasn't letting go of his hand anytime soon.

"I... they couldn't see us, the pulpo, then the wind..." He reached for his hood, and his hand came away black and slick. He stared at it. "I'm not dead," he said. "How am I not...?" He looked up at March, then struggled to sit up. Madame hurried to help him, despite the slime. "Oh. Thank you."

"There is poison in the sting," March told him. "I have

249

healed you, but being...what you are, it will take some time to cycle out of your body. You will be well soon enough."

He nodded to Madame and to me, then left. I figured Aster had to know something about the connection between March and me—after all, he and Madame came as a package deal, and she sure knew more than she was saying—but I'd have to get him alone. I had a feeling she wouldn't make that easy, but I was reluctant to call in my debt marker on something I could probably do myself.

Madame turned to me and said, "Don't lose the flower." Then she hauled Aster to his feet like he weighed five pounds and hustled him the hell out of my room, despite his very weak protestations. "I've got you, my dear boy. You'll be fine, come along."

When they were gone, I wandered back into the bathroom to clean up. Other than changing and probably burning the sheets, I needed a shower, but the slimy black outfit was in the tub. I picked it up with my fingertips and holding it at arm's length dropped it by the door. Maybe I could get Marecy to get rid of it, but I didn't want to bother her again. I picked up the dirty towel to add to the pile, when the gold glitter caught my eye. Gold glitter, just like on Aster's face. I thought it was from the squid, but March had treated it like was Aster's blood. I realized I must have gotten it on my hand when I slapped him. Even though it was that or get eaten, I felt bad about hitting him. I wondered if it was safe to apologize and absently rubbed the strange stuff between my fingers. It didn't feel like blood, it was sandy. Sort of gritty. I held my finger up to the light and squinted at it.

"Nah..." And I understood what March had really meant, and what Madame really didn't want him to say.

It was a tiny golden gear.

Gears. Cogs. Clockworks.

Aster was a construct.

# 31

*Ruby*

I snatched up the dirty towel and held it up for a closer look, and sure enough, it was covered with not only the black slime of the pulpos, but tiny golden gears. Blood. Aster's golden blood.

The next question was what to do with what I'd just learned? Tell no one? Sit on it? Never speak of it?

Yeah, no.

I took a breath. Okay, March knew, but he promised Madame he wouldn't say anything. He also told her unicorns couldn't keep secrets, which made me think that if I broke the news, he would back me up. What would she do? Shit, what would *Aster* do? He had no idea. I thought of how he'd talked about Trade, he thought they were beneath him.

Why would she create something so beautiful, so elaborate, and then keep it a secret?

Well, I couldn't keep this to myself. I decided my shower

would have to wait, pulled on a clean outfit, and went to find the only person I knew I could talk to.

First thing I did was get myself lost.

I was learning the secret to getting anywhere inside or outside the palace seemed to be to concentrate on your destination and ignore your surroundings. It may take a while, but eventually you'd get where you were going. Walls and halls were replaced by trees and gardens, and I didn't stop to look and see if the flowers were blown glass or the benches were real wood. I thought hard about Marly's pretty house and kept walking. Eventually I stood in the little bend of road that I could have sworn her house stood on—I could even faintly smell the petrichor. But there was nothing: not a house, not that huge garden and doorway to the sky…just nothing. It was an empty overgrown lot that twitched and shivered when I looked at it for too long, like the aura you see before you get a migraine.

"Shit," I muttered, and pushed my way in, through brambles and tall weeds, thinking there might be some sort of clue lurking in the brush. Out of the corner of my eye, something moved. A hand—a human hand lovingly stroked my ankle. I stifled a shriek and heaved myself back. Of course, it was only a cluster of dead, curled leaves. Back on the curb, something black and tarry seeped out from under the grass, like high tide does when you live near the beach. I swore again and stumbled backwards, trying to keep it off my shoes.

"Greatest day to you, Child o' Dust." An older fae woman in a rich burgundy robe had come up behind me, and I jumped again. This place was trying to give me a stroke.

I managed to sputter, "Um, great day to you too." I wasn't sure if Child o' Dust was an insult or what the retort ought to be, so I sort of let it hang out there.

"You appear to be at odds and ends," she said. "May I assist?"

"My friend lived here," I began but before I could tell her about tree fingers and dirt blood, she broke into a sunny smile.

"Ah, Queen Melis. The hope of the ages, the bud and the blossom, our queen of salt and wine." Again, I couldn't tell if this was supposed to be ironic or if she was Marly's number one fan.

"Yeah, that's her. Where's her house? It was right here."

"Why, it moved, of course. It's yonder." Yonder turned out to be way on the other side of the city. Way on the other side.

"How did her whole house move? And why?"

"The light. It follows the light. As we all do. Greatest day." And she was on her way, turning onto one of the backwards-folding streets and out of sight in an instant.

So, the houses are like flowers, and why wouldn't they be? I wondered if Marly's house got to move to the sunniest spots, if that was part of being queen of the Whole Damned Place. I straightened my robe and headed yonder, and did my best to ignore how the road seemed to try and get out from under my feet. I kept walking, past buildings that bent down to take a better look at this little lost Child o' Dust, past trees that put their crowned heads together to whisper about me (I'm sure of it), and past open fields where pools of light gathered and blazing banks of wildflowers twice as tall as I was. But I didn't stop. When I got to Marly's house, it looked exactly the same: potted plants on the stoop and that dumbass mailbox. I called to her through the open window. She wasn't home.

I gave a long indignant sigh that no one heard and kept walking.

It felt like hours later when I finally got back to the palace. I tried to get to the royal residence and after a bunch of false starts and backtracking, I finally found Ilex playing some kind of dice game with a few other maids. The dice appeared to be live mice, and judging by her grim expression, she was losing.

"Hey, Ilex, can I talk to you for a second?"

I'd startled her, and she looked up at me, the mice bouncing from her hand and scampering off in different directions. "I missed my shot," she said in an oddly flat voice.

"I guess that one's on me. Sorry."

I led her out of the earshot of her companions.

"How may I assist you?" she asked in that same strange voice. Her eyes looked funny—instead of silvery darts like bright little fish, the lights were pale blue-gray and sluggish.

"Well, first I wanted to ask about your breathing. Are you okay?"

She stared at me, touching her throat with her fingertips. "It is my business."

"Marly is worried about you."

"That is her business."

We were interrupted by cheers and tiny squeaks from

the players and dice. Then I said, "Can you tell me what you meant? When you said you didn't all agree with what Madame?"

She didn't blink or change expression. "I'm sure I don't know what you mean."

I didn't want to get her in deeper shit, so I nodded. " I don't want to make trouble."

She smiled faintly. "My lady queen is in repose. She is well. There will be no trouble."

"No, I mean trouble for you."

A faint line formed between her brows. "There is no such thing."

"Ilex, are you alright?"

"I am at my lady's service, and at yours."

I thought about the woman who had gone toe-to-toe with Madame. This…was not that. "Ilex," I said in a low voice, "I saw what Madame did to you. It's okay. I'm on your side—yours and Marly's."

She stared at me. "I am at my lady's service, and at yours. How may I assist you?"

Sasha was right. Her spirit, the thing that made her who she was—gone. "Can you take me to the queen, please?"

She smiled and bowed, and—like with Amory—one, two, three steps, and we were somewhere else.

This was Sasha's private place, his room. And if I had to pick 'Sasha is comfortable here' out of a lineup, it would have closed the case. It wasn't even a room, not really, as most rooms even here in the kingdom boast at least most of their walls plus sometimes a ceiling. This was the remains of a probably-once-grand circular tower, and it was three quarters open to the dark sky and the Seelie Court above us. No one who spent time here could possibly forget there was a war, and that the Unseelie kingdom had both won and lost. An admittedly lush looking pile of blankets and quilts served for the bed, and a silver tray with the remains of a meal—bottles, plates, and glasses—sat off to the side. Candles surrounded the bed, and they did not flicker, because even though the room was wide open, there wasn't any wind. There also wasn't any other furniture, so I planted myself on the edge of the plush pile.

Despite the vertiginous edges—we were up pretty high, maybe as high as the lookout in Marly's garden, the queen herself looked completely at home, and totally freaked out. She was pacing and smoking just like she used to do after a particularly brutal parent teacher conference. She'd left the cigs behind a few years ago, and it looked like they'd been replaced by some kind of trumpet shaped flower.

She offered me the unlit end.

"No thanks. Is he here?" I looked around.

She set the blossom down and used a silver cup on a slender stick to put it out. "He's in session with the people from the Seelie Court. I don't think I'll see him until the actual party." She put her hands on her hips. "He was right. Madame fucked with Ilex."

"I know. She brought me up here, acted like she was in a trance or something."

"Remember I said we appreciate the strike, and move to the counter? Ilex is the counter.

And I need to decide what to do in response."

"Uh, is it smart to escalate?"

She looked at me like I'd lost my mind. "It's the only way. It's how it's done, here."

"Well, I don't know if this'll help with your land war in Asia, but I have some news."

She made a face and sniffed. "What's that smell?" Then she blushed, remembering me and smelling.

"No, it's fine. It's me, I skipped a shower to get here." I mean, it actually was me that time, so I didn't have to spiral.

She threw herself onto the pile of cushions (carefully out of stink range) and listened as I told her about the hunt, the Field, the pulpos. I told her how Aster got attacked, and how I saved him. And after that, how March saved him again. "Madame gave me a flower. She says she owes me one."

Her eyes lit up. "That'll help."

Before she ordered an air strike, I said, "At first I wasn't sure why my helping Aster put her in my debt—"

"Well, isn't he sort of her ward? Some distant relative?"

"That's what I thought, too. But it's not. It's something else." I held out the dirty, glittery towel.

"Ew, what is that? Pulpo juice? It stinks."

"I know," I said impatiently. "But that's not the only thing." I shook it at her. "Look at it."

"Okay, fine." She took it gingerly between her finger and thumb. "It's got some sparkly shit on it. What is that?"

"It's Aster's blood."

She frowned and held the towel close to the light of the candles. Then she put out her other hand. "Magnifying glass." I'll be damned if one didn't appear. The handle was shaped like a long silver feather, and she held the round glass in front of her eye. "Are these...gears? Little cog things?" She looked up at me, wide-eyed. "So, just to be clear, this is the blood of a construct, not a fae. Fae have blood that looks like champagne, so sometimes it has a gold cast, but there isn't anything like grit or gears in it. And you're telling me this is Aster's blood? Are you one hundred percent sure about this?"

"Yeah. One hundred and ten percent."

I repeated March and Madame's conversation about keeping secrets. "Don't speak it, those were her exact words. She thinks she owes me because she...built him? She's his creator."

"Holy shit. And he doesn't know? You're sure about that, too?"

"That's what she told March. And Aster never said anything that made me think he was hiding something. In fact, he doesn't think much of the constructs at all. What do we do?"

She tossed the magnifying glass over her shoulder, and it vanished—back to the elements. "We have to tell Aster. Envelope," and one drifted from thin air into her waiting hand. She carefully scraped the gears off the towel into the envelope, sealed it, and handed the packet over to me.

I tried to picture that conversation. "I don't..."

"He has the right to know." Her tone was much sharper than the conversation called for.

"Why are you yelling? I'm not arguing with you."

She sighed. "Sorry. It's just...I feel really strongly about coming clean with big secrets. Even difficult ones. Especially those. Something happened to me, and I didn't find out about it for a long time. The...person who knew was afraid to tell me. And it might have made a big difference if I had known what it was."

"Well, that's shitty behavior." I thought of the notes I'd found hidden in the dresser. Funny how two people in her life let her down like that. I figured it was while she was first getting adjusted to her life here at the Unseelie Court. "Some people are just cowards, you know?"

"No, honey. Not cowards. Not like that. People get scared, or they feel like they're to blame, that they're guilty. There are all sorts of reasons, why people do what they do. I was mad, but now I'm not." Despite what Sasha warned me about, deep down the Marly I knew and loved so much was soft hearted. If it had been me, I think I would have carried that grudge to the grave.

"Whoever it was is lucky you're so forgiving," I said.

"Yeah, they are," she said with a smile. "And they turned out to be a really good friend, so it all worked out." She sat up. "But this is all sort of beside the point. Aster absolutely has the right to know. And you have to tell him. You know that. It's the reason you came up here, right?"

I nodded. "Sure. When Madame disintegrates me, make sure Sasha throws me a nice party."

"You make a point." She frowned, thinking. Then she made a face again and waved her hand. "Clean. Sorry, that pushed a boundary but I figured under the circumstances?"

I took a deep sniff of chilly Unseelie air, as me and my

hair were now cleansed of any pulpo juice. "The judges will allow it. Thanks."

"Maybe we can convince him to keep quiet? Until you're back home?" She shook her head. "Or I can just tell him myself."

"No." I stood up. "It's up to me. If it all falls to shit, I can use the flower she gave me." I hoped I didn't have to as I had a strong feeling I would need it for something else. "And I think Sasha will protect me. I think March will too, if it comes to that."

"Shit, I've been so worried about Ilex I didn't even ask. That versette was a whole entire thing last night. You okay?"

"Why wouldn't I be?" I snapped. She raised her brows and began to speak but I cut her off. "He and Amory got what they wanted; it has nothing to do with me. But there's something..." It was so frustrating. *You know*, said the voice in my head. *You know.* "No, I don't know, jeez."

Marly patted my arm like I was a mental patient. "It'll be okay. You'll figure it out. Now let's go tell our Real Boy he's just a Pinocchio."

It turned out Marly had some trouble with the way the fae got from place to place. She said it was like getting seasick times one million. So we had to wait for one of the guards to come up, put her to sleep for what she called her 'traveling nap' and then wait for her to wake up and get ready to move. It only added a few minutes but I can't imagine she enjoyed being carried around like a sack of potatoes. She said she and Sasha were working on it. I got to spend a few seconds enjoying having something she didn't possess, then another few minutes of guilt just to even things out.

Once she was back on her feet, I followed Marly through the maze of hallways, and I couldn't help but notice the way the fae bowed and moved aside to let us pass. The crown carried some weight around here. Even if they talked behind her back they stood at attention to her face. When we got to Aster's place, she magicked up a calling card, and with a wave of her hand sent it inside. He came to the door and let us in.

"You look good," I lied. He did not look good. "How are you feeling?"

"Fine," he replied. His eyes were cloudy, and his hair was tied in a loose ponytail. His normally peachy skin looked gray, but I could see the welts were almost gone, so that was good at least. "I have to sit down. Come in."

Marly and I glanced at each other as we followed him inside. I was starting to think maybe we ought to put this conversation off until he was stronger. "Your place is cute, Aster," I said, and it was; a sort of walled courtyard, an indoor/outdoor situation with elegant dark gray velvet lounge chairs set among a mainly green garden. He was short on flowers but his grass would have made my dad weep—St. Augustine grass was the only thing that would grow in the Florida heat, but it always looked like it longed for death and felt like walking on steel wool. "You'll have to give me some lawn care tips."

He laughed and it turned into a cough, then said, "Really, I can't take credit. It's just how it looks." He shuffled across the soft, perfect lawn and we followed. "I should have asked you here instead of visiting the pulpo. They were more energetic than usual."

"I'm just glad you're okay."

"I mean it," he said, lowering himself onto a chaise. "I don't understand why she attacked. They're usually placid. It was like they sensed an enemy. I can't apologize enough for putting you in danger."

"It's really okay. Until they attacked us it was very exciting." Marly looked at me like 'really?' but I powered on. "Thank you, in fact. No one else here takes me anyplace interesting."

He smiled and leaned back. "I'm honestly starting to feel better. Madame of course has been taking marvelous care of me."

"I'm sure she has," Marly muttered. I kicked her ankle.

"Do you feel well enough to have a talk?" I asked.

He cocked his head. "Talk? About what?" Then he tried to straighten up. "Forgive my rudeness. I'll call for refreshments."

"No," I said, and gently pushed him back down, "let's just talk. About you." He looked completely baffled, and very tired. I had a bad feeling about this.

Marly said, "Describe only the good things that come into your mind about your mother."

"Seriously?" I turned away from her and laid my hand on his. "What do you remember about your family?"

" Nothing at all," he said. "Only what I've been told. They were killed in the Light War. My mother was dear friends with Madame, and she took me in. I was a small child—an infant. It was Madame who raised me."

"Good, that's fine." I said. "What were their names?"

He looked increasingly curious, but answered, "Marguerite and Zin. What's this about, Ruby?"

"Tell me, have you ever fallen and scraped your knee? When you were small, maybe? Or cut your hand with a knife?"

"What? No, of course not. I remain under a charm of minor protection, all children do." He paused. "Madame insisted, although of course I'm not a child anymore. Now that I think about it, I might be the last one under it. And all the charms and spells are collapsing. Because of the light, you know." He gave a sort of smile. "It certainly didn't hold up this morning."

"So you've never seen your own blood. Okay." I pulled out the packet. "Do you know what this is?"

He peered at the tiny glittering gears. "Aren't those... that's what the constructs use for blood, isn't it? Where did you get that?"

I looked at Marly, and she nodded. I took his hand and held it tightly. "I got it from you. This is your blood."

Aster stared at me for a minute, then gave a short laugh. "This is a joke. Isn't it considered rude to make fun of someone when they're ill, even among humans?"

"I'm so sorry," I told him, "but it's not a joke."

"Then a sort of revenge? For my putting you in danger?"

"It's not that, either." I turned his hand up and tapped the little gears onto his palm. "When I slapped you to wake you up—do you remember? —well, your blood got on my hand. This is your blood."

He sat up stiffly, held his hand out, and dumped the

gears onto the grass. "I don't believe you."

"You don't?" Marly's mouth was set in a grim line. She sat down on the other side of him. "You think Ruby would make this up?"

"No, of course not, but..."

She continued. "You think Madame isn't clever enough to create someone like you?"

"Something," Aster said. "She would have told me. Wouldn't she?" But I could see the doubt in his dark eyes.

She held out her hand. "Knife." A thin finger of a blade with a gleaming black handle dropped into it. It looked like softhearted Marly had left the building.

"This is too much, Mar, don't be crazy, come on," I said. "We'll work this out without—"

She sliced her palm open, and a bubble of blood welled up—nearly clear with a faint golden tinge, and bubbles. Champagne. That took me back to a bottle of champagne spilled all over my kitchen floor...only it wasn't my kitchen, and it wasn't champagne...

She turned to Aster. "Now you."

He looked at me with a kind of desperation. I couldn't help him. I couldn't make it not true.

"Fine," he said, holding out his hand to Marly. "You do it. After all, it'll only hurt for a second."

"No, honey," she said, drawing the knife across his palm, "this is going to hurt forever."

# 32

*Ruby*

The three of us watched as a glittering gold seam rose on the palm of Aster's hand. He held it out as far as he could, like he was hoping it would leap off his wrist and scuttle away. His eyes were huge and he was starting to hyperventilate. I reached for his unhurt hand. "Breathe, babe. Let's all calm down, okay?"

"Calm?" he gasped. "I'm a..."

"You're still you," I said.

"There's never been a me," he said. "I'm a lie." He was starting to tremble; he brushed my hand off and struggled to rise. "A... a construct?" The disgust in his voice made my heart ache for him. He gave up and kind of slumped back down, staring at his bright, bloody hand. "Why wouldn't she tell me? Why did...why did she make me?" He gasped. "My mother, my father...they're not really my family at all."

I wanted to tell him they were, that if he remembered

them, they belonged to him, and then I remembered that he said they died when he was a baby. He didn't even have memories. "I'm sorry," I said for the millionth time—I was racking up debt to someone, but at this point I didn't care. But Madame loves you, I think. She raised you. She took care of you—she still does."

He glared at me. "Why do you defend her? How she must laugh, watching me prance about like a real, living fae. I'm nothing at all."

"That is not true," Marly said. "You're you. Look at me." Marly took him by the chin. "What am I?"

"You're...the king's lady. The queen."

She nodded. "That I am. And what else?"

"Human, but not...but also like us?"

"I began my life as a human," she said. "And then I was a vampire for a couple of days." She was? How did I not know that? "And then, it took a couple of months, but now I'm one of the fae. But you know what? Every day, no matter what else, I was still me." She thumped her chest. "Dead, undead, magic, human, fae. In here. And so are you. You're smart, and kind, and look at what you just did. You're brave as fuck. And you've got to be really brave right now."

"Wh... why?" He leaned back on the chaise, looking spent.

"You can't let Madame know, not yet."

"Why not?" we both asked.

"Obviously, she's going to be angry that we told Aster the truth. The event with the Seelie Court is coming up." She turned to me and widened her eyes. "If this got out, she'd need a good explanation."

That was clearly my cue to let her take lead, which was also what Sasha wanted me to prevent. I tried to deflect.

"All we know is constructs—some of them—are working for her. Aster, what do you know about this?"

He looked like he wanted to cry. "Nothing. Nothing at all. All I know is my life was fine—of course, we all worry about the glass, but everything was fine. I honestly didn't like to think too much about things like that." His mouth twisted. "I had the patronage of a great lady and was free to do as I liked. And so, I did, like a little pet." He looked at his hand. The bleeding had stopped, and in another world, he would have a handful of shiny confetti, ready to toss. "I ignored everything that didn't have anything to do with me. So, no, I never heard her making plans." He flung the glitter away with a look of disgust, then looked at me. "What do I do now?"

"We wait, I think," I said. "Let's see what happens at this party." He nodded. I wished I could have read his expression better, but all I could see was someone who felt sick and had too much heaped on their plate.

Marly and I exchanged looks. We both knew what we had to do. We'd have to find a way to use Aster against Madame.

I gently rubbed his shoulder. "At least you know, right? And we are both here for you, for whatever you need." To me, knowing the truth seemed more important than the pain learning the truth caused. I just hoped in Aster's case we hadn't made a mistake. "And you know who you can trust."

"He already knows who to trust. If you were one of the

fae, I would strike you down where you stand, human girl."

Madame stood in the doorway. We were busted. How much had she heard?

"Yeah, well she's under the protection of the king, so power down." Marly had her unimpressed face on, but I was definitely quaking.

"It's fine, Madame," Aster said. He got to his feet. "We were just talking. I'm feeling better, honestly—"

"It's her fault you were so injured to begin with." She turned back to us. "Leave at once." It seemed like she hadn't overheard the crux of the conversation, thank God.

"It wasn't her fault, and I may speak with whomever I like," Aster retorted. Maybe it was the fae version of adrenaline, but he was getting some roses back in his cheeks. "They can stay as long as they like. Maybe it's you who ought to leave."

Marly and I glanced at each other. He was going to spill the beans.

"No," I said, quickly jumping in. "We've overtired you. We'll go." I tried to make my face look like everything was fine. "Aster, let me know if you hear anything else about Lauren C's service, but don't—"

"Leave him alone," she snapped. "He doesn't know anything."

"You've made sure of that," Aster told her. Yeah, he was definitely going to talk. He looked at us and smiled. "Don't worry. Now we all have secrets."

Madame' eyes narrowed. "What does that mean?" He lifted his chin. "No answer for me? I can't say as I approve of this change in your behavior. I'm going to assume it's the poison left in your body and that as it passes you will return to your senses."

He folded his arms and rolled his eyes.

Marly laughed. "He'd fit right in with my ninth graders. We'll be on our way, then. Aster, I hope you feel much better soon." She glanced at Madame expectantly, and Madame managed to make her bow look snotty. With a snort, Marly left.

I quickly curtsied and turned to follow.

"You," Madame said.

"Yes?" I had one foot out the door.

"You won't be able to cower in the king's shadow forever." She whirled in a swish of gaily patterned yellow and pale green silks and stalked off through the far entrance.

"Aster," I said, "Are you going to be okay?"

He looked at me wearily. "I have to think. I'm going to the Eye."

I turned to go, and as his door rematerialized, the last thing I saw was him collapsing onto his chaise, head in his hands.

# 33

*Ruby*

"He'll be fine." **Marly hardly** looked convinced, but it was too late to second guess. "It's just a lot to take in, in one day."

I agreed. "Ideally you get attacked by Cthulhus and almost die and then find out your whole life is a lie over a period of, say, several weeks."

"I still think we did the right thing." She had that look on her face. "What did he say to you? Just now?"

"That he was going to the Eye. Ever been there?"

She nodded. "Weird, but kind of also interesting."

"Can I ask you a question?"

She shrugged. "Sure, I guess."

"Um, just now, did you tell Aster you were a...vampire?"

She sighed and rubbed her eyes. "Yeah. It cleared up. It's a long story. I'll tell you all about it, but things to do first, okay?"

I felt a wave of lightheadedness, just like at Noisette's when the subject of vampires came up, and found I didn't want to hear about it after all. Marly, a vampire? That was too disgusting—and too terminal—to contemplate. She must have meant something else. "Good. Okay. What's next?"

She tapped one finger against her chin. "I don't know yet. Let me head back. Come and grab me later so we can get ready for tonight."

I rounded a corner and almost plowed into Master Greaves. He did the same loose-jointed leap as when he came to my room that first day, but instead of bowing or making some charmingly quaint pronouncement, he took me by the arm and said in a low voice, "It's time we talked, Lady Ruby. Will you be missed?"

Of course, I jumped at the chance to finally ask about his pep rally with Madame, and maybe find out how to snap Ilex out of it. If anyone was looking for me (no one was looking for me) they could just wait. He led me to a clearing in the middle of the palace—at least that was sort of where I put us. It was a peaceful, open space, lined with white benches and with a small pond in the center. Irises like those in Marly's garden dotted the bank. We were alone. I sat next to him on one of the benches and waited to see what this was going to be all about.

"The fête tonight, you know how important it will be? You know the Seelie Court will send its highest representatives? Decision makers, not those who bow and curtsy."

"You mean people who will get things done, not hangers-on. What do you think is going to happen? Have you...*heard* anything?" Oh yeah, so subtle. I was a regular James Bond.

He looked at me pensively then said. "I might as well tell you that your presence at our gathering yesterday was not entirely unnoticed." He saw my eyes widen and patted my hand. "Madame is unaware. I, however, could not help but take note of you and the *re'em*. You both were throwing off a great deal of energy."

To cover my mortification, I said, "Um, did you know that *re'em* is actually a biblical mistranslation from Hebrew? It means rhinoceros. I looked it up." I don't know why I thought he'd be interested, or that he knew what Hebrew was, or a bible, or a rhinoceros, or why I even looked it up in the first place, but it was better than blushing to death in silence.

He smiled. "I did not know that." He paused, gathering his thoughts. "Since you were occupied during our meeting, let me tell you that it is said the Seelie Court have the secret for repairing the glass. Our Lord king will ask for help. We—I do not believe he will be successful."

That tracked with what Sasha told me, and what Marly said about offering up his sword. "But he has a plan, doesn't he?"

"From what we have *heard*, it's more of a gamble." I took that to mean he had been spying on Ilex for information for a while. I decided not to let him know I knew that. "We have placed our hope in the hands of Madame."

"She has a plan of her own." A plan where the constructs would live in their own light. I'd heard that much while I wasn't busy throwing off energy.

"She does. A good plan." For a second the hope on his

face made him almost handsome. Then his rubber-mask features grew somber again. "I believe Madame has the best chance of convincing the Seelie Court to come to our aid, and reverse the darkness. Ruby, I am here today to beg you not to try to stop her."

"Stop her from saving everyone? Why would I do that? And who would listen to me anyway?"

"You will be most inclined to try," he said.

"It would help if I knew what we're talking about. What's the big reveal?"

He grimaced, the face of tragedy. "I am sworn. Unable to speak it."

Of course. If I were Madame, I would have done the same thing. From what I'd learned, breaking a promise was considered a particularly evil kind of lie. The kind with particularly evil consequences. "You said it would bring trouble and grief." He nodded. "But I should let it go on."

"It is not what I would have chosen. But it must happen. Perhaps if I show you what we are facing, you'll understand. Do you trust me?"

I snorted a laugh. "After that performance with Ilex? What do you think?"

He sighed impatiently. "She, like the rest of my folk, are tools. Tools may be broken. But they also may be repaired. Any damage taken by Ilex will be undone as soon as what's to come is over. This I promise you. There. Have I gained your trust?"

I cocked my head at him. "What do you think? You yourself said you'd be unreliable. And what do you mean, 'show me?'"

"It will be unpleasant for you. Uncomfortable. But I will be by your side and will let no harm come to you." That sounded suspiciously like Aster's going-on-a-fun-outing idea, and I'd seen how that turned out.

"What do you want me to do?"

"Stand up. Face away from me. And hand me your medallion."

I leaped off the bench and away from him. "No dice, pal. I know what'll happen. My head will blow up and my brains will run out my ear holes."

He shook his head, becoming anxious. "I will not let that happen. But you must see what we face if we fail."

I swallowed. "You won't let me die, or go deaf? Or go crazy?" After promising me a quarter million times, I agreed. I had to see, right? I did as he asked, and he stood behind me. I closed my eyes, and as I lifted the medallion off, he took it from me, and immediately covered my ears with his hands. Just for good measure, I clapped my hands over his. I could feel the thick silver chain twined through his fingers, and hoped like hell he wouldn't drop it. The noise was bad, but bearable—like being in the front seat at a demolition derby. I opened my eyes.

The gentle afternoon light was gone, and I shivered convulsively in the bitter cold darkness. I looked up as best I could without moving my head, I could see a few slivers of twinkling glass; high, cold, and as dim as the distant stars, and shedding just as little light. We were standing nearly ankle deep in ash, which drifted through the air and left greasy soot on our hair and clothes and faces. The garden and the benches were gone. The pond was a seeping pool of sludge, the same black ooze I'd noticed outside Marly's place. The plants were dead—ghostly white stalks and brittle leaves that rearranged themselves into grasping, boney hands. We stood on the remains of a broad boulevard in what looked like a bombed-out city. At the far end of the rubble-strewn street stood a big fountain like in a town square. The basin appeared to be full of slowly moving, quivering jello, which gave off a chilly blueish light. Close to my feet, a tiny grey and white spotted frog crawled onto a rock, and as I watched a beetle the size of my palm scuttled out of the ash, gripped the little frog with its pincers and slowly began to tear it apart. I looked away

"Where the fuck are we?" I couldn't hear my own voice, but Greaves did. He spoke right into my ear. Meanwhile, the jello in the fountain had humped itself over the lip and was oozing in our direction.

"We are in a place called Verdant Home. It was once a happy community. This is what waits for all of us if the light fails. This is our future if we fail."

I took a shuffling half step and a cloud of acrid dust blew up, and when I sneezed both our hands slipped off my ears, and the sound hit me, and it was awful. I tried to scream but took a huge gulp of sooty air in and began to cough instead. He replaced his hands in less than a second, but I was choking. Right away, Greaves jammed the medallion back over my head and I fell on my butt—was I sitting in ashes? No. I was on the grass. The pretty pond, the grass, the trees, they were all back.

"Why?" I wiped my streaming eyes and struggled to catch my breath. "Why didn't anyone tell me?"

"Until now, there was no need." He looked embarrassed. "I did not withhold this from you out of malice. But you had to see it before tonight's events. There will be no slow descent, no gentle going. What you saw? It's close and gets closer every day."

I shook my head, and started to ask him a question, but the ash caught my throat again. Finally, I wheezed, "Is this all a lie? Or an enchantment? Is that...hell...what's really all around us?"

He sat back down on one of the clean, ornately decorated benches. "It will be. If you look in the shadows, you can already see it."

I had seen it. I thought of the ooze at the edge of the street and the quivering creature in the fountain. This was really happening.

He looked at the sky. "Everything we are comes from the light, and as long as it lasts, so does our home—and so does my own life. But as the light diminishes—"

"The shadows take over." I shuddered.

He nodded. "So, you see, if Madame is not successful, soon enough our home will be nothing but ash, and the things that live in ash. You must not stop her."

Then it dawned on me. "She owes me." He looked at me, curious. Of course, he didn't know. "She owes me a debt. If I tell her not to do...whatever she has planned, she'll have no choice but to stop." I knew this was leverage, but after what I'd just seen, I didn't have the heart. And he did promise that

Ilex would recover.

He rubbed his face. "This is worse than I thought. I was hoping to simply stop you from trying to interfere. This could cause the entire plan to fail. Please, please, do not stop her." He took my hands in his own. "You will not thank me later, but you must promise me. Swear it."

"Wait." I remembered why I was here in the first place; what March and I had promised each other. "I won't swear on anything that'll hurt Marly."

He sighed. "No. This has nothing to do with her."

"Then I swear," I said. I could still smell the reeking ash. "I swear it, I won't stop Madame. Hell, I'll even help her, if it means stopping…that."

He released me and sat back, looking tired. "I doubt that, Ruby. I don't think you'll want to help her. Not at all."

# 34

*March*

**M**ud and green. That was mainly what March remembered about that spring, and that war. It was an indulgence, he knew, to relive memories so long past, because all the mortals and most of the xenos he met and loved and fought were dead and (except by him) forgotten. An indulgence because while he felt everything all over again, there was no pain when it was over. It might have happened to someone else. It was merely interesting.

Mud; that was from endless feet—men and women—and endless hooves and wheels moving back and forth across what had once been meadows and fields. And green; because in that cool and gentle northern place, things that grew could only be slowed, never stopped. He was on the edge of the battle at the moment, on a hillside slick with mud and blood, with the queen by his side. The screaming had died away. He thought it was almost over.

"You don't have to be here," she told him. She looked at him with grief and pride. "Why are you still here?"

"I am sworn to him, Lady. And so, to you."

She gave him a penetrating stare. "That I needed you to protect me was never anything but a polite fiction. You don't even carry a weapon." They both knew he didn't need one.

"I swore that as well, long before we met. And you may not need my protection, but you have it anyway."

She nodded and sighed. "I know. I'm glad it's you, here. Now."

It was a strange thing, being a knight without a sword, but if he held one in his hand, he might have had to use it and that was unthinkable. He thought the king's advisor knew he wasn't what he appeared, but then again neither was the strange old man. And he *had* sworn himself to the new king, one drunken evening long before, because the boy was radiant with the kind of glamor that was fully human, and March found himself unable to look away. The king was clever and young and he loved his land and his people and his pretty fair-haired queen.

March loved the queen as well, but only until she moved on to another brave and handsome warrior who suited her better. That knight was long gone, the king was no longer young, and they were about to lose the battle.

"I could...intervene," March said. He knew if he changed into his real form and went forth, the armies would fall to their knees and the tide might well change.

The queen wiped tears from her cheeks, her manner turning brisk. "No. This is the Matter of Britain. This must happen now so other things will happen later." She managed a smile. "You'll probably live to see them."

"And you?"

She looked away. He didn't know exactly what she was, but she was no mortal, that he knew like he knew the paths of the stars. It was strange, thinking on it, how many otherly people the king drew to himself.

From the muddy valley, a shout went up from the clot of exhausted men, struggling to lift their swords against each other. He and the queen looked down in time to see the dragon banner, lovely white and gold, dip and spin and finally fall. The queen lowered her head and for a moment he could almost feel her grief. He raised his hand, thinking to comfort her, but let it drop. Eventually she looked up.

"It's time for you to leave." She looked past him, back towards the safety of the vast and darkening forest.

"Come with me."

She smiled and touched his cheek. "I release you from your vow. Go."

She was right, of course. It was time to leave. Every time he involved himself in the affairs of men, and those who lingered close to men, he found himself in deep and perilous water. He thought he might travel east, to lands of endless grass and sky.

Returning to the present, he wondered if Gwenhwyfar still lived, and where she might be now. "March?"

A different queen stood before him, no more human than the last.

"Are you lost?" Marly asked.

He shook his head to clear away the memories, and gave her a weak smile. "In a general or specific sense?" He looked around. "I keep losing my way. I think I'm on the right path, but then...nothing looks right."

She nodded. "It's this place. It did a number on me until Sasha helped me figure it out. The trick is to concentrate on where you want to go, not on where you are. So even if you come across, like, the replica of your bedroom when you were in middle school, just walk on by." Then she smiled. "That would be pretty startling, in your case. Where are you going?" She winced, probably thinking she'd overstepped. "It's none of my...Never mind." But a queen's prerogative was to change her mind, he supposed, and she continued.

"No. You know what? It is my business. You know Ruby could see you two last night, right? Were you trying to be a dick?"

"A...why would you call me that?" Was she trying to be rude? Dicks were nice, but the way she said it wasn't.

"I know how you feel about her," she continued, "and I know this is awful and hard for you and all that. But was sticking your tongue down Amory's throat in public a helpful way to act?"

He looked at his feet. "She told me to leave her alone. That what we did was a mistake." Then he looked up. "Did she tell you we—"

"I heard about a make-out session in a dark hallway." She sighed. "And here I thought the Unseelie Court would slightly less resemble high school."

"I am trying to respect her decision. I feel as if she is

starting to remember me and who we are to each other. I understand the magic in the kingdom is degrading, and so the enchantment she is under is starting to crumble. But I must let her come to her memories in her own time."

"And in the meantime, you've got someone to keep you warm."

He let himself look offended, then resigned. "It is in my nature to accept what I am offered."

Marly quirked a grin. "You're just a unicorn who can't say no."

He frowned and lifted his chin. "Well, Ruby is keeping company of her own, isn't she?"

Marly's eyes widened. "Are we really going to talk about Aster right now?" He could clearly see the idea of snapping off his horn and shoving it up his ass surface in her head like a bright fish, and then dart away. "Okay, let's talk about Aster. So, do you still hate that guy?"

March cocked his head., He counted Marly a friend but he sometimes found her conversation exhausting. Unicorns, in general, were not subtle. Why did she ask him what she already knew? Unless she knew he knew…Bah. "As it happens, I don't. I've actually found some things out. About him."

She smiled; curious, kind. "Really? What sort of things? You seemed so mad just now."

"I… can't say."

"Can't?"

"I literally can't say. I made a promise. That carries a lot of weight here. As you know."

"Okay, well, how about this? If I guess right, just nod

your head." Before he could argue, she continued. "He's a construct. You found out when you saved him from the pulpo attack. Madame made him for fuck knows what reason and never told him. And she made you swear you wouldn't say anything about it or say anything to him. Am I close?"

He sighed. "How did you find out?"

"It was Ruby that figured it out. She wound up with her hands covered in golden gears, and put it together."

He narrowed his eyes. "So, this whole conversation was you basically being a…dick."

She laughed. "Yeah, I guess. I was pissed at you last night on Ruby's behalf, and honestly, I don't know if she was mad, into it, or didn't care at all. I'm guessing a lot of one and a dash of the other two. And she wasn't the only one. Don't blush, honey. It's in your nature."

"So," he said, wanting to move things along, "what do we do with this information?"

"Ruby came to me because she trusts me. My advice was to go to Aster and tell him the truth, and that's what we did."

"What? You told him? For what purpose?"

"A couple. First of all, he deserves to know the truth. Poor thing was fucking blindsided. We totally had to talk him off the ledge—I mean, get him to calm down. You know what he thinks of constructs—we had to remind him he was a person, no matter what's in his veins. He's still himself, right? I think we got through to him. He understands he can't tell Madame what he knows, not yet. I told him why it was important, but I didn't try to get a promise out of him."

"He's not bound, not like I am. He's going to confront

her, isn't he?" He paled. "Madame will—"

"Will what?" She had a look of curiosity that was almost clinical. "What do you think she'll do? See, that's the second thing. Personally, I think she'll be so consumed with rage that a little human and the king's new whore outed her secret, it'll put a serious foot up the ass of whatever she had planned with the Seelie fae."

March gasped. "You would use Aster?"

"You're damned right. He's a loaded gun, and based on his reaction, he is going to go off hard. He may take her out completely. Or he may slow her down long enough for us to buy some time. Sasha has a plan of his own, we just have to let him do his work."

He gave her a long, appraising stare. "Then what is Aster? A person? Or a weapon?"

Marly ground her teeth. He could feel her impatience. "Why do you think she made him?" He didn't reply, because he didn't know. "That woman is the queen of the long game. She knows the Spire of the Seelie Court is a collector."

"Everyone knows that. So was Sasha—he tried to collect me."

"Yeah, well, what if she made sure she had something in her back pocket. Something shiny. Something to trade."

He raised his brow. "Aster, in exchange for the throne."

"And the glass repaired. We know she's already got the backing of most of the constructs. Throw in a new generation of pure fae babies and the court will fall in line. Sounds like a pretty good deal."

"Except now Aster knows what she's up to, and maybe

can stop her. He does know all of this? You told him what you think Madame plans for him?"

She took a moment to reply. "I told him everything I know."

He felt great pity for the boy. He knew what it felt like to think the world was one way and being utterly wrong.

"And Ruby? Does she know all this?"

"Only the first part. She doesn't know the why. And no, I'm not going to pull her aside and tell her, because she doesn't need to know and because she's got a soft heart." He had to agree. It would be well within Ruby's nature to fling herself between Aster and whatever Madame had in mind. But Marly had apparently given this quite a bit of thought, because she continued. "And I can't risk you coming up for air long enough to tell Amory. Promise me, the same one you made Madame. You won't talk."

He nodded, then folded his arms. He thought fleetingly of Gwenhwyfar and the cost of the crown. "This court could do worse than having you as its queen, Marly."

"Thank you."

She looked grimly satisfied, and he realized she thought it was a compliment. She said, "Listen, if you're looking for a place to gather your thoughts, I hear the Eye is a good place to visit."

A place of calm. And where he'd met Amory. "The Eye? Yes, that is a good idea. I'll do that."

She turned to go. "Strike, counter strike," she said softly.

"What does that mean?" he asked.

She looked back, smiling. "Not a thing. Nothing at all."

# 35

*March*

**M**arch left Marly's side wanting to find his new and interesting friend Amory and tell him everything he'd learned. Of course, he couldn't. For one thing, Amory was busy.

"I'll find you before this whole boring thing starts tonight," he had said that morning between kisses. "Meetings. You know."

March decidedly did not know. He had never attended a meeting. It conjured an image of white men in those choking ties sitting around an oval table and barking at each other like dogs. But even if Amory abandoned every meeting he had, it wouldn't matter. He promised Marly, he promised Madame; he couldn't speak about Aster.

He thought about the number of promises piling up. He didn't care for the feeling, the obligation. It was like hands on him; grasping, plucking. And, as he usually did when he was feeling itchy and restless in his spirit, he wandered. Dressed in his human body, he found walking helped him sort things out. On his current walk, he remembered to pay attention to where he was going.

While he worried about the direction Marly seemed headed in (he could easily imagine blood, and not her own), he had to admit her plan was an interesting—if not pleasant—one. Madame struck him as the sort of person who always assumed they were half-a-valley-and-two-rivers ahead of you at all times. He could imagine her shock at having her secret spread out for everyone to dine on. He then thought about how Madame acted at Aster's bedside. Her fear looked genuine to him, but then, along with being that giant step ahead, he knew perfectly well she could look or act any way she thought might do her good in the future. Just because she shed a tear over Aster didn't mean Madame wasn't planning on using him as currency later. Of course, if Aster refused to serve as her currency, she would lose her leverage, giving the advantage back to Sasha, whose plans were currently only his own.

With humans, March usually could tell what they would do, in a given situation. These people, these fae, were opaque.

Even Marly, whom he thought of as a friend, with her new eyes and her new crown, he wanted to but couldn't say her heart hadn't changed.

Thinking about Marly led him to think about Ruby. He wondered how long before the magic used to blind her to their past would wear away. She said he was a mistake; that what they'd done together, however briefly, was a mistake.

Had she meant it? He was a poor liar, and couldn't always spot one coming in his direction. He could only assume she meant what she said, and wait, and hope.

He turned a corner and found himself staring into the limitless void of The Eye. Marly was correct, it was a good place to gather one's thoughts. And it appeared he wasn't the only one who thought so.

Aster was kneeling at the edge of the black expanse, head bowed, and his hands thrust into the emptiness. From his elbows down, they had taken on the characteristic of mist. March didn't hesitate, he grabbed Aster by the shoulders and hauled him backwards, where he landed with a thump.

"What's wrong with you?" Aster scrambled to his feet, angrier than March could recall seeing him—or any of the fae, really. "Why did you do that?"

"I... thought you were going all the way in," March told him. "I was trying to save you from disappearing."

"Save me? From the Eye?" Aster's anger began to cool as he realized March simply didn't understand what he was doing. "Did you think I was in danger?"

"I see you weren't. I apologize for laying hands on you."

Aster pursed his lips. "Thank you. It's fine." He paused. "Just so you'll know, I was contemplating. This is where we go for peace and reflection."

Reflection. Hadn't Amory said something like that? "How does it work? What is the Eye, anyway? If you don't mind my asking."

"I don't." He thought Aster looked relieved at having something other than himself to talk about. "Its where used things go. We also come here to give the Eye things we don't need anymore, spiritually speaking."

He understood the metaphysical part, being well-versed in the application of prayer. "Used things? You mean, actual things?"

"Of course." Aster held up his hand. "Say you want something." A wide brimmed, plum-colored hat with a swooping ostrich feather (also plum) appeared. "But it's not quite right. You would have preferred aubergine. And you don't feel like fixing it, you'd prefer to start over." He tossed the hat into the Eye, where it disappeared in a quick burst of pretty violet sparks.

"It's...is it for your trash?" It made a certain sense—unneeded items and unwanted thoughts.

"In a way. But nothing is really trash, is it? It goes back to the beginning, and we re-use it to create something new. You do know how our magic works? It's all based on balance. To make, something else somewhere must be unmade. There is no hat, in other words, without a hat."

March tried to recall if he'd seen any fae anywhere wearing a hat. Maybe Aster had seen it in one of his reality shows. "You're looking much better."

"I'm feeling almost back to normal. And I must thank you again, for saving my life." He laughed bitterly. "My life. I suppose you know?" March swallowed and shrugged. "What is that face? Did you speak with Madame about the peculiarity of my existence?"

He struggled—would this be considered a breach?

Aster laughed again, this time more cheerfully. "By the

grimace, I'm guessing she did. Allow me to release you from her promise—after all, I'm the subject, I should at least have that right."

March sighed with relief, thinking this place came with far too much calculation. "Thank you. Yes. I saw your blood—it got on my hand. I confronted her, and she told me..."

"What did she say? Exactly?"

"Just that you are her most valued creation." This was a lie on his part, but a well-intentioned one. It might even be true. "I want you to know I think it's very brave, what you're doing." Aster gave him a curious look. "It can't be easy for you, knowing the reason why Madame made you, all those years ago."

Aster said, "Go on."

March knew humans enjoyed confession, and imagined the fae felt the same way. If he let Aster know he understood, gave him space to talk about it, it might ease his unquiet mind.

"She's a very clever woman. I have lived a very long time, and it wouldn't occur to me to plan for something so far in the future." Aster didn't reply. "Knowing how the Spire would love to have someone like you that they wouldn't be able to resist you. I mean, you are pretty flawless. And I'm sure once they've made the trade, things will improve for everyone. It's exciting, isn't it? Imagining a new life? It's supposed to be quite beautiful, the Seelie Court." He glanced around. "Brighter, at least."

"Trade?" Aster stammered, "trade...me?" From the stunned look on his face, March could tell he had made a mistake. *I told him everything I know,* Marly had said, not, *"everything I suspect."* She had lied to him, or rather been just vague enough to skirt the border of a lie. Either way, she'd used him. He'd get back to that, in time.

"No," March said firmly, although he knew it was too late. "Certainly not. How could I possibly know what she has in mind? Well, I ought to go, I am expected, I suppose I'll see you..." he began to edge away.

"Wait, stop." Aster grabbed hold of his sleeve. "Please. Please, tell me what you mean."

Not for the first time, he wished he were far away. "We know she has something planned to undercut any deal the king might try to strike. We know the Spire is a collector of the rare and unusual. And you are that, aren't you?"

Aster laughed, a little wildly. "Only a day ago I would have given anything to be considered special. Look, my life has meaning after all. Do you think—" He paused. "I was about to ask you if you really thought her capable of doing something like this. But how would you know? I know her best, I think; better than anyone save perhaps our Lord King."

"Is she, then? Capable?"

"To gain the throne? To throw down and humiliate the king? To do that, she would be capable of anything."

# 36

*Ruby*

**W**hile **I made my way** to Marly's house—it had moved again—I had plenty of time to think about what I'd seen, and what I'd learned from Greaves. When I told Marly about the dead city—hilariously named Verdant Home, she nodded, looking grim. Clover pressed his bulk against her, almost knocking her off the couch.

"Pet," he said, sounding worried.

She pushed him off and righted herself. "I'm fine, baby," she told him, and he settled on the floor at her feet. "Sasha took me there. It was pretty bad."

"It was maybe the worst thing I've ever seen. Like that scene in Event Horizon but in real time." The acrid reek of ash still burned my sinuses.

She shuddered. "Ugh. Sorry. It's not a secret—I think everyone knows. We just don't like to think about the future—about what happens if the lights actually really go out. When the shatter happened it was just one pane that exploded and that was bad enough. Sasha says if we can get the Seelie Court to help us fix the panes, this place will start to heal. That future will never happen." She smiled. "We'll create our own future."

"You're honestly, seriously into him, aren't you?"

"He's a lot different than when I first met him. I think he's changed. Whatever happens tonight, I've got his back. Are you on board?"

"Mar, I can't go against Madame, I swore."

"Let's define 'go against.' It doesn't stop you from taking our side if the Seelie Court agrees to Sasha's terms. And if not, you can sit on your hands. You'll either help us, or do nothing." She gave me a sharp look. "Am I right?"

"God, I hope so."

"Pet," said Clover. I think he was hoping for the best, same as me.

She sighed. "He told me if he's successful, he'd deal with her once and for all. I don't know what that means, but..."

"Yes, you do." We stared at each other for a minute.

"Mistress." Ilex entered with a graceful bow. "It's time."

Clover rose to his feet, whining. He backed away from Ilex. Marly put a reassuring hand on his neck, smoothing down the raised feathers.

"Ilex," Marly said carefully. "How are we doing? Excited about tonight?"

Her smile was sweet and blank. "I look forward to continued service."

We glanced at each other. Marly cleared her throat. "I've

got this. We'll meet you out front in a few minutes."

"Shall I fetch Clover's collar?"

Marly smiled down at him. "He's got to sit this one out." She stroked his head. "Sorry baby. We think the Seelies might be intimidated. I thought that was the idea, but Sasha doesn't want to freak them out."

"As you like." Ilex bowed again and left, and Clover, now calm, sat back down at her side. She bent forward and rubbed her forehead.

"She was my best—my only friend here for a long time. She taught me how to smoke *paf*." Her words caught in her throat. "She made me coffee—she found coffee because she knew I liked it. Now…"

"Master Greaves said she'll be fine."

She lunged forward in her seat, her eyes shooting sparks. "What did he tell you? Do not fuck with me on this."

"What? Why would I…?" Then it was my turn. "You're not the queen of me, so settle fucking down. Got it?" Clover rose onto his haunches, prepared to defend his mommy against my raised voice. "Of course, I'm going to tell you, jeez."

She sank back down, and he did too. "I'm sorry. I'm… I'm…I honestly don't know what I am right now. Just please tell me what happened."

"That's practically the whole reason I'm here. Sasha was on the money when he said Madame just wanted to shut her up for a few days. Master Greaves said she's still in there. She was damaged, he said, but she'll be back to normal…" I paused, wanting to be exact. "As soon as what's to come is over. That's what he said. What he promised. *Promised*. I know what that means. And I think he feels bad about squealing, for what it's worth."

"At the International Bank of Queen Melis, a nickel, because I am, in fact, the queen of him. When this is over, I'm going to have a crack at him and see what falls out." She snorted. "Damaged my ass." I took a second to be thankful I wasn't him.

Then she gave herself a shake, and got up. The liquid silk of her black gown rippled down and out, revealing the blood red layer underneath. Her pearls glowed against her collarbones, and even though her green boots didn't go with the dress, she somehow pulled it off. She always looked elegant to me—of course, to me, tall = elegant. But tonight, she looked like a goddess. She went to the window and opened the birdcage, and the flock of little lights that made her crown did a lap around the room like a flock of agitated birds, then settled against her chest. "Shh, it's okay fellas," she cooed. "I've got you."

"Those things love you."

She smiled, looking around her room. "I get a lot of love here, believe it or not. Here, lift your arms so I can fix your sash." I'd gone with a wallpaper looking blue and white floral-patterned robe, the sort of thing the slightly dowdy sister of the starlet wears to a red carpet—pretty but not flashy. "They're called a chorus. That's their collective name. And I don't love them wandering around in my hair, but aren't they pretty?" She straightened up and stroked the lights, which gathered under her chin. "Come on, boys. Here we are." She lifted them over her head and they hung in the air like a firefly chandelier. Once they had settled, she raised her hands and a gorgeously creamy white velvet cape materialized around her. As she lowered her arms, golden roses bloomed and their vines trailed themselves over her shoulders and down her back.

She took a deep breath and turned to me. "What do you think?"

I grinned. "Somewhere a drag queen is missing her best look. Nah, you look…I mean you look like a queen. A real one."

"Whatever happens tonight, I want you to know I'm really glad you're here. You're a shit bodyguard but I've sure as hell missed you." She reached out and hugged me, and I held on tight.

"Is it going to be okay?" I asked.

She took a long time to answer. "Let's go to a party."

But the way she said it, it sounded like "war."

# 37

*Ruby*

The ballroom was filled to capacity—I couldn't see the far walls. Instead of gossiping or drinking and waving their chopsticks around, everyone looked still and tense. They were all waiting. We were all waiting. The fae all got up to bow to Marly as we went by, some graciously, some grudgingly.

We found our table, although to this day I don't know how Marly spotted it. Anyway, I sat next to her. We all got to our feet when Sasha came in, leading the Seelie delegation. At the head was the Spire, a tall and very fair fae, with long white hair and a heavy looking white gown. Sasha told me the Spire was to be addressed as 'they' and then informed me that ideally I wasn't to address them at all. Of all the fae I'd seen so far, this one looked the most like they could have stepped out of a story book. Before Sasha could speak, there was a flurry of activity behind them, at the entrance to the ballroom.

"How dreadful, we're late." Madame sailed in with a bunch of her friends, trailed by March and Amory. Madame bowed before the Spire, and then her gaggle did the same. March watched Amory bow and seemed to copy it. They all found seats nearby. Still no Aster.

"It is my honor, " said Sasha after shooting daggers at Madame, "to present The Spire, who speaks for the Seelie Court."

The Spire stepped forward. "How kind of you all to come out and honor our fallen sister with us." Their voice was smooth and mellow and utterly captivating. They didn't resemble Lauren at all, but the warmth in the voice, that was the same. "It has been too long we have been apart from our cousins. It is just a shame that the premature death of our sister was the force that ended up bringing us together. I hope to honor her we can finally move forward from the grievances of the past. Thank you for hosting us tonight."

Madame popped back up and made a pretty little speech apologizing for being late and holding up the works and how glad she was, etc. While she was talking, I whispered to Marly.

"What if Aster doesn't show up?"

Marly was smiling and looked utterly carefree, like we were at the prom and she knew the election results. "He'll show." She sounded pretty certain. She caught me watching Amory, who had one arm slung over March's shoulder and was whispering in his ear. March lowered his head, smiling at whatever Amory said to him. "Are you okay?" I didn't answer, and she squeezed my hand under the table. "If it makes you feel any better, he's as fucked in the head about this whole thing as you are."

"Yeah, I feel great now." *It's none of my business where he spends his time. Or with whom,* I reminded myself. *I don't even know him. I don't even like him. I definitely didn't like kissing him.* So why did it feel like someone jabbed their thumb into my heart?

By this time, Sasha had not only started talking, but apparently said my name. I jerked my head up. He took pity on my blind panic, because he repeated himself. "I was hoping you, as one of Lauren's friends and her contact in the human world, might tell the courts a little about your time with her."

I slowly got to my feet. I desperately wanted a beer or something, but nothing appeared on the table. *Tell the truth. That's all you can do now.* I looked around the ballroom and at the ocean of black eyes, bright with their drifting lights.

"Lauren was...Lauren was the most different person I'd ever met. Different from me, I mean." The Unseelie fae were paying polite attention. The crew from the Seelie Court were laser focused. "Until I met her, I didn't know anyone who was so...completely enthusiastic about life. She was never bored. She was never cynical or jaded. Everyone she met, everything she did, she learned from with a passion. And I learned so much from her."

I remembered all our lunches, where I tried to explain human life, and she reacted like it was the best book she ever read. Or the best reality TV show. "I learned that even things that suck can be a lesson. I learned to pay attention. I learned that even a sliver of a sea shell could be worth a fortune. And a Target bathmat can spark joy." I smiled, thinking of her and her best of all-time haircut, and to my surprise felt my eyes fill with tears. "I tried to teach her about the human world, but I also learned about the fae from her, too; that you weren't all scary." I glanced at Sasha and he gave me a tiny nod and smile. "She was the best ambassador the fae could have hoped for." I turned to face Madame. "Because of Lauren, I believe the truth is greater and stronger than a lie, even if you don't call it one. I miss her. I wish I was more like her. Um, thank you." I sat back down, wiping my eyes with the back of my hand.

"That was beautiful," Marly whispered. Noisette's look was pure murder. I'm sure she thought it should have been her speech to give. March watched me, looking serious. Amory, with one arm still draped around March's shoulders, had his hand to his mouth, but I could still see his smirk. He was laughing. At me. I shot to my feet.

"Also. Hearts and emotions aren't toys. If your intentions aren't pure, if you're coming from a place of anything but the best intentions, a human will come for you, and you will not win...is another thing that Lauren taught me. Thanks. Thank you." I sank back into my chair. Amory hadn't moved his arm but he sure wasn't smiling anymore. Sasha leaned forward. "Well spoken."

The Spire stood and faced me. "Lauren enjoyed her time with the humans. She was emphatically in favor of greater communication between our realm and yours. Perhaps at another time we can explore this idea." Wait, did that make me the human rep? Another time, to be sure. They turned to Sasha. "It is time to discuss terms. Have you given more thought to our proposal?"

I saw a muscle in his jaw twitch and clench. "I have. And I could continue to give it thought until the last bit of glass shatters and falls on my head and my answer would be the same. It will always be no."

# 38

*Ruby*

"**W**hat does he mean, no?" Marly whispered. She'd gone pale. I think she was counting on the offer of the sword (and the implied offer of the glass) to be a slam-dunk, cutting Madame off at the knees. By the look on her face, she wasn't expecting this.

"Oh." The Spire put a sad look on their face. "How disappointing. And it was such a good idea, too. I really thought we had come to a *fruitful* place in our bargaining."

"That which you seek to bargain for does not exist." Sasha looked grim.

"Does not exist or, does not exist yet?" The Spire leaned forward. This was an important point—what it meant, I didn't know. Just looking at them, you would think the Spire was the good guy—good person, that is. Dressed in white, with soothing words and a calming voice. Sasha, in black armor as always, looked like the villain. You never can tell. The Spire continued. "Is it worth your kingdom to hold such a treasure back? I assume you have spoken to your young bride about this decision, as it involves her?"

"This lady has not—"

"Of course he has," Marly snapped. And that was the moment I saw the look on Sasha's face—how much he truly, for real loved her. Not for his kingdom or what she could do for him, but for her, herself. "Of course. Do you think my lord king wouldn't include me in the most important decision of the future of the kingdom?" I knew she was totally winging it, but the Spire looked convinced. I wondered mightily what she was agreeing to. She got a sly look about her. Usually that meant she was about to win a bar bet. "And isn't it the law that once an item is off the table, it is no longer to be mentioned? It doesn't exist."

The Spire looked a little shaken. "I did not mean—"

"So keep me and mine out of your mouth."

I think Marly and I figured out what they were bargaining for at the same time: something priceless that involved Marly and didn't exist yet. Something Sasha couldn't be persuaded to part with, not even with everything that was at stake. It was the reason she was here. It was the future, the one that they would create together. Her expression when she looked at Sasha confirmed it. I wanted to jump up and applaud, but hey, I can read a room.

The Spire sighed. "Then you have nothing. How very sad. Well, the speech about Lauren was nice, so this wasn't a complete waste of time." They lifted their finger and the

Seelie fae all got to their feet. "I leave you and your court to sink into the darkness."

"Wait." Sasha looked at Marly for a long, tender moment, then turned back to the Spire. "I have a counter proposal. May I convince you to hear it?"

With another finger flick, the Seelie court settled back down. The Spire rested their chin on their folded hands, leaning on their elbows. "I am listening."

"I offer this." He drew his sword and held it up. The slender glass blade caught the light and made it glow as if lit from within. "As I did in our session." The Spire began to shake their head, but Sasha wasn't done. "And along with it, I offer myself." As he said it, he took Marly by the wrist, holding her back. "I offer myself as your hostage for as long as you require. I would leave this good lady as my proxy, to rule in my stead."

I could hear her whispering, "Noooooooo" but I don't think the Spire heard.

"How interesting." The Spire motioned to one of their guards, who bent to listen. Were they going to go for it?

Madame cleared her throat. "If I may, I have something I think you'll find more to your liking than playing host to my lord king. He can be quite disagreeable." She was making her move. Where was Aster? "I have something to bargain with."

The Spire looked up, cheerful. "Madame, I have wondered when I might hear from you."

"Traitor," growled Sasha. "Withered stalk." He turned back to the Spire. "She has no authority to speak."

The Spire inclined their head. "She sat at the bargaining

session that ended the last war. Even I wasn't there for that. Does our law not provide that gives her the right to be heard? Is your law not the same?"

"It is," Sasha admitted, "but you might as well listen to the howling of beasts."

Marly and I looked at each other, wide-eyed. If that was all he had, he had been outplayed.

She smiled around the room. "May I continue? What if I offered you something special? Something absolutely unique."

"Don't listen to her lies" said Aster who, at last and thank God, stood in the arched doorway. "Yes, I said lies. There is something I must say."

The Spire sighed. "Are all your negotiations like this?" They waved the assistant away. "Very well. If your lord king has no objections?"

Sasha had very fucking much no objections. "Speak."

I could see Aster swallow hard and take a deep breath. "I am not what you all think I am," he began. "And Madame knows it, and has known it my whole life—if life is what we want to call it."

She laughed, a bright and brittle laugh. "I am forced to report my poor Aster is on the mend from an attack by a pulpo—the human girl was at fault, of course. And everyone knows how their poison affects the mind."

"Humans? Or pulpo?" The Spire asked. Oh, weren't you clever, Gandalf the Bitch?

"Are you still on that?" Aster asked. His eyes glittered. "You know she wasn't at fault."

"Really," said the Spire. "Ought this to be continued privately, between you two?"

"No." Aster stood straighter. "It should have started that way, though. Madame, perhaps you can tell us all why you built and breathed life into a construct and allowed it to live among the court as one of their own?"

A murmur went through the room, although if the fae were horrified at her deceit or rubbing elbows with the help, or just wanted more of the story, I couldn't know.

"Do not go down this path," she said, in a low and quaking voice. "You will regret it."

"There's nothing I don't regret," he said. "It is my belief that she created me and raised me alongside all you real folk, in hope of this moment. In hope of using me to trade with. I do not wish to be—I will not be used as property. If you take me, it will be as a prisoner, not a gift."

Holy shit, was that why she built him in the first place? If this was what Master Greaves warned me about, I couldn't stop her from trading Aster away. Marly watched intently, nodding to herself. March looked like he was about to faint, for some reason.

"Is that what you thought?" Madame sounded sad rather than angry, which should have been a tip off. "As if I'd ever let you leave my side."

"You have no right of control or ownership over me. Not anymore."

Everyone in the room, from the Spire to Sasha to the Trade folk who had—oddly—set down their trays and were watching very carefully, held their breath and waited to see what Madame would do.

"I had hoped to never tell this story, "said Madame, "and now I find I must share it with strangers. Who among you remember Marguerite?" Quite a few of the fae said they did. "My dearer-than-sister. Lost in the Light War along with her husband, as were so many of both of our courts. You may not remember her son, Aster." Of course, that set off a sort of quiet ruckus. "I saved the child—an infant, one of the last infants, I suppose. He was grievously wounded. I took him to the Belly, to my shop, and I set to work. If I had stopped to think, I would have thought only of the dead, so I did not stop to think. I didn't even stop when poor little Aster's heart quit beating. By then, I had put together something new. Something beautiful and alive. You are a little bit of your parents still, Aster. And a little bit of me. You are one of a kind, and I would never trade you away."

Poor Aster strode to her side and dropped to his knees. He had tears in his eyes. "Why didn't you just tell me?"

"I always meant to, but by the time you were grown you were so perfect, I didn't see the need." She paused. "Do you really think I'd concoct a plan from the day your mother died that would somehow pay off now? Am I such a villain?" He broke down in sobs, and she gently stroked his back. "There, there."

Marly was gripping the edge of the table. She was white as a sheet. "Fuck. Fuck. I was wrong. What did I miss?"

"You knew about this? And you weren't going to tell me?"

"There wasn't time, and I was afraid you'd jump in, and

I'm sorry. But I was wrong. Goddamn it, what did I miss?"

Madame looked up again, ice cold. "As we were saying."

"Oh, you're not done?" The Spire's eyes were bright with amusement. "What a fine entertainment. We should have come down here ages ago. Yes, please, do continue." Did they really think this was some kind of performance? Maybe they did. Maybe they all watched the same reality TV, and this was some prime drama.

"What about something you've never seen before?" she asked. "You're a collector, are you not?"

The Spire admitted they were.

"No need to be coy. Your collection is the envy of the kingdoms. I have something no one anywhere in any plane or realm could compete with. You would be a legend."

The Spire smiled. "You already have my attention. Please conclude the roasting and get to the carving."

"How would you like a unicorn?"

# 39

*Ruby*

Everyone looked from **Madame to** March, who had been whispering with Amory. Feeling the stares, he looked up.

"What?" he asked.

"Are you sure?" The Spire was thrilled. "This is uncommonly generous."

"It is our pleasure. He's all yours," Madame replied.

"What now?" March began to rise from the table, but Amory, who still rested his hand on March's shoulder, dropped what he'd apparently been hiding in his sleeve. It was a child's daisy chain, and he caught it with his free hand and quickly looped it around March's neck. "Sorry, beautiful." Amory kissed him on the cheek. "I did try to tell you, more than once." He got up and strolled to Madame's side, and handed her the end of the floral rope.

"March," hissed Marly, "get the fuck out of here. Change.

Run."

He looked at her, panicked. "I can't."

"Rube, use the flower." Marly was frantic. "Madame, she owes you, use it."

From across the room, Master Greaves and I locked eyes. It wasn't Aster at all. This was what he was trying to tell me. This was what I couldn't stop, if I wanted life to come back to this place. This was the choice I made, and this was the promise I had to keep.

"I can't." I said.

Marly hissed between her teeth and the look she gave me was pure poison. Instinctively I put my palm across my neck to protect my throat because wasn't she a vampire, once?

She noted my gesture. "You should be so lucky," she snarled. Then she tried to get out of her seat, I guess she was going to do what I wouldn't and save March somehow, but Sasha still held her arm. She looked back and forth between us; she was furious. Sasha would pay, later. I guess I would, too.

"He is temporarily in a sort of magical stasis," said Madame. She allowed Amory to lift her hand to his lips and smiled up at him. "For easy delivery."

"He will be our honored guest," said the Spire with a twinkling smile. "You're certain? If it were me, I'd hate to give him up."

"Of course, he will be missed. We adore him. Let this serve as a symbol of our willingness to work towards a better...a brighter (if I may) future for both our kingdoms."

"This is delightful, Madame, better than anything I had

envisioned. We can begin working on repairs to the glass as soon as we have our new friend installed. We'll endeavor to make him comfortable. So many people will want to see him. Tell me, how do you get him to turn back and forth? Is there a special word?"

"He's not your pet." I turned to Madame. "This is some bullshit—"

"Why does the human speak?" the Spire asked. "Does she come with the unicorn? Are they a set?"

"No," March said. "Leave her out of this."

I could barely stand to see the grief and disappointment in his eyes, and I looked away.

"Oh well." The Spire gave a shrug. They leaned towards one of their courtiers and spoke briefly. The courtier rose and went to stand behind March. "A word of advice, Madame, because we will be working with you in the future. As far as the Seelie Court is concerned, you have assumed the throne. Let me be the first to acknowledge Queen Tournesol, Ever Fragrant Prima Fleur of the Unseelie Court."

Madame—excuse me, the fucking Queen placed her hands over her heart and bowed her head. Then she said, "And the advice?"

"No kingdom may have two rulers at odds, as you and the Lord King remain. If I were you, I'd do something about that. With our complete support, of course." And with that, the entire Seelie entourage, along with a stunned looking March, vanished.

*What have I done?*

"Traitorous cow," Sasha sneered.

Madame laughed. "I agree with the Spire. It's long past time we cleared out the old underbrush and let new green grow." She turned to Sasha. "We don't need you. Or your... her. And tell me, what good would one little half-fae hybrid monster be, anyway? How does that help us? With the light back, our ladies will bud and blossom once more. The garden of Unseelie will thrive. Our magic and our power will flow and restore our land and our bodies." She turned to the crowd. "Now you must decide. Who shall rule?"

Noisette was the first on her feet. Her face glowed with passion and intensity. She'd been waiting for this moment for a long time. "I vow my hands and my eyes—and my heart and my gifts to our new and rightful queen." She turned to face the crowd. "Tournesol!"

When the cheer went up; *Tournesol, Tournesol*—thin at first but growing in volume, I knew it was all over for Sasha. Madame took it all in for a minute, then turned back to him. "It appears a decision has been made. Enjoy your stay in the human realm."

"But they'll get sick," I said, forgetting to keep my mouth shut. "They can't live there."

"How unfortunate for them. They'll just have to be careful where they lay their hands."

"No," I said. "They won't. Because you're going to make sure they're fine." She glared at me. "Yeah, you know what I'm talking about."

"Now, you want to use it?" Marly said. "Good. Because I cannot go back to oven mitts."

I turned to Madame. "Perhaps this would be a good time

to balance the books, Madame Queen. Don't you owe me a debt?" She growled something through her teeth. "Was that a yes?" I couldn't save March, but I could make sure Sasha and Marly didn't drop dead from iron allergies. "I would like you to create a ...potion—" I paused and turned to Sasha. "Is that the right word?"

"Near enough," he agreed. "It will serve."

"A potion. One that keeps both of them healthy and wards against anything environmental, physical, biological or, um, emotional that could make them sick or injure them. Or anyone around them." I frantically ran over the terms in my mind. These bitches live for loopholes. "Something that will last as long as they are, uh, exiled to the human world. No, strike that. As long as they remain in the human world. And if they return to court, it won't hurt them there, either. Something that won't hurt them in other ways, or hurt their friends. Something without side effects. Something that won't hurt the baby. If there is one. Or any baby, ever."

Madame gave me a look that should have turned me to cinders, but finally she snorted and said, "As it is owed, so it shall be paid. Check your pockets."

I remembered something else, and I had to be sure. "And what do I owe for apologizing?"

She looked at me blankly. "I beg your pardon?"

"I said I was sorry a bunch of times. What is my debt?"

She turned to her companions. "What is this human going on about?" She looked back at me. "You have been listening to fairy tales."

"That's not a thing, Rube," Marly said.

I turned to her. "Mar, I know you're mad." It was more than that. I think if Sasha hadn't been holding her back, she would have come for me.

"I'm not mad at you," she said, and I sure as fuck hoped she meant it. "You can't break a promise, here. That *is* a thing, but it's fine to apologize." She frowned. "Who told you that? No, I'm just thinking of all the people I'm going to kill." She was still looking at Madame.

I nodded. Sasha could try to contain her all day, but Marly saw her future clearly, and it involved blood. "We'll take care of each other."

"We'll take care of our own," she said, "No more secrets, that part is over." Then she got a strange look on her face. "It's over. Maybe..." She spotted Ilex hanging back with the other constructs. "Hey Ilex. I guess I'm not your mistress anymore. But come over here, if you don't mind."

Ilex only hesitated a moment, then came forward. Her face was puffy, and it looked to me like she'd recently had a good cry. But her eyes were her own.

Marly said, "So, you want to go on an adventure with me?"

"My Lady." They joined hands. "I do not wish to disappoint, but my place is here. I only regret I will not get to meet your beloved Aunt Harriet."

Marly nodded slowly. "Maybe someday. You two will have a lot to talk about." She sniffed a little. "I love you."

Ilex smiled. "Better than coffee?"

Marly gasped with sudden dismay. "Clover."

"Do not fear for him. It will be pleasant to remain in the

company of another who loves you."

They shared a long hug. Then Marly stepped back and turned to Madame. "If anything happens to Ilex, so help me God I will come back here and cut off your hands." Madame raised her eyebrow and nodded; game recognizes game. "Anyone else?"

"Me." Aster left Madame's side and stood with us. "I want to go with you. I want to go where I can trust people."

"You still don't trust me?" Madame put on her best heartbroken face, and she was so good, I wanted to fall at her feet.

Aster seemed to have gotten over his melt down. He stood tall, smoothing the bronze silk of his robe, and looked down his nose at her. "Your story was touching, but my life is still a lie. I'm sorry about your friend, but she has nothing to do with me. I thank you for raising me so well, whatever your reasons. But I wish to try and find a new way to live. If they'll have me."

"We'll be lucky to have you," I said. I was so proud of him. And then to Madame, "Will you let him go?"

She smiled sadly. "I thought you and I would build a new world. Aster, is this truly what you want?" He nodded. She held out her hand and he went to her. "Then, go." And she reached up and stroked his cheek with the flat side of a long, thin blade of grass. Then she drew its edge across his neck.

He frowned. "I don't..." When he touched the line the grass had left, his throat opened and all the bright golden blood in his body came pouring out. The lights in his eyes dimmed and went dark. He dropped to his knees, then fell to the ground. We stood, shocked. I clapped my hands over my mouth.

"There," said Madame. "Now he is free."

"You...you killed him." I could barely speak. "You loved him."

"I made him," she sneered. "And now I have no further use for him. After all Ruby, you said it yourself. We're not the nice ones."

# 40

*Ruby*

**M**adame tossed the blade of grass on the ground, its purpose served, and stepped over Aster's body. "I believe you'll find James waiting at the gate to take you to your new home, the human realm." She cast an eye at me. "You, too. But a word first."

I didn't appear to have a choice. Sasha and Marly, ashen, left the hall hand in hand without another word. The fae, who just an hour ago had been Sasha's subjects, drew aside to watch them leave. Noisette was grinning like she won the lottery, and I couldn't help but notice the fae folk drawing away from her. I guess there was an upper limit on crazy, even in this crazy place. After the cheer that had gone up for their new queen, I wasn't surprised that no one made a move for Sasha, or against Madame, who had acquired in the last couple of minutes a construct guard. I saw Master Greaves at the back of the hall, standing with the rest of his people. They were embracing. Some of them were weeping. I think he was, too. He got what he wanted, there would be plenty of time later for regrets. One day he and I would have a conversation, that much I knew for sure.

"What did you offer the Trade folk?" I asked. I couldn't take my eyes off Aster's silky hair, spread out on the shiny floor. He lay in a pool of golden glitter, almost like a pool of champagne, almost like Lauren, and now both my friends were dead.

"We still have need for servants," she replied, "but they will be citizen-servants, and may advance in rank."

"May?"

"Too bad your debt is paid; you could have used it to negotiate on their behalf. I wonder if you have more pressing things to worry about."

"And I wonder if you'll find ruling is as much fun as being a scheming, murdering bitch."

She laughed. "I imagine I'll find out." Then she paused, and looked me up and down. "What if…"

"Nah, you're not sucking me into a guessing game."

She smiled. "No games. Just wondering. What if I could bring him back? If you wanted me to, what if I could retrieve your unicorn?"

"He's not my—"

"I imagine the Spire would pout, but perhaps the ex-king would serve in his place. It's what he himself wanted, isn't it? I'd even allow the conditions you imposed remain in place for…her."

"You'd let me take Marly home and she'd be safe there?

And March would be free?"

Isn't that what you want?" She looked at me, expectant. " Imagine plucking our former king whole from your friend's life. You would all be free. What would you say?"

I could feel sweat on my neck, turning chilly. "I…" Marly would never forgive me. Never. I could not fuck her over again, because this time she might do something worse than yell. And March was probably fine—they seemed really invested in him. It wasn't like we had some great bond or anything. "No." I said. "Let it stand."

She practically hummed with delight. This was obviously what she wanted me to say. I waited to find out why.

"I feel as if there's still something you wish to ask me. We won't see each other again, so I grant you one truth, no debt accrued. Would you like to know about March?"

"I just want to go home." I felt sick—both the nausea that I'd come to expect, and the knowledge that somehow, I'd made a horrible mistake.

"That's not a question," she said like I was on Jeopardy, and I have never been closer to murder. I took a deep breath and unclenched my fists.

"What are March and I to each other?"

"Finally," she said. "Here we are." She opened her arms for me to approach, and I hesitated because I am not an idiot. "Oh, come on, I assure you, you're safe." She smiled. "A promise, from me."

When I was within reach, she grabbed my arm and spun me around so she was behind me, like Master Greaves had done. I guess this was standard ops for bullshit magic. She put one hand flat on my stomach, and the other over my mouth. "It's like you know him," she whispered in my ear, "if only you could remember. Am I right?"

Since my mouth was covered, I just nodded. My head was full of her sweet floral perfume. I felt dizzy.

"It's very like a thread, isn't it? Begging to be pulled?" I nodded again. "I am partially holding back the spell cast upon you right now, so you can hear and listen and understand. And like every other piece of magic here in the Unseelie kingdom, the spell is starting to degrade. Oh, it has a long way to go, but the little fish in your mind are certainly nibbling around the edges. Yes, human girl, you know him. Perhaps 'know' isn't a strong enough word. How about this; you loved him. In fact, you loved each other, as well as a mortal can claim to love a creature like that, or he can understand what it means to love another. First you saved his life, and then he returned the favor. It's a long story. And it appears his affection for you lingers...or at least it did until someone new came along. Wasn't Amory a lovely distraction? It would never have lasted, of course. His heart is and remains yours alone. But what about you? Magic, little human. You're under an enchantment that has erased him from your memory. More than that, it turns words of love and remembrance to gibberish. I believe some vomiting was also involved. It turns out you aren't ill; you aren't mad. You're just trying to recover your life, with sadly little success. And because I am feeling generous on this glorious day of my ascension, I will let you remember this conversation."

And it was true. I knew it was true. It wasn't déjà vu, it

wasn't this place that drove me to him. It was my own past, just out of reach. Then I thought of how I'd treated him, how he told me about the person he'd once loved, and how I let him go. I wanted to die.

She released me and I fell to my knees, gasping. "Bring him back. I changed my mind." Marly would forgive me, in time. I'd make her understand.

She laughed like I'd made the cleverest joke. "Obviously I can't do that. It's done and done. I was just curious to see what you'd say."

She was right—"what *would* you do, what *if* I could." It was just one last little game. "Why? Why would you do this to me? To us?"

"Me? My dear, I had nothing to do with it. Excellent question, though. Who would do such a thing?" She smiled, and I wanted to slap her. "Ask the king."

# 41

*Ruby*

**N**eedless to say, it was a quiet car ride home.

Marly had her chorus of lights in her lap, gently stroking them to keep them calm. Sasha stared out the window. I didn't know how to ask or where to start, so along with the return of my nausea, yay, I sat in silence, fuming. I was angry at Sasha for fucking with my mind, I was angry at Marly for letting it happen and not telling me. I was also angry at Marly for having the nerve to love the man who tore apart my mind and ruined my life, and I was also, also extra mad at Sasha for being exactly who I thought he was—duplicitous and cruel. The stories about the fae were right; Lauren was the exception. Poor Aster was just a victim. Sasha, Madame, Amory, the fucking Spire—they were the vicious, ugly rule.

Mostly I was mad at myself for thinking any of these people were my friends. I kept seeing the look on March's face as that rope of flowers tightened around his neck. He turned to the one he loved for help. The last thing he saw was me, letting him down. I wasn't his friend, either.

"Get some rest, Ruby, you earned it." James said to me as he opened the car door for me. "You brought your friends back home alive."

"Not all of them," I said.

"You'll figure it out," he said. "Your heart will show you the way."

Isn't it always when someone tries to be nice to you, that's when you can't hold back the tears? He hugged me in my driveway and let me cry while the ex-royalty stood by, looking uncomfortable. Good, they should.

Finally, I pulled myself together. "Thank you for your advice. I wish I'd done better. But the thing you said about apologizing? It turns out not to be true."

James looked curiously at Sasha. "Does an apology not put the speaker into debt?"

Sasha looked even more uncomfortable. "I might have, um, implied that…"

"What for?" Marly asked. "Why would you make that up?"

Sasha shrugged. "I just don't like hearing 'I'm sorry, my Lord this' and 'forgive me, my Lord that' all the time. Makes me feel obligated to say 'oh, it was nothing.'" He got a little huffy. "Sometimes it's not nothing."

"Nothing? Are you telling me…" James folded his arms and his look turned menacing. I braced for action; which one of them I'd step in front of TBD. "Since my remaining debt appears to be 'nothing,' *lord king*, in the future find someone else to cart around your narrow elf ass."

"I am not an elf," Sasha replied with a sniff.

James just laughed and shook his head. "You're not a lot of things." He looked back at me, flipping the keys between his fingers, and his look softened. "Good luck with this one. You know how to reach me, if you need to travel."

After he drove off, I took a deep breath and let the two of them into my house. Everything was the same—exactly the same. I picked up my phone, right where I'd left it on the table, and turned the screen on. Only a few hours had gone by since I put on the king's medallion and left for my "vacation."

"Ask the king," I said. "That's what Madame said to me, in case you were wondering. 'Ask the king.'"

"Ask me what?" Even with his human-appearing eyes installed, it was hard to get a read on him.

"I think you know." I felt bile rise, burning the back of my throat, and forced it away.

"Madame," Sasha mused. "She wanted you to say that to me. I'm wondering what she put in your head."

I laughed, and it sounded crazy. "And I'm wondering what you took out of it. My head. She told me what you did. How you went into my memories and took March out. I still don't remember my time with him, but I know it's true. Isn't that funny? Finally, someone told me the truth, and it wasn't either of you." I pulled off the medallion and threw it on the floor. "I think you both should leave. You have your potions, so good night and good luck."

They looked at each other, and to my surprise they didn't

look guilt-stricken at all, only sad and tired.

Marly touched the back of Sasha's hand, then picked up the necklace and set it on the table. She turned to me. "Did she say why?"

"Does it matter? It was just another shitty trick from a shitty person. And you, you're supposed to be—"

"Stop speaking." Sasha still commanded the room like a king, even if he was in exile in my living room. I stopped speaking. "I would have thought by now you'd know better than to take what that woman says at face value. Think, Ruby—is it to her benefit if we stay together, we three? Or is it to her benefit that you cast aside your dearest friend?"

He had a point.

"Here." He pulled something out of his pocket and handed it to me.

"You mean to tell me you had this on you the whole goddamn time?" Marly barked. "You

told me you couldn't fix it. Damn it, Sasha."

"I said it was as fixed as I could make it at the time." He still sounded calm. "There would have been consequences."

Before she could yell some more, I jumped in. "A pebble?" I held it up. "What is this?"

"It is a rock from the river of time," he said. "And if you want to know the whole story, the reason I tumble bank goldfish, blue copper bird."

I glared at him. "I guess your spell is still in place because that made no kind of sense, and I still feel like shit. Thank you, your Highness."

He didn't seem quite so calm anymore. He rubbed his

face with his palms and then said, "Just swallow the stone, Ruby."

"Eat a rock? You're out of your mind. Fuck you."

"Although I am pissed at him," Marly said, "and we're going to talk AT LENGTH about his shitty, lame-ass plan, you should do what he says."

"You'd agree with him about anything."

"Ruby, look at me." Marly reached for me, and I squirmed back, but she grabbed my hand in hers. "You feel like you're going to barf, I can see it. Deep breaths. We can end this. It's time to fix things." I nodded and tried to breathe through the sick feeling. "It's me. The one you can trust. You know that. And I think you should swallow it." I looked at the stone in my palm. It was smooth, about the size of a tic tac. It wasn't like I would be powering down a Flintstone vitamin.

"Will I understand? Will I feel better?"

"You'll understand, all right. And you won't feel sick anymore, I promise."

"I do trust you," I said to her. "Okay." And I dry-swallowed the little stone. At first, it felt like I choked down a boulder. It was stuck in my throat and made me cough, and I struggled not to throw it back up. Then, I found myself sitting on the floor. And then, and then....

Everything that hurt me fell away.

A dark street, a late night. A shining light coming from the most beautiful thing I'd ever seen. A man who was so much more than just a man.

And then images flickering by, going so fast I couldn't make them all out. I didn't have to, because they were my memories and they were settling back into place, in my mind, where they belonged.

Drinking at the bar, laughing. Sex so gorgeous it lifted me off the bed and surrounded me with a kaleidoscope of color. Eating take out Chinese food with his fingers—I got that one right. Slow dancing under a smiling moon. Roses.

And then a knife, and blood, and darkness. Then Marly was a vampire—and yeah, it got better—and then Sasha was there, and the *kitsune*, and March, who was losing his mind.

It kept going, because the memories Sasha buried kept rising, the mist was clearing, and finally I remembered everything.

The last things to return were the memories of the time I'd just spent at the Unseelie Court, rewritten with my mind now whole. I could see myself walking into the big ballroom for the first time and seeing Madame.

"Shoulda grabbed that chopstick and stuck it in her fucking eye," I muttered. I saw March appear on the scene, and it's so funny how you can smile and cry at the same time. And then, horrifyingly, how he told me about the woman he loved and lost, and all I had to offer was 'Too bad dude, at least she's not dead.' And finally, my half-hearted flirtation with Aster. Poor Aster, who never saw it coming, what happens when humans show up. It wasn't like his reality TV shows, not at all.

Marly rooted around in the fridge and got us all beers. She sat with me on the couch, and Sasha took the armchair.

I sniffled back tears. "I understand why you did it, Sasha, you saved him from coming unstuck in time. I take back most of what I said. But what happens now?"

Marly squeezed my shoulder. "Yeah, you mentioned consequences? And they had better be dramatic."

He nodded. "They may very well be. It wasn't my intention to punish you, or him. I never thought you'd see him again. How could I know you'd both show up at my court at the same time?" We all said "ex-court" in our heads. "Madame planned this most carefully. She sent for March already with a plan in place to use him. Aster was a misdirection; the truth of his creation was something she almost certainly put in your path."

"She didn't send us out hunting that day, though." And then I remembered his hood, his favorite; a gift from Madame. The gift that failed and gave him away. Son of a bitch.

"No," Sasha continued, "but she knew one way or another you'd figure it out."

"It was you, though." I turned to Marly. "You're the one who put it together, about him being the trade."

"Yeah, and I was wrong. It was so obvious, and I missed it completely. Like you said, babe. Aster was a distraction, just like Amory. The difference is Amory is still there." Marly and I locked eyes. Good ol' Amory, he was on the list for sure.

Sasha said, "Now March is back in your memories, and you are back in his, for that's how my spell was written. What do you suppose he'll do, knowing how he was used by Madame and knowing that you remember him?"

"He'll tear the Seelie Court in half, and she'll be next." Marly smiled.

I said, "He told me a story about the last time someone

put him in a cage. It was like...in the Dark Ages? To cure the villagers of a plague. He..." He'd been betrayed that time by a woman who was supposed to care for him, too. "...he doesn't like being locked up."

Sasha nodded. "I'm sure he doesn't. Well, here are the consequences you asked for. The Seelie Court may find they have a very angry, very determined and very powerful captive. Or they may find they have a cage containing a madman who once dreamed of being a unicorn."

Marly flopped against the back of the couch and took a long drink. "If I didn't know you'd never do something like this on purpose, I'd say the timing is pretty convenient."

"Yes," he replied, "you caught me. I set this whole thing up—losing my throne and cast out of my home, just so I could break the spell and activate the unicorn now. You're far too clever for me."

Instead of dumping her beer on his head, she grinned and leaned over and kissed him. "I know. Know what else I know?" We waited. "You may know, and March may know, but the Spire doesn't know you two actually know each other. Hmmm, know..." She paused. "Ever say a word so much it doesn't sound right anymore? Anyway, I think I remember the Spire also saying something about you being some kind of representative for the humans."

I nodded slowly. "Thank you, Lauren."

She lifted her bottle. "To Lauren C. There's our in. And Ilex is back in her head and in place. Now all we need is a plan." She looked over at Sasha, shaking her head. "You're not in charge of it. Offering yourself, my ass."

Finally, we couldn't keep our eyes open, and I gave them the bedroom. I stretched out on the couch. The old, familiar streetlights slanted through the blinds. "I remember you, March. I remember everything. Just hold on. I'm coming to get you."

# 42

*March*

White. Everything was white. Even with his eyes closed, the brightness leaked through.

March opened his eyes. He was face down on the floor. It was marble—good marble, veined with grey and gold, and lit from beneath.

He sat up. It was hard at first to judge the size of the room because of the almost unbroken whiteness, but it was just that; a room. The walls, also gently glowing, were featureless, and bowed out a bit in the center. More white above his head. Unlike his forest glade at the Unseelie Court, his new hosts had given him some furniture. At least, of a sort. He recognized the silhouette—Louis Quatorze. Two chairs, a chaise or couch, a coffee table, and an enormous plank of a bed. But they were silhouettes only. Each piece looked carved out of heavy glass. No. He ran his finger over the rococo curls on the leg of a chair. Not glass, Lucite. Smoky gray transparent Lucite. Probably given a touch of color so he wouldn't walk into anything and whack his shin—after all, he was too valuable to risk injury. He looked up at the chandelier which was overly large for the size of the room. He could see it wasn't intended to shed much light, but break the plane of the otherwise blank ceiling, which might have brought on vertigo. It was black, shiny, and resembled the spine and ribs of a large undersea creature. He thought the room looked like a particularly chic nightclub from some time in the late 80's.

He got up and moved to the edge of the hard, undecorated bed and took stock. He had only what he came with: the robe in shades of brown and gold and green; his beloved work boots, given to him by Ercilia, which held trapped in the cracks of their leather the dust of his travels; and, underneath, soft cotton undergarments, which Master Greaves had made for him after he complained that the Unseelie Court was chilly.

It was chilly here, too.

He looked down and with a shudder brushed away the shriveled remains of the flower rope that bound him.

Amory.

He knew he ought to be very angry about the whole thing, but honestly, Amory had told him flat out several times. *Madame has eyes and ears everywhere. Careful where you place your trust, in fact, perhaps you ought to trust no one at all.*

He hadn't realized what sort of a warning it was at the time, of course. He was only enjoying the relief of simple desire. He knew Amory wasn't interested in his magic; he had plenty of his own. And beauty? The fae was certainly not lacking. And the thing, that thing he couldn't control that drew humans to him whether they wanted it or not—it didn't have an effect on the fae. He could confess to himself that after the confusion and pain of seeing Ruby treat him like a stranger, and then worse, a mistake, giving in to Amory's pursuit was a balm. *Ruby will remember me in time*, was what he'd told himself, *and I have something to do while I wait.*

It was all a lie, of course. A set-up. But he couldn't help but think it was one Amory took a special pleasure in, as he had. In fact, just thinking about it made his cock twitch. He was glad of the loose robe and wrapped it around his knees.

"You," he said, looking down, "are going to get us killed one day."

He checked, and no, he didn't feel any guilt over it, just some regret that he could no longer just have what he desired without consequence or introspection.

He decided to think about the events that brought him here, instead. In focus, carefully, so he might understand what happened and who he ought to blame (other than his own, careless self.) Madame, obviously. The reason she'd sent for him, the real reason. She told him at their first meeting: *I brought you here because you are supposed to be beyond price.* Not a lie, not even a misdirection. The bald truth. And the Spire apparently agreed. He was worth the price of a kingdom, and the kingdom of the Unseelie Court was to be saved. He wondered what Sasha's counter play would be; he didn't seem the type to give up and slink away. And Marly, she'd gotten the taste of power in her teeth. She'd have something to say.

Strike. Counter-strike.

He tried not to be disappointed in Ruby. She didn't know him. Why would she have leapt to his rescue? A part of him had hoped at that moment her memories would have breached the dam of the magic, and she would have...tried? Said something? Done something other than look sad and then look away? It wasn't like she had some leverage, a debt or something, a thing to use against Madame. But a word would have been nice.

He transformed his body with a sigh, and as always wondered why he waited so long. He walked to the white expanse of wall, and touched it with his horn. In a moment he'd be on his way.

Nothing.

Whoever arranged for the cage knew what they were doing. He turned back into his human form, thinking he could at least deprive the Seelie folk of a show. After all, they knew what a man looked like.

He found he was tired and stretched out on the comfortless bed. As his eyes drifted shut, something moved in his mind. Something changed. He went to look, and as he did, the still and colorless pages in his memory slowly came to life.

"Oh, you're back," he said, and gladly ran to greet her...

...holding her close in the orange light of a sodium street lamp

...kissing her for the first time in her little house

...showing her color and light and pleasure and love

...walking single file in the woods, arguing about Gaia (he backed away from that one)

…telling her he'd find a way to come back to her

He hadn't, but someone had. And if he could find her in his mind, then her memories must be restored as well. So, the spell that repaired his mind was broken. He gingerly eased out of the days and nights of his memory and back onto the hard bed. This was now, and he didn't feel confused or disoriented. So far. So that was good. So far.

*You've done some things, Ruby; you and Sasha and Marly. You've changed things. The counter-strike has begun. Let's see what happens next.*

He leaned back again and folded his arms behind his head. Out loud, he said to the Seelie fae, who were, he assumed, watching him through the walls, "I'll be free soon. And you had better decide where you want to be when I get out of here."

Smiling at the thought, he closed his eyes and slept.

Ruby and March will be back!

Look for The Glass Sword: New World Magic Book Five in late 2023.

If you enjoyed this book, please consider leaving a review—thanks!

# Acknowledgements

As I said up front, I owe so much to the various talents of Cait, Gen and Other Jenn, the Drunk Mythology Gals, who held my hand (and sometimes my hair) as this book went through its various incarnations.

A bouquet of flowers and a parade for World's Best Editor Carly, who is always right.

A handful of glitter (which might be construct blood) for Aurelia, who made the covers even more delicious.

The teachers at Yoga District who keep my urge to kill at a manageable level (mostly.)

My gang: Antigone, Matthew, Michael, Vanda, Mike, Tony, Chris.

Frida the Destroyer and Onion, who both get cookies.

My family, but mostly Dyon.

# Also by Kim Alexander

**New World Magic:**

Pure
The March Effect
The Great Shatter
**A Poisoned Garden**

**The Demon Door:**

The Sand Prince
The Heron Prince
The Glass Girl
The River King

# About the author

Kim Alexander grew up in the wilds of Long Island, NY and slowly drifted south until she reached Key West. After spending ten rum-soaked years as a DJ in the Keys, she moved to Washington DC, where she lives with two cats, an angry fish, and her extremely patient husband.

Please visit her at kimalexanderonline.com

www.ingramcontent.com/pod-product-compliance
Lightning Source LLC
Chambersburg PA
CBHW070534260626
47161CB00002B/374